Christmas in Angel Harbor

Christmas in Angel Harbor

Jeannie Moon

Christmas in Angel Harbor

Tule Publishing First Printing, October 2020

The Tule Publishing, Inc.

First Publication by Tule Publishing 2020

Cover design by Lee Hyat at www.LeeHyat.com

This is a work of fiction. Names, characters, places, and incidents are products of the author's imagination or are used fictitiously. Any resemblance to actual events, locales, organizations, or persons, living or dead, is entirely coincidental.

ISBN: 978-1-952560-90-3

Dedication

For the librarians of the world.

Some gifts aren't under the tree.

Chapter One

NOVEMBER ON LONG Island was unpredictable. Kind of like a woman.

One minute she was giving you attitude, the next she was warm and charming. The ever-changing weather showed that Mother Nature could be one moody customer. Within a week she could bring rain, sun, gale-force winds, warm temperatures, frost or snow. It was a far cry from the sunshine and warmth he'd left behind in Hawaii, but with each strike of his foot on the pavement, with each mile behind him, Dan Gallo was glad he'd come home.

Avoiding his life hadn't done anything to help the anger that still swirled inside him, at least not yet. There was a chance he'd start to settle once he established a new routine, but even when that happened, he wasn't going to tell anyone where he was. He'd left a string of pissed-off people since he'd gone off the grid, but Dan didn't really care. Angel Harbor, where he'd spent the first twenty-two years of his life before leaving for law school, was the perfect place to hide in plain sight. He was staying at the family house where his sister lived with her husband and kids. She was thrilled that he was going to be around for the holidays and gave him the small guest cottage to use for as long as he wanted.

The main house was a grand lady. An old Victorian with

gingerbread trim, it was located just outside of town up a long hill that gave the upper floors spectacular water views. His cottage, while not big, was roomy enough and suited him fine. Compact and recently renovated, it had a bedroom, a living room, and a dining area with a small kitchen. It was the perfect place for Dan to get his head on straight and plan his next move.

Whatever that might be.

Long Island was steeped in stereotypes. Sure, there were McMansions where there used to be open space, and it was too crowded for its own good, but it really did have a lot to offer. With stunning and varied coastlines, history, agriculture, and great downtowns, at its core, the region was really just a bunch of small communities connected by their presence on a long skinny stretch of sand that jutted out into the Atlantic Ocean. Weighing all that, he didn't know why he hadn't come home sooner. The big plus? He'd been gone a long time, and no one really recognized him. If someone did, his current situation often made the person uncomfortable enough to leave him alone. Mostly, he could be anonymous here. Something that definitely appealed.

Pulling back his stride to take the hill, he turned onto Main Street and allowed the peacefulness of the view to seep in. Only a small breakfast place and the local deli were open this early, and the smell of bacon and eggs frying on a griddle wafted toward him. He'd already run three miles in the sleepy neighborhoods around his sister's house, enough to justify an egg sandwich from his favorite deli.

Turning toward the park, he figured he'd do a lap on the paths along the harbor to assuage any guilt that might crop up once he indulged in a breakfast that he'd thought about far too often when he was away from Long Island. Sure, he could get an egg sandwich anywhere, but not like this one. It was the little things about home he'd missed most. He'd learned the hard way that a good life was a collection of small experiences. While big and flashy might impress in the short term, the millions of tiny details about an experience were what mattered.

Maybe it was his age. Once he passed fifty, Dan's tolerance for nonsense dropped to zero. He liked things simple and uncomplicated. It was one of the reasons he'd sold his apartment in New York, and bought the house in Hawaii. The constant crush of people, the endless busyness, exhausted him. His beach house on Oahu was peaceful and quiet, but the solitude brought him no peace.

His reputation was as an enigma, a mystery man who only showed up when a book or a woman necessitated his presence, and his agent played it up. His latest author photos were black and white art shots that had him shadowed and sinister-looking.

As he ran, he observed his fellow early risers. He nodded to a pair of elderly women who were walking almost as fast as he was running. Their pace was impressive as they power walked in the morning chill, barely sparing him a glance. He could use that little slice of life. The story that was swimming around in his head needed the people and locations Angel Harbor provided. No more murder and mayhem. No more blood. Even if it did sell, Dan was done with it.

The sun decided to break through the low clouds, and from its position, just above the horizon, it cast tendrils of light over the water. Everything shimmered and sparkled in response. He stopped, taking a deep breath as he took it all in.

This place was his next book. He wasn't sure of the plot. He hadn't fleshed out the characters, but Angel Harbor was the setting. Turning, he could see clear up Main Street. It was idyllic, almost too perfect, but that's what he was in the mood for, and no one was going to tell him otherwise. Not this time.

From where he stood, he could see the candy shop, the toy store, and the local tavern—all three were decked out in holiday glitz way too early for his liking, but he had to give them a gold star for effort. In addition, he spied a few restaurants, an art gallery, and a tea shop getting in the Christmas spirit. But it was the bookstore, sitting quietly on the north side of Main Street, that captured his attention. It held so many of his memories. It lived in an old house, a two-story clapboard structure, painted a deep gray, that had converted nicely to retail space decades ago. It still exuded the same friendliness and warmth that had welcomed him when he was first figuring out how to tell a story. He could see the large-paned front windows displaying a variety of books for kids and adults, and the wraparound porch held a quartet of weathered rocking chairs that invited visitors to sit down and stay for a while.

"Keep your eyes open to possibilities." Isn't that what Mike Fallon had always told him? The former owner of the bookstore was a fountain of good advice. Whether it was about writing, or school, or girls, Dan had embraced Mike's philosophy for a very long time. Until he didn't, and that's

when his life seemed to get away from him. He was so caught up in *the life*, that Dan forgot to live.

He'd spent hours in the store as a teen, writing in his notebooks, and hiding out from his jock friends to avoid being labeled as a nerd. They wouldn't understand why he wrote, and he didn't want to explain it to them. They were good guys, but putting words on a page was a lot different than executing a strategy found in a playbook.

Some of his quirkier habits developed when he was working at the round table tucked in the corner of the history section. Dan still wrote the first three chapters of any book longhand to get in the flow with the characters. He liked to use a cheap, blue ballpoint pen for the task, so a few years ago he bought a gross of the things and never traveled without at least a dozen in his bag. He always remembered how Mike would let him stay after closing to keep working, while the older man was cleaning up from the day. He made Dan promise that when he was famous, he'd come back and have a signing in the store.

He'd never gotten there, and the guilt of it gnawed at him. He was a multinational bestseller, which meant he got his way. Always. He could have pressed his publicist to arrange a signing at Harbor Books, but like so much else in his life, he didn't take the time to think about anything outside his own self-centered interests. Yeah, there were a lot of regrets rooted in that store. Dan would have to try and vanquish a few of them.

Done with his run, he made his way to the deli, and as soon as he walked in, the smell of bacon, eggs, and strong coffee filled his head. A group of men dressed in jeans, work shirts, and jackets were talking and laughing as they collected their coffees and sandwiches. The way they exchanged pleasantries with the woman behind the counter, Dan could see this was just a regular morning for them, and he found he was a little envious of the closeness and the routine. Each one nodded at him as he walked by, and he recognized Billy Scalino, one of those jocks he went to high school with. Billy's eye widened in surprise when he saw Dan, and he offered a pleasant greeting.

"Nice to see you, man." That was all he said, but Billy's greeting was indicative of the town as a whole. People were nice here. That didn't mean they wouldn't tell you where to go if you pissed any one of them off. Dan shouldn't have been surprised at the friendliness of the greeting, but a lot of years had passed between then and now. These men had better things to do—like making a living and raising their families—than to worry about some guy in the deli.

If he was going to do justice to his new book, a knock off the pedestal the industry had put him on would be useful.

In his head the story was starting to take shape. It wasn't going to be like anything he'd ever done, and he had plans to start today. Now that his setting was shaping up, the specifics had a place to go.

JANE FALLON MADE herself a cup of burnt sugar tea and let the smell of caramel and vanilla drift over her. She added a dollop of local clover honey and inhaled the sweet steam. As flavors mingled, Jane knew that, quandaries aside, it was going to be a good day. Maybe even a special one.

Something had been buzzing around her for the last week. She felt like there was a familiar presence in her space. Eerie and comforting at the same time, a sense of familiarity in the feelings had her wondering exactly what the day might bring.

With Halloween in the rearview mirror and Thanksgiving a couple of weeks away, Jane knew it was time to start prepping for the Christmas shopping season. Her vendors had been calling about last-minute orders, but the stock room was already overflowing with goodness. She had holiday cards ready to go out today, an ornament tree with a selection of gorgeous hand-painted decorations, gift books, pens, kids' books and puppets ready for shopping season. She was sorting out the decorations, which she would start putting up right before Thanksgiving.

A cold snap was on the way, and she was hesitant to let her uncle Joe, who was turning seventy-six in a few days, climb up on a ladder when temperatures with wind chill dipped to the single digits.

The bell over the front door of the shop jingled and right on time, she was greeted by her mom's sunny grin. Still an active part of the shop, even though it was officially Jane's, her mother kept her hand in some of the day-to-day operation.

"Good morning," Kathleen Fallon sang. "Wow! It's chilly! I think the temperature dropped ten degrees since the sun came up."

Unwinding her long, multicolored scarf, her mother hung it and her big wool coat on the hook just inside the office. She wore her unofficial winter uniform of jeans, duck boots, and a chunky sweater in navy blue. The woman looked like a coed, even with the mop of curly gray hair that framed her face. Jane hoped that in twenty-five years she'd be as eager to meet the day as her mother was.

"I know. I just checked the weather. It's going to be bitter tonight." Jane poured her mother a cup of her favorite Earl Grey tea, no sugar or milk. "I'm thinking I'll decorate inside a bit today."

"Good plan." Blowing on the hot liquid, her mother took a sip. "It's going to get warm again, well relatively, by next week."

"It's supposed to be beautiful in Santa Fe," Jane said, reminding her mother of the spa retreat she would be taking with her friends the following week.

"I know, but I'm still here for this round of cold. You know, I'll miss you and everyone in town terribly, but I will not miss the nasty weather once I move south for the winter." Gripping the mug with both hands her mom took another sip of tea. "What else are you checking off your list today?"

"I pulled some new mysteries for Dave's mom. If he comes in, they're right on my desk in the back."

"He's very sweet picking up books for his mother."

"He is, but that's the only thing I've done so far. I guess we'll see what the day brings. Was Chloe excited to see her friends at the groomer?"

"As always." Her mom had dropped Jane's Collie off for her monthly spa day. Normally at the store, Jane would miss her furry coworker today, but there was plenty to do and it was better the dog wouldn't be underfoot. Jane knew her mother would be prepping the children's room for the holidays, setting up special displays and putting out stashes of holiday favorites. After thirty-three years teaching kindergarten and first grade, the children's room was her mother's domain. Jane, on the other hand, spread her love of genre fiction and paper goods around the shop. Beautiful journals, pens, stationery, and cards drew in a lot of customers looking for unique gifts. There was a large selection of planners and calendars, and every week a group of women gathered in the common space to swap ideas and planner tricks. The shop carried all the big bestsellers, but Jane filled the shelves with her favorite mysteries, romances, historical novels, and memoirs.

Harbor Books was an institution in their little town. One of the oldest businesses on Main Street, there had been many changes since her grandfather opened his book and stationery shop during the Great Depression, but the Fallon family had adapted to each challenge.

Over the last twenty-five years, she'd brought the store to a new level—ironic because she'd never planned on owning the store, or making her life in Angel Harbor. But here she was, and as she faced a brand-new phase of her life, Jane wondered what was up next.

"Are all Tara's college applications done? I know she had some early deadlines."

"Finally," Jane sighed. Her seventeen-year-old daughter had complained through every one of them, agonizing over each essay. But now that most of them were done, tensions had lessened in the household.

Tara had always been stubborn. Curious and determined, she hadn't been easy to keep up with. Her daughter had shifting passions, jumping from one activity to the next. That all changed when she took a creative writing class at the beginning of her sophomore year. Like someone flipped a switch, it opened a whole new world for her daughter. Her talent—her passion—for the written word was the spark that moved her. She made good friends in the class—brilliant, creative kids like she was—and they brought her into the theater program, completely changing her trajectory. Jane's appreciation for the arts—and for Tara's gift—was rooted in her training in archeology. A civilization's art and literature told the story of its people, providing a view of the past that was deeper than historical events could ever show on their own.

"She's going to be fine, you know." Her mother was the endless optimist. Her years in the classroom made her secure in her belief that her granddaughter would figure things out. Of course, in her mother's eyes Tara could do no wrong, even when she was at her moodiest.

"I don't know what she's going to do with a writing degree, but what do I know?"

Mom chuckled. "The same thing you did with an archeology degree. She'll find her way."

That wasn't very comforting. While working in Scotland as a researcher with a renowned archeologist, Jane got the call that her father, Mike Fallon, had died. The staff job that was supposed to launch her career, the PhD program she'd had her sights set on since she was a freshman undergraduate, were both mothballed. Her dad's death pulled her home and it irrevocably changed her path.

Her friends, her career, her aspirations were gone. Jane had adjusted, pivoted into a new role, but there was always an inkling of regret.

She took up the mantle at the bookstore and moved back in with her mother, who was devastated by the loss of her husband. Eventually, Jane married badly, and divorced quickly. However, the bright light in all of it was Tara.

Once the baby came, there was no returning to her dream of traveling the world and learning about ancient civilizations, but she never doubted that her little girl was an amazing gift, and always would be. Difficult times and all, Tara was at the center of everything she did. Jane would never regret becoming a mother.

"You're drifting," her mother stated quietly. "Where's that boat headed today?"

"Nowhere." Jane shook off her wanderings with a smile. "I'm going to drift myself into the stockroom. I want to double-check my gift inventory."

From the sidelong glance sent in Jane's direction, her mother didn't believe her. There was no reason she should. Her mom was many things, but clueless wasn't one of them. She could always tell when the people she cared about were brushing off her concern. "Right," Mom said. "You make sure you have enough crystals and bookmarks."

"You forgot the journals and dreamcatchers," Jane retorted as she walked to the back. The gift section was an ongoing tease with her mother. Jane had set aside a small corner of her shop to indulge her need for beautiful things. The section was called *Modern Artifacts.* Not that books weren't beautiful, but the color and light brought in by the locally crafted candles, crystals, textiles, and paper goods made her feel more connected to the world outside her small corner of it. "Tracy should be in soon. She can give you a hand with the children's room."

Her best friend, Tracy Kelly, had been a fixture in Jane's life since they'd landed in Mrs. Sherman's kindergarten class at Woodbury Avenue School. Obsessed with the large playhouse and the endless possibilities the magical classroom provided, Jane and Tracy had a formed a bond that was more sisterhood than anything. Jane was an only child, and Tracy had brothers, so the two girls grew up together, weathering every storm along the way. In the toughest times, they were there for each other. When her last child had left the nest for college five years ago, Tracy transitioned from part-time employee to Jane's right hand at the bookstore.

Once in her office, Jane picked up a heart-shaped piece of hematite. The stone, a gift from her friend Claire, was smooth as silk and cold to the touch, at least initially. After a minute, a tingly warmth would radiate up her arm. It grounded her, and spending a little time in the quiet, holding a piece of the earth, let her collect her thoughts. Her grandfather called it woolgathering, and Jane found comfort in it. The dreams of her youth may not have come to fruition, but she couldn't help thinking that the course change was for a reason. Understanding that didn't stop her from ruminating, and sometimes feeling sorry for herself, but she no longer wondered what could have been. Life had a funny way of putting you where you needed to be.

After she breathed out several times long and slow, Jane's

eyes were drawn to the crystal angel that sat on the shelf above her desk. Setting down the stone, she reached for it. It belonged to her father and before that to her grandfather. Each of them kept it in the bookstore, right in this spot.

Tradition was beautiful, and Jane respected the Fallon legacy, doing her best to keep it alive and well.

But changes were coming, and Jane knew there was no way to stop them.

Chapter Two

NEVER IN HIS writing career had Dan felt like he didn't know what he was doing. Even in the early stages of his career, after he'd drafted his first book, he had confidence in his ability to tell a story. Maybe it was hubris, arrogance even, but he didn't doubt himself.

It was probably because he'd always stayed in his lane. He wrote crime thrillers, procedurals. His dad was a cop. Dan was a litigator. The genre fit him, and he was good at it. But it was time for him to leave his comfort zone and write something that challenged him to dig deeper, to bare more of himself.

Something from his heart.

This book needed to do more than entertain, it had to inspire his readers. Comfort them. He'd spent a lot of time gutting victims; now he wanted to help people heal.

He had no idea exactly how he was going to do it, but coming home was the first thing he'd done right in a long time.

His sister was ten years younger than he was, and in addition to her career, she wrangled a pack of small humans whom Dan rather enjoyed. Never having had any kids of his own, it was a novelty to have their voices as his background music. Looking out of the cottage window at the long, hilly driveway, he saw the three of them charging up from the school bus. Backpacks thumped against their legs, or on the ground. A lunch bag was dropped and retrieved. And on cue, just as they got to the side porch, a yellow Lab burst through the door and pounced. The dog's tail wagged faster and faster with each squeal from the kids, and Dan took in every inch of the chaos as it raced toward him.

This was why he'd come home. He didn't need late-night ride-alongs with the police and gloomy solitude. He needed a bunch of loud kids and a mess of a dog. His new book was about a small town. About families. And the only way he was going to get in touch with the story milling around inside him was to embrace the crazy.

His nieces and nephew were giving him exactly what he needed, not only for his story, but for this point in his life. Dan was tired of being at odds with himself, of fighting for his peace of mind. He knew somewhere, deep down, was his happy place, but he was still struggling to find it.

He came to the door of the cottage and Tammy the dog bounded over when she spotted him. Large for her breed, the dog's coat was more creamy than yellow, making her stand out against the colorful fall leaves like a scoop of vanilla ice cream. The joy that poured off the dog was palpable, and Dan could only smile at the rest of the chaos that ran his way.

"Uncle Dan! Uncle Dan!" The chorus of small voices almost drowned out Lindsey Buckingham's screaming guitar. Music often set the tone for his writing, and in this case, it was about the character's memories. *His memories.* That's what was going to make this book different. Special. And a damn big risk.

"Did you get your words today?" His oldest niece, Ella, was his taskmaster. Every day since he'd arrived, she checked with him, holding his feet to the fire and asking about his plan for the book. She was brainy and artistic, with a lovely sweet soul. He figured she was going to run the world someday. She'd be disappointed if he told her all he had were impressions and feelings surrounding what he wanted to do—the words were fighting him.

"Not as many as I'd hoped. I was thinking a change of scenery might be in order. Does anyone want to go to town and get some hot chocolate?"

"Meeee!" All three kids raised their hands and bounced up and down on the stone walkway in front of the cottage. Even the dog barked.

"It looks as if we have a consensus. Go inside, and check with your mother. If she's okay with it, we'll go in…" he looked at his watch "…thirty minutes."

The kids didn't need to be asked twice. With giggles and rapid-fire chatter, they dashed into the house. His sister would either be pissed at him for messing up their after-school routine, or thrilled for an hour of peace to collect herself after her own long day.

His sister was a doctor. A family practitioner, she worked four days a week, and tag-teamed the kids with her husband who was a teacher. It was a crazy life, but they always sat down for dinner together no matter how busy things were. Their life was a collection of routines, and those predictable patterns provided a safe haven that made the family the center of everything.

Since he'd arrived a few weeks ago, he'd taken a seat at the table, and there was nothing better. Following the kids into the house, he heard them all talking at once, an excited rush of syllables merging together like a human symphony. His sister was picking words out of the cacophony and finally shushed all of them, directing her gaze at him.

"I got Uncle Danny, town, and hot chocolate out of that. Perhaps you can explain?" Her eyes narrowed like a mom, but her mouth ticked up in the corner like the little sister he knew. She was always full of fire and energy, and even though she had an MD at the end of her name, Melinda Gallo Beck hadn't changed a bit.

"I thought I'd get them out of your hair for a little while. I need to stretch my legs and they need to burn off a little energy." It sounded like a reasonable plan to him. He doubted she would object.

"So, you're going to sugar them up?" One eyebrow shot up inquisitively, but the sparkle in Mel's eyes was pure mischief.

It was only a little sugar. He wasn't going to have them mainline cookies and ice cream. "It's a hot chocolate and a trip to the bookstore. How bad can it be? If we go now, I'll have them home in time to get all their homework done before dinner."

"I hate homework." The grumbling came from his middle niece, Jamie, who at eight had the attitude of a hormonal thirteen-year-old. She was sharp-witted and read people like an FBI profiler.

"Yep. Me too," he said. "But you'd better get used to it."

With an eye roll that looked like it hurt, Jamie plopped

down in the chair. "Are we going?"

Dan's sister shrugged and nodded. "Sure. But don't give Uncle Danny a hard time and don't be little beggars asking him for everything in sight. He's not your personal credit card."

Like he wasn't going to buy them something. It was a bookstore. What kind of uncle was he if he didn't buy kids something in a bookstore?

"Yes, I am," he whispered. Jamie liked that and put up her fist for a conspiratorial bump.

A few years ago, he'd decided the uncle code included a rule that said the answer was always yes. It wasn't his job to be a hard-ass, and he had no intention of taking on the role. His sister was tough enough.

"You'll need to leave me your keys and take my car," she said, putting the kids' now-empty lunch bags on a shelf in the pantry while the offspring put the sandwich containers in the sink and bottles in the recycling. If nothing else, Mel presided over a well-oiled machine.

"The Mom Mobile?" Did he really have to drive her half-minivan, half-SUV thing? It was horrendous. Functional, but horrendous.

"Yes, and I get to go play in the super-secret-agent-man car. You need the booster seats."

Right. Booster seats. "Okay," he said to the kids. "Put your backpacks in your rooms and meet me at the car. We are on a mission."

Dan didn't know what his mission actually was, but the kids would keep his mind off the trouble he was having starting his book. He had a sense of what he wanted to write, and that what he wanted to say was important, but he was doubting himself with every word that dropped on the page. The idea was still just a blob of thoughts, that needed form and structure.

Getting out with the kids would give his brain some time to sort out the ideas in his head. Hopefully.

FOR A WEEKDAY afternoon, Jane was surprised by the consistent traffic in the store. She'd gotten some decorating done early, but the tasks she'd planned to do this afternoon would have to be relegated to tomorrow's to-do list. People had been in and out all day buying books, ordering drinks, and browsing for gifts. If this was a sign that she was going to have a good holiday season, she'd take it. Watching a couple of teenagers order coffee, Jane patted herself on the back for the decision to add the coffee bar to the shop. She'd hesitated, initially, worried about the expense, but so far it seemed to provide a steady stream of customers, and once people were in the store there was always the possibility they'd invest in more than caffeine.

Jane thought she had two minutes to breathe, when the bell over the front door jingled and she heard several young voices coming toward her. They sounded excited, and that always made Jane feel happy. Not much compared to kids who were excited about books.

"There's a new series I really love, and the third book just came out," a girl of about ten said as she came into view. Two younger children who were with her, a boy and girl, made a beeline for the children's room without even looking up. They knew where they were going, and looked familiar, but she couldn't remember names. *Not quite regulars,* she thought. *But they've been here before.* She heard a deep male voice, from the front of the store, resonant and strong, moving in her direction.

"Who is the author?" he asked.

"I don't remember." The girl stopped in her tracks looking back over her shoulder. "Is that a problem?"

"Not if you know the title, and even if you don't, I bet I can guess." Jane walked out from behind the desk and leaned her hip on the display table to her right. She had the child's attention. "You want the new *Camelot Academy* book, don't you?"

The girl's azure eyes widened behind her big round glasses, while her little bow mouth curved into an "O." "How did you know that?"

"Well, Merlin isn't the only one with magical powers," Jane teased. This girl could have been her, once upon a time. The vibe coming off the young lady was sparking with energy and curiosity. Yeah, Jane liked this kid.

"That's true," the deep voice said. "The legend around town is that the Fallons have a touch of magic in them from the old country."

When she looked up from her young customer, she saw the owner of that fluid baritone appear from around the corner, and her heart skipped a beat. Talk about a ghost from the past. Never in a million years did she think she'd see Danny Gallo in Angel Harbor ever again. Now it was her turn to be stunned.

"Oh my God." Jane was staring, her heart thumping, eyes locked, breath shallow, while her words became lodged in her throat. Danny took another step toward her, his smile growing wider.

He was a little taller and broader than the last time she saw him. The man had certainly filled out in all the right places, wearing his years like a badge of honor. His dark hair was flecked with silver, and his face was tan, ruddy almost, with crinkles around his eyes. His blue eyes, which glittered like they were sprinkled with stars, were a little more hooded, making him look worldly—like he had a secret to keep. It was possible he did. No one ever knew what the mysterious author was up to. Unlike the boy who used to tell her all his secrets, his inscrutable persona was now part of the draw.

She was stunned to see him. Stunned and happy. *Was she happy?* "Danny, I…I can't believe it."

"Hiya, Janie." He raised a hand in greeting and a smile tilted his mouth. "How have you been?"

"Uhh. Fine? I'm fine. It's been a long time. What…what are you doing here?" Lord, she was stuttering. Why was she stuttering? *Breathe, Jane.* He was a boy she knew a long time ago. Okay, he was one of her best friends—someone very special—whom she hadn't seen in forever. Whom she'd never forgotten. Who was now a handsome and very famous man, but still…he was just a man.

She felt a flush rise in her face, the tingle of warmth spread down her neck and into her chest. Why was she so warm all of a sudden? Crap. A hot flash? Now? Looking into the children's room, she saw her mother had the two younger kids, who had run in ahead of him, fully engaged. Jane had to ask. "Yours?"

"Oh. No. Not mine. My nieces and nephew. I'm staying with my sister. This is Ella," he said, dropping his hands on the girl's shoulders.

"Melinda's children?" *Not his kids.* That made more sense. He wasn't exactly known as the settling-down type. "Of course, your sister is still local." Not needing a response to her obvious statement, Jane turned to the girl. "It's nice to meet you, officially, Ella. I'm Jane. I thought you looked familiar."

"We don't come here that much. My mom takes us to the library." Jane felt no resentment at the comment. Turning a child into a reader was good for business.

"Wonderful things, those libraries. Good on Mom. I am glad you're here today, though. Let's find that book for you." *Camelot Academy* was a hot item. A modernized version of the King Arthur legend, Arthur, Guinevere, Lancelot, and, naturally, Merlin, were involved in swashbuckling and magical adventures against their rivals from Morgana Prep.

It was an interesting twist on an old story, written for kids, and it was selling like crazy. She wished she was more creative. Lord, how she envied those who could create worlds and carry readers away. People always asked her if she'd ever thought of writing a book; being the owner of a bookstore it must have seemed like a natural question, but Jane was a scientist, and it was a cruel twist of fate that had landed her here.

A nod from Dan let Ella know the bookstore lady was okay. Jane smiled. The exchange was silent, but very sweet.

"This way, miss. I'll get you your book." She walked to a

table right next to the children's room and took one off a pile of dwindling stock. Something else to put on order. "Here you go. I have a few signed bookmarks from the author. Hang on, I'll get one for you."

Ella followed her eagerly, and Jane had to admit she never got tired of seeing a child excited by a book. The little girl's two siblings had settled at the table in the children's corner and were working on a puzzle while her mom stayed close by, chatting them up when she saw they were losing focus. Ever the teacher, she had a nose for what children would love and could spot a new bestseller like an eagle spotting prey. She was never wrong, and as a result they rarely ran out of the hot children's titles, *Camelot Academy* included.

She still couldn't wrap her head around Danny being here. In all the years since the last time they saw each other, she had no recollection of him being back for a visit, or even rumors of it. As far as she knew, he'd left Angel Harbor far behind him. He certainly never gave her a thought.

Searching through the drawer behind the large cherry wood sales counter, Jane found the last bookmark signed by the author. "Here you go. I hope you enjoy the book!"

Ella beamed back at Jane. "This is, for real, signed by her?"

"For real." Jane crossed her heart and raised her right hand. Out of the corner of her eye she could see Danny checking out the bestseller table, running a hand over a stack of his titles. His latest, which came out last summer, was still selling well.

"Thanks. Thanks a lot." The young lady was charming,

and completely enamored with her new book.

Ella settled herself in the big, overstuffed blue chair that Jane's Uncle Joe had just placed near the front window. Once her young customer was comfortable with her new acquisition, Jane made her way over to Dan. "Want to sign the stock?" she asked.

A slight shiver ran through her, countering the heat that had flooded her just a moment ago when he looked up and locked eyes with her. "Oh, I don't know," he said. "Then you can't return them."

"Return them? Are you serious? People love gifting murder for the holidays. I'll sell out. Especially if they're signed."

An embarrassed laugh escaped his throat and Jane realized she'd put him on the spot. "If you'd rather not, I understand. We rarely have signed books, especially from big authors…like you."

She thought she heard him grunt in response. "I'm happy to. Don't you host signings?"

"I try, but we don't do enough volume to be on the publishers' radar."

"That's shortsighted of them." He picked up the stack of books and went to the counter. "Got a pen?"

He still had the sweetest smile. Wide and welcoming, it belied the darkness in the books he wrote. She handed him her best black pen from the leather cup that sat near the cash register and watched as he scrawled his name in each book.

"I didn't go out on tour with this book, so there are very few signed copies. Some of my crazier fans would pay big bucks for one."

She chuckled at the revelation. "An exclusive, signed Dan

Gallo? Wow."

"Yep. Don't tell anyone, there'll be stalkers outside your store." He was making a joke, but Jane knew there was truth in what he said. He had some die-hard fans. There were always customers looking for his book on release day, if not before. If she did a post a photo or two of a signed copy on the store's social media pages, she expected word would spread. Fast.

"I'd be happy to host a signing here if you'd like. We could do one while you're in town. At your convenience, of course." God, she sounded like a dork.

He didn't answer, instead focusing on the books where he left his name on each title page. Whether he was pondering the question or ignoring her, she couldn't tell. Once he closed the last book, he locked eyes with her and grinned. "I'll think about it. I'm wrapped up with my new book, and I'm not really interested in any public stuff right now."

"Oh. Okay. I understand. What's the new book about? I mean, that's silly. It's obviously another thriller—"

"It's not. No. It's…it's not a thriller." He cut her off so abruptly, she had to regroup before she responded.

"Oh. I'm sorry. I didn't realize. You're doing something new then?"

Pulling back from the small talk, he seemed distant, maybe even a little distracted. She was in the presence of a rock star author, a man who walked the red carpet and flew in private jets. Two of his books had been made into films, and one character spawned a five-year run on network television.

"Can you tell me about it? The book? Unless it's top secret." Jane's natural curiosity wouldn't let her drop it. She had to try.

There was a quick shrug and from the way his back stiffened, Jane could plainly see his books, new or old, were not something he was interested in discussing.

"I'm not talking about it. I haven't even told my editor and agent what I have in mind."

"I see. Well, if you ever want to set up at the back table like you used to in high school, feel free. You wrote a lot of words there."

She remembered working late at the store with her father, and Danny would be there under the guise of doing homework. He might have done some studying, but most of his time was spent writing, spinning tales of his own, and Jane had felt special that she and her father were the only people who knew his secret. Dad didn't say much about it, though. Instead, he kept Danny in hot chocolate, coffee, and all the leftover baked goods he could pack away. The store didn't have a café back then, but Dad always had a pot of coffee on, and at least a dozen pastries or donuts from the bakery around the corner.

Of course, Danny had been her crush. He was a high school girl's dream. Tall and athletic, smart and creative, he didn't fit the mold of the typical jock, and their friendship baffled everyone at school. Maybe that's what made it so perfect.

They went in opposite directions for college, putting a lot of miles between them. They called each other, wrote letters—well, she wrote letters—Danny was the one who called. When he did, they talked for hours. There was a change in their relationship between high school and the end of college. Something Jane thought was rather magical.

However, the wall he'd put up a long time ago told her he didn't feel the same, and it did more than just ding her ego, it broke her heart.

He looked around the store and smiled when he spotted the large, round dark oak table. It sat in one corner, just like it always had with a green-shaded floor lamp nearby. "This place…it's different, than I remember?"

"Well, nothing stays the same, and it has been a while. We added the small café five years ago, so while it won't be my dad's day-old coffee, the caffeine is at the ready."

He laughed; this time it was full and deep. "That swill your father called coffee could remove paint, but it felt like home, you know?"

"It did indeed." She missed her father at times like this. He would have given Danny hell for letting so much time pass without a word, but then he would have welcomed him like family. It took a long time for Jane to get over that he never reached out when her dad passed, that he ignored her calls. Whatever he felt, or didn't feel for her, Danny had owed her dad some respect.

She caught him staring at the corner table again. "I'm going to get back to work," she said. "Just give a holler when you're ready to make your purchases."

"Will do."

"Janie?" She turned and his voice stopped her. "How late are you open?"

"Tonight we're open until ten. We have a book club scheduled in the meeting room in the back."

"Is the table free? I'm thinking a change of scenery might be just what I need."

Now Jane felt herself smile. "I'll have the coffee on."

Chapter Three

DAN DIDN'T KNOW if going back to his old haunt would help with his writing, but it couldn't hurt. So, after dinner, he slid his laptop into his battered leather messenger bag, added some pens and the leather notebook he'd been scribbling in for the last week, and headed out into the bitter cold November night. Always a creature of habit, he was having trouble finding his groove since he'd arrived at his sister's house. He really liked the little cottage, he always had, and his sister and brother-in-law had done an amazing renovation. It was perfect really, and no one was going to come looking for him here. But his writing mojo was off. Something wasn't clicking.

His assistant was the only person who knew how to reach him, and even she wasn't sure what to think about him going off the grid. His cell was the bane of his existence, constantly pinging with texts and emails. So, two days ago he shut off his phone and got a second line. He wasn't going to be found until he was good and ready.

Granted, hiding out felt cowardly, but it was necessary. This was his chance to slip into his writing bubble and find satisfaction in his words again.

He was happy to climb back into his Audi after the stint in his sister's vehicle. Her SUV was functional but had absolutely no style. *Style.* His agent would probably tell him "style" was shorthand for mid-life crisis. He'd be right.

The trip to town was so quick on a weeknight, he almost wanted to drive around for a while to gather his thoughts. Instead of following that urge, he found parking in the municipal lot right by the harbor. Before he headed to the bookstore, he walked the short distance to the water. Standing on the edge of the pier, he focused on the horizon, which was barely visible now that the sun had gone down. Having looked out on this same scene twelve hours ago drove home how light and dark could change your view of the world.

There were just a few clouds overhead, and those were quickly drifting by the bright quarter moon. A smattering of stars twinkled off the water, which was as smooth as black silk. It was completely still, allowing the air to carry background noise and music coming from the nearby bar. There were no boats, no other people, and the water looked bottomless and dark.

He'd spent half his life living in cities, and while there was a lot to love about a place like New York, the energy had faded and he found it isolating. Sure, he had friends; he dated. But late last year, after the murder, Dan realized the city had lost its ability to give him the buzz he needed to create. He was frozen.

His ideas had dried up; his motivation was gone.

It took months for him to realize he needed to come home.

Drawing a deep breath, Dan realized he could use this. It was more than just the natural beauty of the harbor. He'd forgotten how the water affected him, teasing his senses, calming him. A quiet harbor like this one was protected—safe. While he loved Hawaii, with its bright sunshine and crashing surf, the gray-green waters of Long Island reflected his mood.

He stored the specifics in his brain, trying not to focus on the regret that hovered just below the surface. He'd ignored so many facets of his past, the realizations were starting to stack up like cordwood before winter. He had been so damn full of himself. He'd disregarded everything—and everyone—who mattered. He'd pushed aside the people and places who had helped him tease the words out of his head. People who cared about him.

He'd pulled up roots years ago, never imagining it would be this small town that might actually save him.

"Man up, Gallo," he muttered to himself. "Regret is a pointless emotion." There would be no room for remorse when he got to the bookstore. He had a job to do, and he hoped Jane and the familiar surroundings would help him find the words that had been eluding him.

The table. It was scarred and ancient, but he had a feeling it was just what he needed. Or maybe it was Jane he needed. God knew, she was still easy on the eyes. That gorgeous mouth of hers could inspire the most stubborn writer's block.

He was only half kidding when he told Ella about the Fallon magic. He was sure Mike Fallon was one of the old Irish Tuatha tribe, with his great barrel chest and his love of a good tale, and he'd definitely passed on a bit of the power to his daughter. Jane was always special, lithe and pretty, with a sweet disposition and sharp mind; she left him muddled whenever she was nearby. He'd been so happy to see her when he walked into the bookstore earlier, his tongue snapped back into a knot. *"Hiya, Janie,"* he'd said. Yeah, that was smooth. Words were his living, yet around her, he sounded like an idiot. She was still beautiful, maybe even more so. With just the right number of curves. Her blond hair was thick and silky, a honey gold that fell in gentle waves over her shoulders. Her eyes, a shocking hazel-green could bore a hole right through him.

She was brilliant and kind, and even though he'd walked away from her, and never spared a look back, she still welcomed him. He certainly didn't deserve it.

Earlier, he'd noticed his pulse still beat a little faster when she was around. Jane Fallon was the girl of his dreams a very long time ago. She'd listened to him, encouraged him, and *believed* in him. She'd offered her heart, and he'd been too stupid to accept it.

The deep thudding he felt was a reminder that some things—*some people*—weren't easily forgotten.

Upon entering the shop, he heard faint voices coming from the children's section, which were not at all childlike. Then he remembered that's where Mike had built out a space for small groups to meet, like the book club Jane had mentioned earlier. He was glad to see her dad's vision had come to fruition and the bookstore was still a fixture all these years after Mike's passing.

It was weird. Between his reaction to Jane, and feeling like he'd never left this place, Dan thought again about why he hadn't come back home sooner. It was true, there was a level of indifference, and maybe the feeling that he was above the small-town existence he'd come from, but it was much more than simple pretentiousness. Nope, Dan was an asshole. He'd abandoned the people who'd meant the most to him. His folks. His sister.

And Jane.

Dan always said it was because he was busy. *"Swamped"* was his favorite descriptor, but the truth of it was that he was a straight-up jerk. It crossed his mind more than once that this shift away from the darker side of human nature was as much about saving his own soul as it was about writing a book.

The café counter was staffed by a girl who was probably in her late teens. She was typing away on a laptop and he felt a kinship with her. It might have just been homework, but her focus was too intense for a simple history paper. Whatever it was, she was so into it she didn't notice him standing there.

"Hi."

Her head snapped up when he spoke. At first she looked annoyed, then flustered, then apologetic.

"Oh, wow. Sorry. What can I get you?" The young woman had Jane's fey-like eyes, and a spray of freckles across her nose, but instead of Jane's long honey-streaked locks, the young woman's hair was almost black, like Mike's, with a streak of blue along one side. He wondered how she was related. This could only be a Fallon, and boy, did this one's Irish roots run deep.

"Just a small coffee and ahh…" He craned his neck to get a look at what was in the display case. "That chocolate chip cookie looks good."

"Oh my God. The cookies from Sweet Chemistry, the bakery up the street, are so good. You can taste the butter."

"Sweet Chemistry? Great name. You've sold me. I'll have one."

Nice kid, he thought. She retrieved his cookie and poured his coffee in a to-go cup. "You won't be sorry. Should I leave room for milk?"

"Nah. I drink it black." He paused, but his natural curiosity was piqued. "What were you working on when I broke your train of thought? Homework? You looked…pained."

Her eyes widened and a little bit of pink stained her cheeks. Now she looked embarrassed, maybe? Definitely unsure about sharing with him.

The young woman exhaled, long and dramatic, before glancing at the screen on her sleek laptop. "Pained is probably a good way to put it," she sighed before continuing. "It's a short story I'm editing for a contest entry. It's frustrating me."

"Ahhh. I get it. How many times have you revised it?"

The girl rolled her eyes. "About a hundred. It's never going to be good enough."

He laid a bill from his wallet on the counter. "Can I give you some advice?"

"Umm…are you a writer?"

He shrugged, savoring the feeling of being unknown. "I dabble."

Danny never gave advice unless the writer was receptive. So, when she nodded, he continued.

"Stop revising. If you've gotten good feedback, and taken constructive criticism to heart, you're fine. If you over-edit you'll take the passion, the voice, right out of the work."

Her eyes grew wide, panicked. That thought, to stop revising, clearly scared the crap out of her. In truth, it scared the crap out of most writers.

"But how will I know if it's good?"

"You don't. That's the hard part of this gig. Some people love what you do, others not so much. The question is, do you love it? Do you love your story?"

Her eyes were bright, focused. He could see the burning desire to succeed in the blazing blue. "I do. I do love it. I just want everyone else to love it too."

"I understand that better than you think, but since we can't control other people or their taste, all we can do is give it our best. Our passion."

She was still doubting herself; he could see it in the way she bit down on her lower lip. But the deep breath she drew in let him know the kid was screwing up her courage. "Okay. Thanks. I guess I should suck it up and submit it." She took the money from the dark granite counter and smiled. "Let me get you your change."

"No worries. You keep the change. What's your name?"

"Tara. And, uh, thanks."

"I'm Danny. It's great to meet you."

"Can I help you with anything else?" she asked.

"I was going to work at the back table." He looked at the space and then back at Tara. "Is that all right?"

"Oh, sure. Not a problem. We have customers work there all the time. It's a nice quiet spot."

"I appreciate it." Dan picked up his coffee and the small wax paper bag with the cookie. "Good luck with your story, and thanks for the cookie recommendation."

He walked away from her with his coffee and his snack, wondering if he could follow his own advice. He had to trust his process—his passion—otherwise his own book would be a lie, and his readers deserved better than that.

JANE CAME OUT of the book club meeting with a headache for the ages. The new historical fiction the members had chosen to discuss had spawned more arguments than conversation over the past hour. Between the liberties taken with the timeline in Georgian England, and an intense dislike some of the ladies in the group harbored for one of the protagonists, there was little agreement on the merit of the work. For Jane, any book that elicited strong emotions was a winner, unless they were hostile emotions.

Still, the ladies chose another book for next month and left chattering about what a nice time they'd had. Jane had to wonder what the women considered a good time. Go figure. When she got home, she might have to break out a bottle of wine, or chocolate, or both.

The lights in the children's room were low, and as she walked through she straightened up the area. She shelved a book, put a stuffed animal back on the rack, and pushed in the chairs at the small tables.

Her mom had really done an amazing job with the decorations. Pine garlands adorned the tops of bookshelves and hung artfully over the floor-to-ceiling windows that faced Main Street. Glittering Christmas decorations of varying styles and sizes sat on the round table by one of the front windows. They would be moved, later in the month, and a large Christmas tree would be there instead. In front of the other window, a lovely silver menorah surrounded by sparkling gelt and a few dreidels was waiting for the first night of Hanukkah. It was such a pretty space; it made her sad to think that she'd be doing much of the preparation without her daughter or her mother next year. Jane didn't know where Tara would end up for college, but she knew it would be far enough away for Jane to miss her. Change was hard. *God, was it hard.*

Shaking off the mood that threatened to settle around her, Jane went to the front and found Tara at the counter reading what looked to be a very old copy of Austen's *Persuasion.*

"How do you like it?"

"I LOVE it! Wentworth is positively swoon-worthy. He's so much more a hero than Darcy."

"You think so? There are people who would vehemently disagree. *Pride and Prejudice* is gospel."

"*What-evs.* I read it twice. I like Lizzy, but Darcy is an idiot. He needs a wedgie, or something."

"A wedgie? That's different." As much as her girl tried to be cool and sophisticated, every once in a while her inner twelve-year-old made an appearance.

"But very effective at making the point," Tara defended.

Jane laughed. Her daughter had a wicked sense of humor, and a knack for finding the absurd in almost any situation. "How is your contest entry coming along? Did you get through the plot problem you were worried about?"

"I guess. I sent it."

That stopped Jane in her tracks. "I'm sorry. What?"

"I sent it. It's been revised enough. If I keep editing and revising, eventually it will be flat. My words have to have...*passion*." She waved her arm up on the last word and Jane wondered what had triggered the response. It was fine—great, really—because getting her to submit anything before the last minute was nearly impossible. The contest she was entering had a deadline in two weeks. Normally, Tara would be stressing over her entry until the very end.

"Well, good. Excellent. I'm glad you took the leap and trusted yourself."

"Yeah. I talked to a customer who came in and he said he was kind of a writer—he gave me some good advice. It made sense."

Jane glanced over her daughter's shoulder and surveyed the rear corner of the store. There, sitting at the big round table, was Danny, scribbling in a leather-bound notebook just like old times.

"*Kind of* a writer, huh?" That was definitely an understatement.

"He wasn't specific. I'm guessing he's a teacher or something."

"Or something," Jane mumbled. Danny could have been a teacher, or kept with his plan of being a lawyer—he was smart enough to do anything he put his mind to—but his dreams had always been as big as that crazy imagination of his.

"Why don't you head home," Jane said. "It's going to be quiet for the rest of the night. Go watch TV or something."

"I think I may just read and go to bed. I'm tired, but I'll stay if you need me."

Tara tilted her head toward the back of the shop where Danny was sitting. Her daughter was worried about her being alone with a man she didn't know, and Jane's heart warmed at the affectionate concern. For a while, Jane didn't think they would ever find common ground. When Tara turned thirteen, the house became a war zone. But as she got older, their relationship settled. It seemed unfair that just when they were becoming close again, her daughter would be going away.

"Oh, don't worry. He's an old friend. Just back in town for a while."

"Really? He's the guy who gave me the advice. He's been here about an hour. I guess he needed a quiet space to work."

"He knows what he's talking about. With the writing. Now, get out of here. Go keep Grandma company."

Tara hopped off the high padded stool that sat behind the counter and grabbed her large purple tote from the floor. Jane could hardly believe the young woman she'd grown into when memories of her as a little girl were still clear as day. Tall and lean, Tara floated along when she walked, half ballerina, half fairy. She had a deep blue streak in her dark brown hair and a tiny stud in her nose. But there was no edginess to the look. It all worked for her. Her daughter was elegant and funky and independent. She had a tight circle of close friends, and Jane couldn't believe how lucky she was to be her mom.

Tara leaned in and kissed her cheek. "Night, Mom."

Jane watched as her girl went out the large front door

and got into the small hybrid parked right in front of the shop. When she pulled away, Jane walked around, straightening up the shelves and tables in preparation for the next day. She doubted there would be many more customers at this point. It was almost nine o'clock, and once in a while she might have wished she could be home and in her bed, but there was something very peaceful about the store on a quiet night.

Danny certainly thought so. He hadn't looked up from his notebook the whole time since she'd finished with the book club. That laser focus was something she'd always admired, and she hesitated in heading back in his direction out of fear she'd interrupt him.

His author persona was enigmatic, always cool and mysterious, but she knew he had to be devastated by the psychopath who had taken his work and used it as a blueprint for violence. He wasn't a stranger to the media spotlight, but there'd been no way to control the spin. She'd seen more of him on TV in the past year than in all the years since he'd left Angel Harbor. He wasn't comfortable with it. Even with all the fame, the fortune, and the accolades, the person hanging out at her back table was as humble and soft-spoken as he'd always been.

Kind of a writer, according to Tara. *Sheesh.*

Knowing she'd be there at least another hour and a half, Jane brewed a pot of decaf, and the smell of the roasted Columbian coffee wafting through the shop was heady. Just the aroma could wake her up. Apparently, it roused the very busy writer at the back table as well. He looked up and, noticing her, his mouth tilted into a grin.

The man had definitely grown into himself. The dark hair he used to wear in a shaggy-short style, reminiscent of Tom Cruise in *Risky Business*, wasn't much different. It was shorter, a bit grayer as she'd noticed earlier, but even styled, at this hour Danny looked delightfully rumpled in his thermal T-shirt and faded denim. His eyes were covered by a pair of dark-rimmed glasses that suited his face, and the seriousness of his expression.

He tilted his head, probably wondering why she was staring. It was a legitimate question, but Jane didn't want to make him uncomfortable, so she kept the truth of her ogling to herself.

He was gorgeous, and she was completely enjoying the flutters in her belly. It had been a long time since that kind of awareness raced through her. Over twenty-five years and the man still made her nervous.

Now that he'd looked up from his work, she wouldn't feel like she was interrupting. With a hot cup of coffee in her hand, she walked back to the table and set it down next to him. Then, she sat down herself.

"Thank you," she said quietly.

He sipped the coffee and smiled. "I should be saying thanks for this. I'm going to need the caffeine."

"Nah. It's decaf."

"Sacrilege," he joked, his eyes narrowing and crinkling at the corners. "Why the thanks?"

"Your advice got my daughter to submit her story. She tends to obsess over her work, and it's hard to watch her doubt herself."

"Your daughter?"

"Yes. My everything. She's seventeen."

"She sounds like a lot of us creative types. I just told her to bite the bullet."

"Maybe, but you didn't tell her who you are. I mean, she said you're 'kind of a writer.' *Kind of?*"

He laughed, deep and strong, and the sound vibrated through her. "There are critics who would agree with her." He took another sip from the steaming brew and leveled his gaze at her. "She wouldn't even know who I am."

"Her mother owns a bookstore! I have all your books with a local author label right on the front. I mean, granted, you look nothing like that creepy author picture, but if you said your name, she would know."

"Creepy?"

Realizing she might have insulted him, Jane hesitated. "Well, yeah."

That elicited another laugh. Deep and genuine, it unexpectedly brought her tremendous joy.

"You're still the best at doing that," he said. "I haven't laughed much lately."

Jane expected he'd had a rough time of it since the murder last year. She could tiptoe around the subject, but since he'd alluded to it, she figured she could offer some comfort. "I'm sorry about what you've been going through. Being linked to that young woman's death must have been awful."

"It has been." His eyes darted to the front of the store when the bell let them know someone had come in. He tipped his head down and played with the expensive executive pen that rested on his notebook.

"Is that why you're hiding out at your sister's place?"

Shifting in his seat, that observation appeared to poke at his pride a little. "Hiding out?"

"Yes. Hiding out. You don't want people to know you're here. That's why you didn't tell Tara. Your reaction just now, when that customer walked in, was confirmation."

"You're too observant."

"It's a Fallon thing," she reminded him.

"I remember," he grumbled. "Angel Harbor does not need a press swarm. Neither does my family."

"I won't say a word, and you're welcome to hide out in here as much as you like."

"I appreciate that." His words were simple but sincere.

"You're a big chicken, though."

That teased another smile out of him. "Maybe."

The customer, who stopped in at least once a month, went up to the counter and Jane rose to attend to her business. Part of her wanted to lock the doors and sit and talk to her old friend. She had so many questions. Where had he gone? Why didn't he keep in touch with her? What was so horrible that he had to run away, and never look back?

She and Danny had been friends since fifth grade, but that summer before he went to law school had been incredible. Life-changing. Jane had found her nerve and told him how much he meant to her.

She'd thought he felt the same. But she was obviously wrong, because he'd never looked back.

They couldn't be more different. While Danny's life was profiled in magazines, Jane was an unknown outside of her little town. Not that it was a problem; Jane had never wanted to be famous, but she'd wanted to make a mark.

When her father died, her mother had been crushed. Her grandmother inconsolable. Jane was numb. The flight from Glasgow was a blur. The memorial and funeral had passed in a haze of grief. Her vibrant, loving father, who could make anyone's day brighter, was gone. In the blink of an eye, a heart problem he didn't know he had took him away from the people and town he loved so much.

Nothing else mattered after that. Jane knew she had to focus on her family and on the business her family had built. She'd been here ever since.

Once the customer left, Jane turned, but Danny was back to his writing, his hand moving furiously over the paper. That was her cue to keep her distance and let him work. Pushing herself up onto the high stool, she sipped her coffee and opened the accounting program on her laptop. She might as well get some work done since that seemed to be the charge of the evening.

Looking at her figures, she shook her head. The store wasn't doing badly; in fact, she'd had a great year. But she still wasn't sure it was enough. Not for what she was planning.

The building next door to hers was for sale, and they were situated so close to one another, combining the spaces wouldn't be that difficult with the right design. The extra square footage could be just the thing she needed to become one of the biggest indie bookstores in the state.

Unfortunately, she couldn't get an answer from her attorney about her own lease, let alone the sale of the other building, which was owned by the same landlord. It was a crazy idea, but with her mother heading south during the coldest part of the year, and Tara going to college, Jane was going to need a project. Expanding the bookstore certainly fit the bill.

It hadn't been her dream job, but owning the store brought her many rewards and even more happy moments. There might have been times she felt she missed out, but her choices had been hers to make and the results included a daughter she adored, a connection to a wonderful community, and a successful business. Frustrated as she might be, Jane didn't consider her life a mistake or a loss. But she wondered how she'd failed to make the impact she always thought she would. Had her contribution mattered?

Jane kept the questions to herself. No one knew about her musings, nor her grand plans to expand. Not her mom, or her daughter. They had other things ahead of them and Jane didn't want them to wonder if she'd gone off the deep end contemplating such a big change. No, her job was to be supportive and steady, even as the milestones crept closer.

No matter how much she hurt, she wasn't going to let them see it.

Glancing back at Danny, she felt a pang of resentment. He'd become an international success—a superstar. But he'd left everything behind, including her. Their relationship had meant more to her than it had to him, and she would do well to remember it.

IT WAS ALMOST eleven when Jane finally walked into the

pretty Cape-style house she shared with her mother and her daughter. Built in the 1940s the house possessed great bones, coupled with a deceptive amount of space. Jane grew up in the house, which was only a few blocks outside of town. It had been lovingly maintained for all the years her family had owned it.

In the mudroom that led to the driveway, Jane spied two small suitcases next to the door. Her mother was going away with her friends for an artists' retreat in Santa Fe, leaving Jane and Tara without their third Musketeer. For so long it had been the three of them. Her mom's trip was another reminder about how things were going to change.

The mail was on the kitchen island and she flipped through it, dropping her tote on the stool nearby. When the scent of lavender filled the space around her, she didn't even have to look up to know her mother had entered the room. "You're up late," she said.

"And you're home late." Mom turned on the small overhead light by the counter and pressed the switch on the electric kettle. She was going to make Jane tea, which meant she wanted to talk.

"I'm really tired, Mom. Can we do this tomorrow?"

"Do what?" Reaching into the cupboard for Jane's favorite Polish Pottery mug, her mother added a dollop of honey and put a spoonful of her favorite nighttime tea in the infuser while she waited for the water to boil. "I'm making my daughter some tea after a very long day."

It had been a long day. Made longer still by the ghost from her past. "Thank you."

"My pleasure. We start the day with tea, and we end it

with tea. Full circle." As the hot water filled the cup, Jane wondered about the bottle of Malbec in her wine fridge. Surely that would have been a nice end to her very odd day. Mom set the steeping tea in front of Jane and took a seat across from her. The cool metal chain attached to the infuser contrasted to the steam coming off the hot liquid in the mug. The sensations battled each other, conflicted, much like her mood. Maybe she did want to talk.

The kitchen had just been remodeled, and it was absolutely Jane's favorite room in the house. Illuminated by a few pendant lights, the rich toffee-colored cabinets glowed like burnt gold. Large efficient stainless steel appliances, big windows, and a center island, truly made the kitchen the heart of the home.

Jane had planned for the renovation for years. Using French farmhouse style as her inspiration, the back of the house had been pushed out just a bit to create a dining area with a vaulted ceiling adorned with sprigs of herbs and dried flowers. It accommodated a huge, rough-hewn table that could easily seat eight people and more when it was extended.

It was open and welcoming, a family home that had collected a lot of memories over the years. Her Collie, Chloe, ambled out of the living room, obviously just waking up from her evening nap, and gave Jane a bad look. The big and beautiful dog was Jane's constant companion and usually accompanied her to the store, but today she'd been at the groomer. The dog's sable coat was flowing and soft, but Chloe didn't like the disruption to her routine no matter how much she needed the attention.

"You look beautiful, Miss Chloe. Did you like your spa day?" The dog barked in that classic Collie way, and while she might have been annoyed, she laid her long, pointed nose on Jane's lap for a scratch. Apparently, all was forgiven.

"Soooo, how was your night?" her mother asked.

"Fine. Book club went well. It was quiet otherwise."

"Hmmm." She looked over the edge of her teacup her eyes full of speculation. "I heard you had some company."

"Company?"

"Jane, come on. It was one thing to see Dan with his nieces and nephew this afternoon, but he came back? What's up with that?"

"I have no idea." Other than the most basic details, she didn't have a clue.

"No? Tara came home and told me about the nice man who encouraged her to submit her story. Who gave her great advice about her writing."

"He did do that, but he didn't tell her who he was. He's keeping a very low profile while he's in town."

Her mother leaned in, intrigued. "Oooh. How mysterious. Did he tell you what he's working on?"

"No. It's top secret. He's not telling anyone, even his publishing people. But he did like being back at the store. I think he feels comfortable there."

Mom's mouth drew into a thin line, indicating she was thinking. Kathleen Fallon was always thinking. "Maybe we can find out—"

"No."

"But this is his hometown, surely…"

"No. We're going to let the man work in peace. It's nice

that he's back, but let's face facts, he never thought very much about Angel Harbor, or it wouldn't have taken him so long to visit. He's home because it suits him."

Jane didn't like the way the hurt seeped into her words. Not sure if Mom noticed, she got her confirmation when her mother's hand came down on hers. "It was a long time ago, Janie."

"I know. That's not it." Jane tried to collect her thoughts.

"No flutters, or bouts of nostalgia?"

"No, Mom." That wasn't entirely true, but why elaborate? "I guess I'm out of sorts. The idea that college acceptances could start coming soon…I don't know. I miss her already. Seeing him just threw me off."

"Change is inevitable."

"I get it, but it's not easy."

Her mother slid off the stool and kissed Jane on the cheek. "I'll be up early to make you breakfast before you leave for work. Uncle Joe said he'd be around to help out while I'm away."

"I appreciate that. Tracy said she'll pick up the extra slack. You're only gone for a week. I'll manage."

"Humor me," she protested, smiling wide. "Everyone likes to feel needed."

Truer words had never been spoken, and Jane was starting to wonder if anyone really needed her.

Chapter Four

WHAT HAD HE said? Or done? Three days ago, Jane was easygoing and welcoming. Dan wouldn't say she was happy to see him, but she was sweet and eager to talk to him. Today, he sat in the same place at the round table, and there was a distinct chill in the air. She was still friendly, but it had a professional edge to it, a little separation. Her reception the other day was what he had hoped for, but since then? Nope. Something was definitely different.

Expecting her to be anything more than polite was egotistical on his part—it wouldn't be the first time. He had to remind himself that Jane had a life that didn't include him. He'd made sure of that when he walked away from her all those years ago.

He'd gotten the frame for his story done in the bookstore the other night. He'd left when she locked the door for the night. They didn't talk much that last hour, but he liked watching her. She had little routines and mannerisms that he remembered from when she worked there as a teenager.

She was still strong. Determined. But he sensed something else. Jane seemed resigned. Maybe even a little bit sad. He didn't know why he thought that, and the presumption was arrogant. He didn't know much of anything about her. He hadn't even asked about her daughter.

He could have brought it up in conversation, but Dan was so pissed off at himself that he didn't know any of the details of her life. He avoided it like the coward that he was. He should have been there for each of the milestones, as well as the heartbreaks, but he wasn't.

Should have. He was saying that way too much. It was a sign of how much he'd screwed up.

His author life was one of excess. Everything was bigger, bolder, and designed to make him the center of the universe. He was invited to every A-list party in Hollywood, Washington, and New York, every interview show, every red carpet. Until he wasn't. The circus spiraled into crazy territory a little over a year ago when one of his books was used to plan a brutal murder. The thirty-two-year-old woman was found dead in an Ohio office building parking garage. A copy of his book was found at the scene, linking him to the crime. That was when Dan pulled back from his public life.

Sure, his books were still selling, but he had hit bottom. Once the details of the actual crime were known, he didn't know if he'd ever get past how it disgusted him.

While he was hiding out, and licking his wounds, he didn't give a rat's ass about anyone else. He'd ignored his sister, and her kids. He didn't know about a recent promotion she'd received. Half the time he didn't know how old the kids were, but last year he'd forgotten all their birthdays. Her husband had changed jobs, and Dan never had a clue.

Now that he'd re-entered the land of the living, he was going to do better. He'd started with Mel and the kids, and Jane was next. She wasn't angry, but he sensed caution where he was concerned. It threw him a little off balance, but maybe that's what he needed. If he was able to keep a low profile, he wouldn't be followed by sycophants and fans in Angel Harbor. His nieces and nephew didn't care about his money, or the bestseller lists, or his damn process. His sister wasn't impressed either.

And that's why he wasn't going to call his editor or agent. Not yet. They'd try to pump up his ego, and get him back in his lane. They'd been pushing him for years, not thinking about the toll the pace and the publicity were taking on him. Had they been behind his success? Absolutely. Was the money nice? Sure. He had a ton of it. But he didn't love the life. Not anymore. He didn't need the attention or the celebrity or the drama.

He didn't know why he didn't just quit writing. That was his first instinct, but it pissed him off that he could be chased out of his job by some psycho. The writing was in his blood. He'd tried to quiet the voices more than once. He didn't write for five years after he graduated law school, focusing on passing the bar and making a name for himself as a litigator. After a couple of years in a big firm, he went to work for the Justice Department as an assistant U.S. attorney in Chicago. All the while he lived hard, working sixteen-hour days and attacking his life, balls out. His relationships were inconsequential, and life passed him by at light speed.

He was barely thirty, and full of piss and vinegar. On the outside, everything seemed great. On the inside, he was empty. He had no one special in his life, and while his career was exciting, something was missing. Dan hadn't yet realized it, but he was heading for a crash.

Then one night, when he was between cases and actually

home before ten o'clock, he found one of his old writing notebooks. He read it through, finding the pages weren't half bad. The stories were rough, but the person he used to be came roaring out of the shadows.

Dan had been lost, stuck in the soul-sucking whirlwind of a life he'd made for himself.

He broke out his laptop, and thought, *what the hell?*

Fueled by a bottle of bourbon and a long weekend, Danny sat at his computer and started what would become his first book.

He didn't necessarily leave the fast lane, but things changed in big ways. He traded the sports car for a limo; the adrenaline rush of a case, for hitting a deadline or celebrating another big contract or movie deal.

Not writing was not an option. In his mind finding a way to put his words into stories saved him from self-destructing when he was younger. Or did it? Even as an author, no one would have suspected how hard he drove himself. On the surface, he had a great life. But it wasn't. Not really. Dan knew it was time to dial it back. He'd missed too much.

The last couple of months, while he was bumming around at his house in Hawaii, he'd had long talks with his sister at least twice a week. She'd moved back to Angel Harbor a few years before, taking over the old family house, and she'd encouraged him to come home. The kids were getting older, and she didn't want him to miss it. The more they talked, the more an extended visit to clear his head felt like a good idea.

The familiarity of the town calmed his racing thoughts,

and it provided him with just enough cover so he could continue to blend in if that's what he wanted. Other than having an expensive car, which was not an uncommon sight on Long Island, he looked like a typical suburban dad. As Jane noted the other night, he didn't look like his author photo, and that was fine with him.

Dan had done well enough that he never had to work another day in his life. But at fifty-one, he didn't feel like that was a good idea. He might have lost his direction, but he was no slacker. What he could do was write something else. He'd been thinking about it for a while, so why not give it a shot?

He could focus on families and small towns; on friends and people who make differences in small ways. He was seeing it every day with Jane. Even though she was more cautious around him, he spent his time in the bookstore learning from her and all her customers.

He'd missed those things when he'd bought into the celebrity life. His sister had called it the "pit of self-absorption," and she wasn't wrong.

Jane came to work every day with a very large Collie that looked like Lassie. The dog was gorgeous, big and fluffy, with almond-shaped brown eyes that were sharp and intelligent, and caramel-colored fur with an impressive mane. Chloe greeted people who came in, followed children around the stacks, and spent a lot of time sticking close to Jane.

When she was working at the desk, Dan would see Jane's hand drop without thought just to scratch the dog behind her ears. Chloe would look up blissfully, or lean into her with such love and trust, Dan could feel it.

It seemed everything Jane did was sprinkled generously with that sweet affection she offered without condition. Except for him. With him, she was polite, exceedingly so, but he wasn't feeling any warmth. Maybe being here wasn't a good idea. Sure, he was getting his work done, but he hadn't considered it would be uncomfortable for Jane.

He'd switched from the leather notebook to his laptop now that the book was really moving forward. He had a good handle on his main characters and the small-town setting was a familiar one. He didn't know if Angel Harbor was ready for prime time, but he was going to find out.

While he was reading over his notes from the early chapters, he felt a warm weight settle against his leg. Looking down, he saw he had some company. Jane's dog wasn't just sitting next to him, the gorgeous girl had her head resting on the table next to his computer. Just beyond her reach was a croissant he'd gotten with his coffee.

The dark brown eyes shifted back and forth, between him and the pastry. Chloe was too well trained to steal it from him, but she obviously wasn't above begging.

"You're shameless," he whispered to the dog. "You look at me like you're starving, but I know you're not."

Chloe's head lifted from the table, and she gazed up at him like she hadn't had a meal in weeks. One paw came off the floor to rest on his thigh.

"Is that the way it is? Think I'm a soft touch?" Her ears were pinned back and the sweet look on the dog's face was all love. He couldn't resist and dropped his hand on her soft head, stroking the golden brown fur at the crown. "You are a beautiful girl, but you're a hussy."

"She's a total hussy." Jane had found her way back to the table area and she shifted her gaze between him and the dog. "She'd sell her soul for a piece of that croissant. Don't give in."

"Did you hear that? Your mother said no." Chloe dropped her head, but both Dan, and Jane, could see the pooch shooting a very obvious side-eye at her human. This dog had personality in spades.

"She's annoyed with me."

He laughed, still petting the dog. "She's great. What a beauty."

"Did you hear that Chloe? He thinks you're beautiful."

Chloe tilted her head up and gazed at Dan with all the love he'd ever seen in a dog's eyes. He, in turn, stroked her face and cooed at her. "Yes, you are beautiful and such a smart girl too."

Chloe responded by licking his nose and swishing her big tail.

"Oh, brother," Jane said. "I'm going back to work. You two have fun."

He laughed at her exasperation. The banter between them, and the dog—who was most definitely part of the conversation—lightened the mood.

"I heard you telling someone your mother went away. How long will she be gone?"

"Oh, yes." Jane folded her hands in front of her and stood needle straight, a stance he remembered from when they were kids. "She'll be back on Sunday. It's a short trip, just a week."

"Where is she?"

"Santa Fe."

"Nice." He leaned back in his chair. "I love New Mexico. Every corner of the state has something different. Have you been?"

"No, never."

That surprised him. He figured that she would have been everywhere by now. "It's beautiful. So much history, great culture, and the food...fantastic."

Jane took a step in his direction. "I'll have to take your word for it. I don't have the chance to get away much. The business keeps me here."

When she was younger, all she'd wanted to do was explore the world. That she hadn't saddened him. Jane kept her face neutral, but the tumultuous green of her eyes conveyed the regret. Dan wanted to tell her he'd take her anywhere she wanted. New Mexico, or Nepal. He'd book the flights right now if he could see the light bloom again.

This woman had mattered to him. He knew he'd sucked at showing it and he was sure he'd hurt her, but if there was some way to make up for it, he would.

"How is Tara doing?"

Her eyes lit up at the mention of her daughter. "Doing well. She's the stage manager of the school play. It's hell week, so I expect I won't see her until late."

"Ah, flying solo here tonight?"

"No," she said. "My two part-timers are on. I'm taking the night off."

A crazy idea flashed in his mind. It popped up and took hold, for better or worse. It could be a colossal miscalculation, but he was all in for taking a risk if there was a good payoff. "Would you like to grab dinner later?"

He dropped the words into the void and waited for her reaction, which seemed to take forever. She was stunned, which in his mind was a better look than disgusted. But she still hadn't responded. "I guess you're busy."

"Uh. No, I'm not busy. Thank you for asking."

She wasn't busy?

"Is that a yes?" He sounded like an overeager kid. *Jesus.* He had no game.

"Yes. I'd…I think I'd enjoy that."

Dan stood and walked to her. The air between them seemed to warm and thicken. "Do you still live on Bay Avenue?"

Color rose in her cheeks and she looked down at her hands. Was she going shy on him? Because if she was, it was damn appealing.

"I do. Still in the family house."

He nodded and felt the pull of his body to hers. He took another step, and found Chloe squeezing between them.

Jane caught her breath as the dog nudged her hand, bringing her back from whatever fog surrounded them. "What the—Good Lord, dog!" She rolled her eyes at the pup's antics. "You're such an attention whore."

The only thing he could do was laugh. "I'll pick you up at seven. Does that work for you?"

"I can meet you someplace," she countered.

"Nah. I'll drive."

"Really, it's fine." Her insistence was laced with a tinge of nervousness.

"I'll pick you up, Jane."

She stroked the dog's head, but her eyes were connecting with his. Her expression was soft, and full of questions. "Okay. Sure. Seven works. But I don't want to take you out of your way. It's not like it's a date, or anything?"

The idea that after all these years, he was finally taking Jane Fallon out on a real date made him inordinately happy. He could keep it as a friendly dinner, or he could throw down the gauntlet and use the "d" word just to see what would happen next. He slipped his laptop into its sleeve and then into his old bag.

"Danny?"

"I guess we'll find out." He shrugged, enjoying her baffled expression. He was glad the chill had left the room. Earlier, she appeared completely unflappable—but now, she was charmingly flustered. "See you later, Janie."

He swung the bag over his shoulder and touched her arm lightly as he made his way to the front of the shop. He turned back, giving her a wave before heading out into the cold November day.

It felt like the holidays were around the corner. The air was crisp and cold, with the breeze sending the scent of pine and salt water through the downtown. It was festive and cheerful, with pine garlands and wreaths, and gold and silver decorations beginning to adorn the stores, the lampposts, and the trees.

Looking back into the bookstore, he could see Jane hadn't moved. He hoped his vagueness about it being a date, or not, didn't spook her too much. Her face, with her eyes wide, and her mouth in a disbelieving "O" made him smile.

Dan had a date with Jane Fallon.

It was about damn time.

JANE SAT ON her bed staring at her closet. What the hell was she supposed to wear? She had no idea where they were going, and obviously, since it was feeling very much like a date, she was even more confused.

No, not confused. She didn't know enough to be confused. What was clear was that she was a middle-aged woman who did not get out enough.

She was so nervous, part of her wished she'd said she was busy or working. But no, she'd eagerly volunteered that she was free, and then she was possessed by some kind of menopausal insanity to say yes to his invitation.

He was due here in minutes, and she was still standing around in her underwear and a pair of tights, unable to make a simple decision. Looking at her reflection in the mirror, Jane ran a hand over her belly and examined the little pooch that stuck out, a reminder of too many cookies consumed at the store under the guise of taste testing. In her head she was hearing glowing affirmations telling her to embrace herself. To accept who she was. Fluffing her hair, Jane didn't hate what she saw. She's was in good shape, not just for her age, but any age. Sure, she'd put on some extra pounds over the years, but she took care of herself. She ran a successful business, had friends and a wonderful family. Still, where Danny was concerned, insecurity rocketed around her gut like pinball.

"This is ridiculous," she muttered to herself. It wasn't

like they were going to have sex or anything, Jane didn't know if she even remembered how. But the person she saw looking back at her was a ticking clock, a reminder of the time that had passed. So much time.

Reaching into her closet, she pulled out a flowing, wine-colored sweater dress and her chunky-heeled black boots. This dress was her go-to and fit almost any occasion. She never thought it would be a first-date-with-Danny dress, though. With a scooped neck and a sweeping skirt, it shaped her in all the right places, and camouflaged the ones she'd rather not have on display. It was a favorite for a reason.

There was no way to know if it was right for the evening, but it was too late to worry about that particular detail. After adding her jewelry, she straightened the neckline and glanced at herself in the mirror. Not too bad. The whir of a motor cut through the gentle quiet of the house just as she zipped on her boots. Headlights flashed into her bedroom window, then quickly vanished, signaling that a car had pulled into the driveway. Looking at the clock she saw it was seven. He was right on time.

This was just dinner. *Just dinner,* she told herself.

If that was true, what was the little buzz flitting around in her belly? They had a history, but it was so far in the past, Jane could hardly consider it relevant. After he'd broken her heart, Jane jumped headlong into her schooling, doing her best to put any memory of the man she had wanted more than anything out of her head. The way he'd just dropped out of her life crushed her, shook her faith. And while Jane was quiet and inexperienced in matters of the heart, she was not a fool. Pining over someone who didn't want her was out of the question.

Instead, she threw herself into her work, taking internships and research jobs wherever she could. Her passport got a good workout, taking her to dig sites, ruins, and museums all over the world. She built an amazing network of colleagues and friends and was considered a rising talent in the archeological community. Jane thrived, forcing herself to forget her heartbreak, burying it like the relics she studied.

When her dad died, it all fell apart, and Jane had been reassembling the pieces ever since.

Back in high school, she was the only one who knew Danny's dreams were as big as his stories. Now, he'd brought her into his confidence once again as he tried to reinvent himself.

Danny was a thoughtful man, who obviously felt things deeply. Sure, at times it was necessary to hold on to the cool kid facade from his youth, but when she watched him in interviews, or on the red carpet at one of his movie premieres, she saw through the practiced charm. All she could see was the boy who toiled in the back of a bookstore to build worlds. They were bound by an old friendship, and by the shared history of a small town that held one of them back, while the other shot forward.

Her doorbell chimed, rousing Chloe from her spot in the corner of the living room. Her pooch scrambled excitedly on the dark wood floors, crashing into a side table, and nearly knocking over a small glass table lamp that had been in the family since their first days in the United States. Normally, the big fuzzball was quiet, very content to hang with her people. But Chloe lived for visitors—all visitors. She and the

UPS man had a little love affair going on. If her dog was ever in the yard during a delivery, he made a point to go over to the fence and love her up. It was the same at the store, where she had a particular fondness for their mail carrier, Elton. The wagging tail and happy bark weren't going to scare off any intruder. Given the opportunity, the dog would invite a burglar in for tea.

"Chill out. We've discussed this. You're too easy." Chloe sat, but the *whoosh-whoosh* of her tail continued excitedly. The dog was incorrigible. After smiling into the hallway mirror for a final check of her teeth for lipstick smudges, Jane opened the front door.

Damn.

It should have been a crime for a man to look this good. She doubted he even made an effort. At the store, when he was wearing a hoodie and jeans, his good looks were casual, boyish almost. Now? The man was gorgeous. He filled the space on her front porch, tall and rugged-looking, in a leather jacket, slacks, and a soft-looking crew neck sweater. There was nothing out of the ordinary, not really. There was something familiar that stirred in her heart, a bloom of awareness that allowed Jane to see past her own fears and insecurities. She sensed neither of them knew what to expect. Normally confident, Danny looked as nervous as she felt. Seeing it on his face, and in his eyes, which now appeared to be a smoky dark blue, pushed her jangled nerves into overdrive. But it also provided common ground.

Shaking off her armchair analysis, Jane chided herself for overthinking. They were old friends. This was JUST dinner.

But was it? If life had taught her anything, it was that

sometimes you needed to question what you thought to be true. Based on the way he looked at her, it was possible Jane wasn't as clued in as she'd thought.

She stood there, hands clasped so tight she thought she might twist off her fingers. The wave hit her all at once, reality crashing into the memories. Jane couldn't quite contain the emotions that she'd been bottling up since he walked into her store last week. Nothing had prepared her for the rush of feelings that filled her head and her heart.

The sharp bark from behind her broke the trance. "Oh. Oh, hi."

His smile bloomed. "Hi. You look…beautiful."

Looking down, she smoothed the front of her dress. "Thank you, so do you. I mean. Um…" He grinned and Jane wondered when she'd lost her power to speak. How old was she? Fifteen? A deep breath helped her regroup. "You look very nice. Handsome."

Danny rubbed his hand on his chin where he had a perpetual five-o'clock shadow. "I clean up okay."

"Come in." Jane stepped back from the door. "I'll get my coat."

Chloe had seated herself in anticipation of some attention, but the dog was vibrating with excitement. She and Danny had become buddies since he'd, surprisingly, been writing in the store every day. When he'd arrive, Chloe would abandon Jane and follow him to the round table, beg for his food, and then, regardless of whether he did or didn't give in, she'd find a corner nearby to curl up. Yesterday, there'd been a spurt of activity during the day and he'd taken her out to do her business while Jane was helping customers.

It was kind and unexpected. Neighborly. But, considering how things had been since he'd been back, unexpected was becoming the norm. Like tonight. He was squatting down, stroking Chloe's face while her Collie looked like she'd found a long-lost best friend. There was such ease. Such familiarity. Jane grabbed her black shawl-collared coat and almost hated to interrupt.

"Who is the sweetest girl?" he cooed. "You're such a good girl."

Chloe's long snout was pressed to Danny's nose while he scratched her jaw just under her puffing cheeks. There were no licks, but her ears were back, her eyes soft and loving.

"That dog is so easy." The comment escaped before she could censor herself, and Danny's response was a loud, bold laugh. He stood up and smiled.

"I believe we established earlier that she loves attention."

"Yes. Shameless."

"I need to watch out for her kind, I guess." Reaching, he took the coat from her hand and held it out for her. Jane wasn't used to such courtesies, but she slipped her arms in the sleeves. She also wasn't expecting her insides to shiver when he lifted her hair from inside the collar, before trailing his hand down her back. *Sweet Baby Jesus.*

Standing behind her he was so close she could feel the heat radiating off his body, and his scent, something subtle and woodsy, completely surrounded her.

The response to his touch was unexpected, putting Jane immediately on guard. She should be beyond this silly crush of her youth. So much time had passed, they'd each lived a lifetime. But with the sparks and heat, there was comfort and familiarity. He seemed to belong in this space, and for a moment it felt like he belonged with her.

Before they left, he glanced around the entry hall. "It's different than I remember."

"It's been a long time, and we've remodeled."

"It doesn't feel like a long time," he confessed. "Not at all."

It didn't. Having him here felt natural, and right.

"Shall we go?"

With a last pat on the dog's head, he opened the door and she stepped outside. The night was cold, and her breath came out in puffs as the moisture crystalized in the frosty air. Using the app on her phone she locked the door and adjusted the inside lights, feeling surprisingly tech savvy. That was until she got a look at the low-slung vehicle sitting in her driveway.

It had tires, so it was obviously a car, but when he pushed a button on the key fob, the headlights went on and the engine roared to life. From the cabin of the car, a cool blue light glowed, making the vehicle appear otherworldly. He settled her into the passenger seat with manners that Jane feared were becoming passé, then went around the front of the car to his side.

She thought about her seventeen-year-old self, sitting next to Danny in his family's old Jeep Wagoneer and driving out to a local beach because he'd heard seals were hauled out on some rocks in the harbor. It was early, maybe seven in the morning, and he'd shown up at her house, knowing her parents would be awake, but it was likely Jane wasn't. It was late November and no kid their age was up that early on a

Saturday morning, but there he was pulling her out of bed.

Sitting so close in the confines of the small car, his smell was familiar. There was a hint of sage and cedar, but instead of generic shampoo, fine leather and bergamot blended with his essence. It brought her right back to that day so many years ago, standing on the beach, with the wind blowing and the sun barely up, watching the silky silver-gray forms of the seals slip in and out of the water.

It was a good memory, one that made her remember the close bond they'd had. Or so she'd thought. Less than a year later, he was gone for college, and moments like that one on the beach were lost forever.

Chapter Five

DAN KNEW HE probably didn't need a reservation for dinner on a Wednesday night, but the restaurant in the next town over from Angel Harbor was an extremely popular foodie destination with a tasting menu he was dying to try. Not wanting to take a chance, he'd called that afternoon and secured a table for them.

Sitting with Jane in the close quarters of his car, he found himself thinking about the community she'd created in the bookstore. It had been an important part of the town when he was a kid, but now, it was so much more. He'd been working there for a little less than a week, enjoying the little rituals that came with a store like Jane's. He liked the ebb and flow of the place, and in the time he'd been there, he was impressed that in the age of online shopping, the bookstore was thriving. Not only was there a steady stream of customers who came in for books, magazines, a gift, and what had to be the best coffee in the world, but there was also an after-school art club, a story hour on Saturday morning, as well as a writers' group, several book clubs, and people who came in, like he'd been doing, to meet a friend, get some work done, or read. He even saw the mayor and the high school principal having an informal meeting over coffee. The store was a treasure, and he was gratified to see the good folks in town taking full advantage of it. Dan wondered if Jane knew what an impact she was making.

He observed people and situations for a living, tuning in to their emotions and motivations. His crime novels could be brutal; learning to watch people and their body language helped him make the books a lived experience. He wanted his readers to feel what his characters felt.

Janie may not have realized it, but her store was that kind of experience. Her shop, full of sights and sounds, was comfortable—like a second home—and Jane treated every visitor, no matter how many times they had been there, like an old friend.

Dan observed people visibly relax in her presence. Her genuine kindness, her openness, were what made the shop special. Being there, soaking up the atmosphere of the shop and the town, was exactly what he had needed to switch gears.

Her head tilted, she was watching the world go by from the window. "I love the new Christmas lights on Main Street. I can't wait until we light up Angel Harbor. The streetlights go on next week, but the big reveal will be right after Thanksgiving."

"I think it will really feel like Christmas to me this year. Between the excitement from my nieces and nephew, to being in a place that's actually cold, I'm getting into the spirit. I helped Gavin with his letter to Santa the other night."

"Oh, that's fun. Did you have fun? I used to love helping Tara with her letter."

"It was great. I don't know if Ella is still on board with

the Santa thing, but she's going to write a letter, just in case. Jamie is thinking an in-person visit is the best way to go."

"Ha! Make sure the kids bring their letters to the North Pole mailbox at the bookstore. We have volunteers from the Chamber of Commerce who compose responses."

"Really? That's awesome."

"Where did you spend Christmas last year? You weren't with your family?"

"No, I was at my house in Hawaii. It's very cool seeing the palm trees all lit up, but it's not the same. Same with Thanksgiving. I love the food there. I mean I really love it, but I just couldn't get into coconut sweet potatoes."

"You never were very adventurous with food." The observation illustrated how close they had been, and how much she remembered.

"I've gotten much better. You'll see," he declared. "I am glad to be here for the holidays. Like I said, it's not the same without family. It took me a long time to figure that out."

"I can't imagine it would be. Last year, we had a house full of people. Some of my cousins came from out of town and brought their kids. We went to the city, and saw the tree, and ice-skated in Bryant Park…"

He held up his hand. "Whoa. Back up. You ice-skated?"

He caught her giving him the side-eye, and then one side of her mouth turned up in a grin. "Okay. Maybe I didn't skate."

"I was going to say, you're not a skater. I seem to remember you and the ice were not friends. You spent a lot of time on your ass."

"That's true. I can stand up now, but I have no ability.

I'd still like to learn, but I'm afraid if I fall, I'll break a hip or something."

He chuckled at the reference to their age. "I don't think we're quite there yet, but I understand the hesitation. I blew my Achilles tendon out a couple of years ago. Partial tear. It took months for it to heal."

"This getting old stuff is for the birds," she snorted.

"Yet it's a privilege denied to many."

It was a sobering thought and she nodded in agreement. Jane's father was only in his mid-fifties, a couple of years older than they were, when he had the heart attack that killed him.

He parked the car in a spot on the street, thankful he didn't have to put his baby in a municipal lot. It was only a short walk to the restaurant.

"Where are we going?" she asked.

"I've been dying to try the tasting menu at Kent's. Are you game?"

Jane's eyes went wide. "Yes! Do you have a reservation? So much for you not being adventurous. The place is always packed. I've been wanting to go, but…"

Her voice trailed off.

"But why?"

A heavy sigh escaped. "Time mostly. My life isn't my own."

Her comment felt like it was part confession, part realization. She was a single parent who ran a very successful business, and that didn't leave her much time for things *she* wanted to do.

Dan got out of the car and circled around to her side to

open the door. He loved that Jane didn't hesitate to take his extended hand when she exited. Looping her arm through his, like it was something she did every day, they started down the sidewalk.

"Did that sound pathetic?" she asked. "I didn't mean it to."

"Not pathetic. You have a lot on your plate. From my vantage point, you're too busy taking care of everyone else to do things for yourself."

Her mouth pressed into a narrow line. "There's some truth to that, I guess."

"Are you happy? It's not a problem unless you aren't. You were always running from one thing to another back in the day." He had a ton of time to himself, and he certainly wasn't happy.

She lapsed into silence, and he gave her time to think as they strolled to the restaurant. Jane always needed thinking time. It was a true gift that she didn't just blurt out answers, and it was why he had always respected her opinion so much. So many people were ready-fire-aim; she wasn't like that. Even when they were in high school, she always took time to weigh out the problem. She'd called it noodle time.

"I'm happy," she finally responded. "I have my ups and downs, but there's much to be grateful for."

He loved her outlook. She, of all people, had reason to be bitter, or angry. Her entire life plan had been turned on its head. But instead, Jane put out goodness. Everything she cast into the universe brought light to the people in her orbit. Her generous offer to let him take up residence in her shop was just one example. He'd have to be blind not to notice that she was a beauty, from her skin to her hair, to those luminescent eyes, she was stunning. Jane, however, was even prettier on the inside.

There were a lot of people walking around town, unusual for the middle of the week. Just before he reached for the door of the restaurant, Dan saw a couple walking past them on the sidewalk glance over and whisper. Normally, he'd smile or wave if there was extended eye contact, but he could tell by their expressions and body language, the people on the street weren't interested readers. Dan's notoriety had devolved into morbid curiosity, and it was out of his control.

Once inside Kent's, they were taken to their table right away—a small banquette set at the rear of the room, giving them a good view of the entire dining room.

Deep gray-green walls served as the foundation for an eclectic mix of lighting and furnishings. Other than the banquettes, which were upholstered in deep brown leather, the chairs and tables were a mix of sizes and finishes. A large bar took up an entire wall, and bottles were stacked in front of a crackled mirror that went all the way up to the pressed tin ceiling. The owners had spent a tremendous amount of time and money to make it look like they hadn't spent a tremendous amount of time and money.

As soon as the hostess took their coats, they slid into the booth and Jane took him by surprise. "That's hard for you, isn't it?"

"I'm sorry? What?" He wasn't sure to what she was referring.

"The way people talk. I mean, it can't be easy." The couple on the street, he realized. He hadn't drawn attention to it, but Jane noticed.

"Ahh. Yeah." He folded his hands on the table and focused on his fingers as he wound them in and out. "I try to ignore it, but it's not fun. I prefer flying under the radar."

"I can imagine." She glanced around slowly, taking in every detail. Ever the scientist, Jane drew information from what she saw. It was always a kick watching her absorb information; he figured after all these years, she was even more astute. "This is really a beautiful place. These pre-war buildings in the village always turn my head. I wonder what kinds of stories are here. If we opened up a wall, what would we find?"

He smiled. They were cut from the same cloth. "I think we're in the same business, you and I."

"You think so? I don't know. I just sell books."

That was possibly the biggest understatement he'd ever heard. "You're undergraduate degree was in archeology, right?"

"Yes. I had minors in classics and biological anthropology."

"Yeesh. Biological anthropology? That sounds like a headache to me."

"It was a headache, trust me on that. I have no idea why I added the biology piece."

"You were never happy unless you were torturing yourself. I think it was an illness of some sort."

"No! That's not true."

"Seriously? Who argued her way into AP Chemistry? You would have aced regular Chem, but no—you wanted a challenge."

"Hmmpf." She turned that little button nose of hers up in the air, feigning offense. "There's no shame in wanting a challenge."

"There's a challenge and then there's being a masochist." Dan was watching her intently, waiting for her to disagree. When she didn't, he continued. "Back to my point, as an archeologist, you pieced together stories from what you found."

"I used science to examine artifacts and material remains of a community or civilization to construct a history."

"You employed science, I use words and my out-of-control imagination, but we're both storytellers." He noticed her use of the past tense.

She was about to answer when the hostess returned to take their drink orders. She was accompanied by the chef, who explained the tasting menu and what they could expect over the course of the evening. Chef asked about food allergies and restrictions, and once he was satisfied that he'd gotten a good read on what they would like, he was off.

"This should be interesting. He seemed very laid-back for a chef. They usually scare the bejesus out of me," she joked.

"The kitchen is getting rave reviews, but you're right it could be an adventure depending on how much ego he possesses. When I was in Paris on a tour stop, my French publicist took me to this ridiculously expensive restaurant in an equally ridiculous hotel. I think it was fifteen hundred dollars for two of us for the tasting menu."

Her mouth dropped open. "Are you kidding? Did that at least include the wine?"

"No! Everything was extra. You wanted truffle cream on something, and it was another hundred bucks. If you wanted the sommelier to pair the wine, which we did, it was another surcharge. I wasn't paying, so I didn't care, but when they brought out one of the main courses, and it was roast *pigeon*, not squab, pigeon, I lost it. I think I laughed for five minutes. Offended the hell out of pretty much everyone."

Jane shook her head in disbelief, clucking at him like his nonna used to do. "Such an ugly American."

"Come on. They called it a delicacy. It's a freaking pigeon. The same birds that would sit on my terrace and leave a mess, but now I'm looking at it on my plate, with its little toasted pigeon feet sticking up…I'm sorry, it was weird. And funny."

She was giggling now. Her smile was wide and bright, and her eyes flashed with amusement. "That is funny. I mean, oh my God, what a visual, the little…f-feet—" Jane stuck her index fingers up in the air and waggled them.

That was the end of her composure. Dan watched as the burst of laughter exploded from her belly, and he went right along with her. The ache in his chest was wonderful, freeing, and watching Jane trying to catch her breath was only making him laugh harder. The pure joy in her features, the abandon with which she cut loose, made his heart happy.

Finally, Jane gasped, sucking in air, and shushed him when she noticed the other diners were staring. "We're so classy."

"We might end up eating pizza at your house if we don't settle down."

Jane nodded and dabbed at her eyes. "God. I haven't

laughed like that in a long time," she said.

He hadn't either. And it felt really good.

JANE COULDN'T REMEMBER the last time she'd had so much fun. The meal was sublime, a combination of tastes and textures that brought her senses to life, but it was the company that made the evening special. She had missed her friend.

In high school, they'd hung out, studied, talked on the phone for hours, but they hadn't considered themselves a couple. They were close, but that particular line had never been crossed.

It was the summer before Danny went to law school, and Jane took off to Lapland in Finland to work on a dig before she started grad school. They'd been inseparable, and she thought things had changed between them. If it was possible, they were closer than they had ever been.

Like before, long nights were spent in the back of the store. They'd talked about everything from families, school, friends, and their dreams. He wasn't writing as much, but he still talked about it, about the stories that he wanted to put on paper. Jane knew the secrets he shared meant something. He'd trusted her, and that trust had been at the root of their relationship.

A relationship that obviously meant more to her than it did to him.

With the delicious dinner behind them, they left the restaurant and stepped into the chilly night. The streets had quieted, and surprisingly, snow was drifting from the sky. It was just a flurry, but it made everything a little more magical. Securing the top button of her coat, and flipping up the hood, she felt herself smile.

"Do you mind if we walk a little? I want to let that meal settle."

Jane looked up at him, his features softer in the streetlights. "I don't mind."

He offered his elbow and as she did earlier, Jane slipped her arm through his. It wasn't intimate, but it was romantic, and Jane had to push the wistful lightness swirling through her back down into the little space in her heart where it belonged. Danny wasn't going to stay in Angel Harbor. He had a life to return to, and Jane wasn't going to suffer the fallout from unrealistic expectations.

"We spent the entire meal talking about me," he said. "What about you? You've got a thriving business and a daughter. You know everyone. How has it been putting down roots in town?"

How did she answer that? Her life plan had essentially blown up before it even had a chance to get moving. Jane was on the cusp of her dreams when she was shaken awake by the loss of her father. Not only was she grieving the man who had encouraged her every step of the way, but all her goals and aspirations were yanked away at the same time. The loss was brutal.

Jane adored her mother—she was a good woman who'd been cast adrift after her father's death. She and Dad were true soul mates, but there was no question in her mom's mind that Jane would be the one to keep the business alive.

Her mother was still teaching and owned 51 percent of the store, which meant at the time, Jane couldn't sell it if she wanted to. Not to mention, she was easily guilted into doing what everyone else thought was the right thing.

In spite of feeling like she'd missed out on the life she'd planned, Jane would never regret her choices or having her daughter. Whatever had happened, Tara was her prize.

"My daughter is my greatest gift and my best work," Jane responded truthfully.

"She seems like a great kid. Looks like you at that age except for the hair. Her dad…"

"Is not in the picture. He never has been."

"Never?"

"No," she said curtly.

Danny nodded and let it drop, making Jane feel bad for being so short with him. He didn't know what had happened. How could he? So she did something she never did…she talked about her ex. "He was a history professor at the state university. I was trying to keep up with some grad classes while I ran the store, and I met him at a department colloquium."

"You don't have to tell me if you don't want to. I didn't mean to pry."

"No, it's okay." She gripped his arm tighter, forcing herself closer. "Ari was handsome and charming. So smart. I could listen to him for hours. We met, really hit it off, and were married within a year. I was pregnant three months later."

"That does not sound like you. You're always so careful."

"Right? I shouldn't have rushed it, but I was in my early

thirties, I'd barely dated, and I thought it could work. He seemed happy where he was, secure."

"I'm guessing that wasn't the case."

"You would be correct. As soon as the lines on the stick turned blue, our marriage went south."

"I'm sorry, Jane."

"Stuff happens." Jane never talked about her ex, about the hurt, about the crushing fear. "When I was just out of my first trimester, he took a visiting professorship in California. You know, just for a few months."

"A few months?"

Jane breathed deep. It amazed her how hard it was to talk about what had happened, even after all this time. "It wasn't a few months."

Danny reached his other arm across and took her gloved hand in his. "It became permanent?"

"A tenure track position. He never came back."

Danny stopped and turned to face her. "I'm sorry. What? Never?"

"Nope. He's never met his amazing daughter."

"Sonofabitch."

"That's accurate." Uncomfortable with the way he was looking at her, she motioned that they should start walking again. "On the plus side, his family was quite well off, and he invested a substantial sum for Tara when she was born. He didn't want anything to do with her, but as a result of that investment, my daughter has a trust fund that will give her the freedom to go to college debt free, and have a nest egg."

"That's nice, I guess, but I still can't believe he just left."

"Believe it. She doesn't even carry his name. She's a Fallon."

"It must hurt, though," he said kindly.

"Sometimes. Personally, I know I dodged a bullet. He was charming, brilliant beyond words, but Ari is an arrogant snob. I feel bad that Tara knows her father walked away. I tried to couch the truth, but I wasn't going to lie to her. Money aside, that's a bitter pill."

Silence descended, and the light snow made it all the more poignant.

"What about you?" she asked. "Any exes?"

"I've had relationships that didn't work out, but I never married if that's what you're asking."

That was a shame. It would have been nice if one of them had been able to make a go of marriage. "Married to your work, I guess?"

"I don't know if that's it." Danny moved the arm she was holding and looped it around her shoulder, pulling her close. "I'm glad you were free tonight. This was nice."

Jane looked up. His smile was sweet and genuine, revealing the lone dimple in his right cheek. "I'm glad I was free too."

"Your store is hopping. I'm so impressed. It's much more than retail space."

"It is. It's part store, part community center. The town depends on us. I'm thinking about expanding. You're the first person I've said that to out loud." She hesitated. The evening had been lovely, and Jane didn't want to spoil it.

He noticed. Danny's pace slowed and he turned to her. "What?"

"I don't want to talk about it." That was a lie—she did

want to talk about it. She wanted to tell someone, if only to let go of the feelings she'd been carrying around. But not here, not now with the quiet streets whispering to her to enjoy this moment.

"Too late to stuff that one back in the bottle. What gives?"

Jane was at war with herself. She had so much to be grateful for, but life as she knew it, the one she'd nurtured all these years, was going to change and she didn't know if she was ready.

"I said 'us.' There's not going to be an us in a few months. Just me. I bought my mother out of the store last year, and she's going to spend the colder months where it's warm, do some traveling. Tara will be going to college at the end of the summer." Just the thought of it brought raw emotion to her throat, so she urged him back to their walk before she completely broke down. She was excited for her mom, and for Tara, but that didn't mean she didn't hate how it was going to affect her.

"Change really sucks sometimes."

"It really does," she agreed. "I don't know. Nothing is sitting right with me. My whole life feels like it's in flux."

"Is there something else?" He picked up on her worry.

Was there? On paper, everything seemed fine, but Jane wasn't so sure. "I can't get an answer about my lease. I should have seen the renewal by now, but I haven't. My attorney has been trying to talk to the landlord, about the existing space and expanding into the small house next door, but he keeps getting the runaround. He said I shouldn't worry."

"But you are worried."

"I've always had the new lease in hand well before the old one expired."

"When is that?" He still had his arm looped around her as they walked. She found the contact wonderfully comforting.

"The end of February."

Danny took a deep breath and she could see his brow furrow as he thought. "From a legal standpoint, you have plenty of time."

"Oh, I know I do." He was absolutely right, but that did nothing to quiet the sinking feeling in her stomach.

"But?"

"I don't know. It's just…a feeling. That's all. I'm probably worrying for nothing."

"You've always had solid intuition. Is there some reason you think they won't renew?

"Not specifically."

"How long has the store been there? A hundred years?"

Danny's question made Jane think about the photos of the bookstore over the years that graced the walls in the shop. It had been a remarkable evolution and the memories eased her into telling the story.

"Almost. The Van Velt family has owned the building that houses the store, and the one next to it, since the mid-thirties. The original Mr. Van Velt, whose name was Charlie, was friends with my grandfather. He leased him the building because he believed in *Daddo*. He agreed that Angel Harbor needed a bookstore, and that a new business starting up during the Great Depression would give the town hope.

Charlie Van Velt knew Paddy Fallon would take good care of the property, and he did. Over the years, any improvements that were made have been at our expense, but the Fallons didn't mind because the place was home."

Out of the corner of her eye, she could see she had his full attention, so she kept going.

"Mr. Van Velt left the building to his kids, and they left it to theirs. The whole time, the lease stayed in effect."

"Wow. That's unheard of."

"One of his great-grandchildren said pretty much the same thing. The family left Long Island in the late eighties, I think. The man, Charlie's great-grandson, came by the store last summer when they were on their way to a wedding at a vineyard out east. He was pleasant enough. Looked around, bought a book."

They arrived at his car just as she finished. The proverbial lump wedged in her throat while tears gathered behind her eyes.

"So why are you worried? It sounds uneventful. Is the landlord losing a ton of money?"

"No. My rent is right where it should be in this market. The building has been paid off for years."

"Then what is it?" His words, kind and without judgment, brought a swell of emotion.

Jane looked away. "This wasn't my choice, you know? I was going to do research and teach and discover amazing things. The store just *happened.* When my dad died, it became my responsibility. Now my whole life is here, and everything is changing. I'm probably worried about nothing, but what if—"

Danny didn't respond. He just let her ramble, and Jane figured he was spooked now that he knew she was a breath away from falling apart over something hypothetical. The last thing she expected was for him to pull her into his arms and hold on.

"Come here."

He didn't offer platitudes or advice. He didn't try to distract her. What Danny offered was compassion and understanding, and perhaps most importantly, he offered friendship. His body provided support, physically and emotionally, and a strength that Jane gave in to because it just felt good to be held. His chest was hard, his breathing steady and his arms gave her a sense of safety she only now realized she'd missed. Jane wasn't a helpless woman. She was the one who people called on when they needed help, so having someone take care of her was as confusing as it was comforting.

She didn't want to move, relishing the feel of him. How long had it been since she'd let someone else bear a bit of the load, even for a little while?

She was always the one who stayed strong, who figured things out. But this was different and Danny must have sensed that.

Taking a step back, Jane smiled up at him. His hair was lightly dusted with snow, and his mouth ticked up at the corners. In his eyes she saw the boy she knew and the man he had become. It was a contrast and a complement at the same time. For her part, Jane was just happy she had the chance to be with him again.

"Thank you. For dinner, and for listening to me. It was

nice to be able to lean on somebody."

His smile grew wider and he pressed the button on the key fob, letting her into the car. When he got in on the other side, he leaned over and without warning, kissed her gently on the cheek. It was a peck, nothing more, but the sweetness of it damn near made her cry.

"You were always the strong one, Janie. You listened to me for hours and hours, helped me find my voice, read my stories and you never judged me. You can lean on me anytime you want."

Her heart swelled remembering how they were when they were together. There was always a feeling of well-being when she was with him. That hadn't changed. But what about when he left? She didn't say that to him, even though it hung over her like a dark cloud. Danny wasn't back in Angel Harbor permanently. Jane appreciated his kindness more than she could articulate, but lean on him? Maybe she could in the short term, but Danny's time here was finite, and the last thing she needed was for him to break her heart all over again.

Chapter Six

WHEN HE PULLED up the driveway to his cottage, Dan saw a glow from the stone patio Mel and Peter had installed on the side of the house. Connected to the dining room by French doors, the crowning glory of the outdoor room was a huge river rock fireplace, surrounded by a collection of comfortable seating. The garden that encircled the whole yard had been replanted with yellow, orange, and red mums, which now had a very light glaze of snow from the flurries earlier. Dan's house in Hawaii had a view of the Pacific, but the warmth of this backyard on a chilly fall night beat it hands down.

Tucked together under a plaid blanket on a double chaise were his sister and brother-in-law. They each had a steaming mug in their hands and were gazing quietly at the yellow-orange flames behind the mesh screen. He didn't know if this was a romantic moment, or if they were just exhausted. When Melinda yawned wide and loud, he had his answer.

"Long day?" He found a seat on the other side of the hearth, feeling the fire's heat immediately.

The two of them nodded in time with the other, looking like they had been to hell and back.

"The kids were *difficult* tonight," Peter said. His emphasis on *difficult* was a tell. His brother-in-law taught middle school science and not much spooked the guy. Considering he worked in a place that was a vat of cooking hormones, to hear the kids were "difficult," meant they were far worse.

"Oh, boy." Dan had seen the normal bickering you would expect from three siblings, but it was never so bad that his sister had the tortured expression of a refugee from a war zone. Tonight, as she sipped whatever was in that mug, her face stayed frozen, her eyes fixed.

"Yeah, they started fighting the minute they sat down at dinner and didn't stop until we closed them all into their bedrooms two hours later. That was after Ella blew a gasket and dumped water on Jamie's head. There was sporadic screaming through the walls until about forty minutes ago. It was heated." Peter chuckled, but it was that nervous *I-need-another-drink* kind of chuckle.

Hearing that Ella—sweet, docile Ella—had lost her temper proved once again, you never really knew a person until you pushed all her buttons. It was probably good for the family to see she had limits.

They sat quietly for a moment, Dan not knowing what to say. He didn't have kids of his own and didn't feel qualified to weigh in. He looked down at his hands, trying to think of something wise or pithy, when his sister broke the silence.

"How was your date?"

Dan looked up to find Mel staring at him, waiting for an answer.

"Uh. Good. We had a nice dinner. Took a walk."

With a wave of her hand she motioned for him to go on.

"And?"

And? What did she want to know? "I'm not sure what you expect to hear. We had a nice time. It was good to get out."

Peter pulled a bottle of Glenlivet from a basket next to the chaise and poured a finger in a glass that appeared from the same stash. He handed it to Dan, who accepted it, but he still didn't know what to tell them.

"Well," Peter began, "Jane Fallon does not date. More than a few men in town have tried to get her to go out with them. She's not interested."

"I don't see how it's relevant." Sipping the Scotch, Dan was surprised at how happy that revelation made him. "Jane has a very full plate."

"Obviously, she found time for you." His brother-in-law was never cagey. He was getting at something.

"She did. Just lucky, I guess." *Damn lucky.*

"So, it was dinner. You aren't trying to rekindle your old romance, are you?" Mel asked.

Where the hell had that come from? "We never had a *romance*. We were very close friends. We still are...friends."

And maybe a little bit more. Hopefully.

Not knowing which of his statements triggered it, his sister burst out laughing. "Are you serious? You two were inseparable. Of course you had..." Melinda trailed off and leaned in, locking her gaze on him. "Jesus. You can't be that obtuse. Do you really think that?"

The truth was he never really thought about it much until recently. So, the answer to the obtuse question was probably "yes."

Before leaving for law school, Dan knew his relationship with Jane was more than friendship. Mel was right. That summer, they had spent every minute they could together, and while things never got physical, they were bonded on every other level. Then he left.

He never came back, even though she'd admitted to him that she wanted more. *Felt more.* A relationship with Jane would have upended both their futures. They were thousands of miles apart, and it's not like they had cell phones to keep in touch back then. Long distance was truly long distance. It was an impossible situation that would have ultimately led one of them to give up on his or her dream, for the other.

"It was complicated." Yeah, that was lame.

"Complicated? No. You were an ass."

"Mel, this is in the past." He knew he'd been a jackass, but that didn't mean he wanted to kill the buzz from his evening by rehashing all the ways he'd screwed up.

"For you it's in the past. But Jane lives with her father's death every day. Every single day. Mom and I went to the funeral, you know. We brought meals. Everyone in town helped out at the store."

"The Fallons have always been loved in town. That doesn't surprise me."

Mel looked away. "Well, you know what surprised everyone? That you were nowhere to be found. Everyone knew you and Jane were close. She asked Mom a couple of times if she'd heard from you."

"Who did?"

"*Jane.* She was grieving, Danny, and you didn't even

send her a card."

"I'm not proud of myself." His sister was right. He should have called, visited…something. There were a lot of "should haves." Too many.

He was an idiot, and a heartless one if he actually had the guts to face the truth. There were so many times he'd picked up the phone to call her, but he never did. Jane would have changed his world, and he wasn't man enough to take the risk.

He never fully got over his feelings for her. Acknowledging that, it made perfect sense that when he had hit rock bottom, he cast the lifeline in her direction.

JANE HAD HIT that strange place in her life where her child was trying to act like the parent. Her daughter was sitting at the kitchen island with a cup of steaming tea and her schoolbooks spread out in front of her. The way she glanced up, her blue eyes hooded by her lashes, made Jane feel like she'd broken curfew.

"There you are. I was so worried! For all I knew you were dead in a ditch someplace."

"Very funny. Obviously, I'm fine."

"Don't you sass me, missy. Are your fingers broken that you couldn't call?"

Jane hung her coat on the hook by the back door and smiled at her daughter who was having some fun at her expense. "Sorry. I left you a note."

"Yes." Tara picked up the note and waved it around.

"*Out to dinner*. That's all! Not a word about where you were, who you were with, or when you would be home."

"What-*ever*." Jane played along, rolling her eyes and clucking her tongue for effect. "I get it. But for the record, you're not the boss of me."

Tara laughed and pulled a large gray-blue porcelain mug from the cabinet and poured her old mom a cup of tea from the matching teapot. Jane settled into a chair at the island knowing she was going to long for nights like this when Tara went off to school. The more she thought about it, the more her heart hurt.

Her baby had been a real handful. She walked early, talked early, and knew what she did and didn't like. That had never changed. To this day, Tara was one of the most stubborn people Jane had ever met. She was also one of the most determined.

Her girl never gave up. If she set a goal for herself, she worked until she achieved it. Once that goal was reached, she set the next one. For someone who was so artistic, she was as methodical as any scientist Jane had ever met.

While she sipped her tea, Jane watched Tara's body language. She was fidgety, fussing with her fingers and rubbing her temples. It was obvious her daughter had something on her mind. Jane had a feeling she knew what it was. "So, how was the last dress rehearsal, Madam Stage Manager?"

Tara sighed, long and dramatic. "Oh, you know that old saying: bad rehearsal, great show?"

Jane nodded, knowing what was coming. "Yeah."

"If it's true, we're going to have an amazing show! A Tony-worthy show." Her sarcasm wasn't the least bit subtle, betraying the worry she was feeling deep down.

"Ouch. That bad?"

"It was a disaster. Actors were missing their cues, stage crew was a mess, the sets aren't done... Are you sure you want to come? Hennings is ready to bolt. I think he may move his family to the Yukon or something." Their faculty director was prone to the dramatic, but in this case, it sounded like the reaction was appropriate.

"What kind of mother do you think I am? I'll be there."

"You're a glutton for punishment, Mom. Grandma won't be home, will she?"

"No, she's having such a good time, she's not coming home until Sunday."

"Good. She'd have a stroke."

Jane laughed. That was the truth. Her mother was a former stage actress, and while she could recognize that the students were just students, she had no patience for shoddy preparation. Jane on the other hand was more forgiving, relishing the strength and leadership her daughter was showing.

"I can't do anything about the cast, but I'm running drills with the crew after school tomorrow. I won't see you until after tomorrow's show."

"Not a problem. I'm working tomorrow night. I'll be there on Saturday with Tracy."

"Okay. Be kind." It must have been one horrible rehearsal if Tara had to remind her own mother to be nice.

"No worries."

Jane sipped her tea, letting the warmth of the fragrant liquid ease through her. Tara wasn't looking up, but Jane sensed there was something going on inside that head of hers. The girl's brain spun at warp speed, especially when she was in a story.

"How was *your* dinner?" Tara asked finally. Glancing up, her eyes were bright and inquisitive. *Nosy girl.*

"It was…it was very nice. We went to Kent's. It has a tasting menu. Different."

"And this Danny guy? You're old friends?"

"Uh, yes." They were. That wasn't a lie. "From high school. And after."

"I called Aunt Tracy."

Fuzznuts. "Really? Why?"

"Because you went on a date, with *this* guy." Tara spun her laptop around with quite the theatrical flair, and there on the screen was Danny's website, with all his dark, sexy gorgeousness right there in front of her. The reaction to him, the fresh memory of how he felt, rocked her to the core.

"Did your aunt give me up? Because really, I'm fifty years old. I think I can go out to dinner with an old friend without it becoming a federal case."

"Mom! Old friend? He's a famous writer, and you went out with him!" Tara was somewhere between giddy and horrified. "He's Dan-Freaking-Gallo! He's right up there with…" she waved her hands around "…Stephen King and Nora Roberts!"

"I'm aware of who he is; however, it was NOT a date." Jane kept her eyes steady, but her nerves were rattling like she'd been mainlining coffee.

"No? You look very nice."

"So? Because I put on a dress, that makes it a date?"

"You're wearing makeup."

"I wear makeup almost every day, and besides, I had to cover the racoon eyes, didn't I?" Jane did not want to go around in circles about this. She especially didn't want to do it with her seventeen-year-old.

"Stop it. You don't have raccoon eyes. Did he pick you up?"

"Yes, but—"

"He *paid* for dinner?"

Crapola.

"Yes," Jane whispered. "He did. Can you stop now?"

Her daughter folded her arms and leaned back in the chair. She was such a know-it-all. "Welp. What did we learn here this evening, kids?"

Chloe barked in response. Everyone had an opinion.

Jane pressed her forehead onto the cold granite countertop. She was much happier when she was living in a state of denial. Turning her head to the side she locked eyes with Tara. "Okay, maybe it was kind of…"

"A. Date. HA!" Tara leaned in, only inches now from Jane's nose. "More power to you, Mom—he's hot. I mean…" She paused, grinned. "For an old guy."

Jane sat up, not appreciating the "old guy" comment. "That's not nice."

"So, um…did he kiss you?"

"Excuse me?" *On the cheek, she thought. And he held her. God, did that feel good. He was all warm, and strong. But it was just two old friends, and he was offering her comfort after hearing her tale of woe. Reading anything into it was courting disaster. He was being kind. That was all.*

"Not going to tell me?" Tara was really pushing her luck. Jane didn't know how she felt about this sudden burst of interest in her life. It was sweet, in a way, but it was also annoying. Thinking about it, if she asked Tara the same questions, she'd get some serious pushback. "Mom…?"

"It's NONE of your business. But no, he didn't. So, no date."

Tara stood and smiled, her eyes glittering in the soft light of the kitchen. She was looking more beautiful and more mature than Jane had ever seen. Her girl was a strong, articulate woman and it had happened in a flash. "If you say so, Mom."

"Don't be fresh."

"I won't, but I do have one more question." With an about-face that made Jane sit back, her daughter's teasing subsided, and gave way to a giddy hopefulness. Tara was back to twisting her fingers. "How long do you think he's staying in town?"

"I don't know. He's working on a new book and wanted to go off the grid. I don't think it's going to be much of a secret in town, but don't broadcast it. As far as how long? Through Christmas? But that's a guess."

Nodding, Tara took a deep breath, appearing to ponder what she was going to say next. There was almost a hint of hero worship. "Do you think he'd, I don't know, talk to me about writing? I just want to pick his brain."

Yeah, definitely hero worship.

"I'm sure he would. He was asking about you, by the way, about your aspirations. I'm sure he'd love to talk shop."

Tara nodded, doing her best to stay cool when she was

obviously having an internal freak-out. "That would be really great. Really."

"I'll mention it to him. You can chat after the play wraps."

"Okay. Um, thanks." There was nothing quite so wonderful as seeing the joy dancing in her daughter's eyes. Talking to someone with Danny's stature and success was like a fledgling guitar player talking to Jimi Hendrix. "I'm going to bed," she said.

"I'll see you in the morning." Jane leaned into her daughter's kiss goodnight. As Tara left the room, Jane remembered something she wanted to say and called her back. "Hey, Tee?"

"Yeah?" When she walked back in the kitchen, her phone was in hand.

"Make sure you call your Aunt Tracy to fill her in."

Tara raised an eyebrow to go along with her wry grin. "Not necessary."

Just then, as if in response to some cosmic stage direction, Jane's phone rang, and the caller ID told her it was none other than Tracy. Her timing was impeccable.

"Night, Mom."

"Night." Jane looked at the ringing phone and resigned herself to the fact that she was in for a very long conversation about a boy. Some things didn't change. "Hey."

Tracy took a deep breath and began. "Tell me everything."

Chapter Seven

DANNY STOOD OUTSIDE the bookstore thinking about what his sister had said last night regarding his relationship with Jane. He'd enjoyed dinner; it was the best time he'd had in ages, probably because whatever was simmering between them had deep roots that had the potential to go way deeper. But Mel was right—he had to make some amends before this went any further.

When he came back to Long Island, he had one goal, and one goal only: to write his next book. Reconnecting with people, especially his sweet friend, wasn't something he'd considered. Or had he? The time he'd spent at the bookstore over the past week had been the stimulus he'd needed to trigger his creative brain. Getting back to his origins, as well as a pure process, was helping the words flow.

Was she part of that? Was Jane his inspiration? Her presence calmed and settled him; there was no denying the special magic she possessed. It forced him to think about everything he'd missed because he'd walked away from her.

The town was acting like a character with a full and complete life. It had feelings and moods, and Danny should've remembered how those moods could mess with him. Even the weather could play games. His time living in Hawaii had made his body less tolerant of extremes, so the cold snap had kept him from running. He'd missed the time outside, using his sister's treadmill instead. But it wasn't the same. Nothing was the same since he'd come home.

Cold be damned, he thought. In defiance he sat in one of the rocking chairs on the bookstore porch. The bite from the wind, the draw of the icy air into his lungs was a shock, a fantastic natural jolt. From where he sat, he had a bird's eye view of Main Street with all its emerging Christmas finery. The town started off by wrapping the antique-style lampposts with pine garlands and topping each with a deep red bow. Every tree, no matter what type, was being decked out with lights. As Jane had noted, it wasn't even Thanksgiving yet. This was going to be some party.

His mind drifted to the night before, when Jane confided in him. Whatever her dreams had been, the bookstore was her life now and it was easy to see that she put her whole heart and soul into making it a success. Logically, he knew she probably had nothing to worry about regarding her lease. The landlord could easily see that the building was in great hands. Jane and all the Fallons who came before her pumped a lot of money to keep the timbers in the old place strong. Danny wondered if he should offer to have his people check things out with her landlord. Maybe that would take a little pressure off. That way Jane could focus on her daughter and her business. It was a small thing he could do to help. The time he'd spent here recently showed him exactly how important Harbor Books was to the town, and to him.

She'd created something special. Sure, her father ran a great shop, but Jane? The place vibrated with her goodness. Whether she wanted to admit it or not, the bookstore was

Jane's destiny, and Angel Harbor was better for it.

Lost inside his own head, Dan didn't notice that someone was standing next to him until a steaming mug of coffee slowly passed under his nose. Turning his eyes in the direction from whence the coffee came, he saw Jane. With her hair lifted gently by the chilly breeze, she was snugly wrapped in a plaid blanket shawl to ward off the cold.

"Thank you." It was all he could mutter. She was a goddess. A beautiful goddess who gifted him with caffeine.

"You look like you have a lot on your mind," she said.

That was an understatement. "You know us writer types," he said. "We're always thinking too much."

"I've heard something about that. Is that who you are? The brooding artist?"

"I don't know about brooding," he said. "I'll take thoughtful, even contemplative, but I don't brood."

Jane smiled that beautiful smile, the one that went clear to her eyes, and Danny felt his stomach do a little turn. She was still the prettiest girl he'd ever met. Her slow, deliberate movements were so graceful, it was like watching a dancer. She sat down in the chair next to his, crossed her legs, and started rocking. Back and forth, back and forth, the rhythm was hypnotic. She didn't say anything, just lifted her chin and looked out at her town.

"I had a nice time last night," she said. "I got the third degree when I got home, but it was a lovely evening. Thank you."

"Who debriefed you?"

"My daughter. First she gave me a hard time about going out and not telling her where I was, who I was with, or when

I would be back. Then, she started asking all kinds of questions about our dinner."

He took a sip of his coffee and watched her expression carefully. Jane was being very cautious about what she revealed to him. Interesting. What was her game?

"What did she want to know?"

Jane took a deep breath, and he damn near died when she started chewing on her lower lip. "She wanted to know if our dinner was a date."

"Ah. What did you tell her?"

She smiled and turned her gaze in his direction. Bright and happy, Jane's eyes opened her heart to the world. Danny could watch her all day.

"That I'm not really sure. That's the most honest answer I could give. She had quite a few specific questions that seemed to bring her to the conclusion that it was, indeed, a date."

Danny leaned back in the chair and started to match Jane's rhythm, moving back and forth, the gentle motion lulling his brain. There was something very intimate about this time they were having together. It felt similar to the embrace they'd shared last night.

"For what it's worth," he said, "I think it was a date. Our first official one, and long overdue. For the record, I had a wonderful time as well."

"I see." Jane's cheeks turned pink, and he wanted to think it was a reaction to what he said, but to play it safe he was going to blame it on the cold. "I'm still not so sure." Her voice had a light, flirty lilt that was musical. It was incredibly attractive. He could listen to her all day.

When Danny looked over, he found her staring at him, a tiny grin on her lips. "Why aren't you sure?"

"I don't know. It felt like something was…missing." She stopped rocking, and stood, pulling her wrap tightly around her. "Don't stay out here too long—it's cold."

"I won't. I'm just going to soak in the morning for a while."

Jane dropped a hand on his shoulder and let it stay there for a moment. Through his jacket he could feel her kindheartedness, her energy. Everything about her seeped into him and jolted his body with awareness. The woman was dangerous.

"I was thinking about ordering lunch later rather than eating the yogurt I brought with me," Jane said as she reached the threshold. "Would you like me to add something for you?"

"That sounds good." Danny's eyes were fixed on her. She held the doorframe with her hand, leaning in almost, with one foot inside and one foot out. Her cheeks were pink from the cold, giving her skin a young, dewy quality. Her hair, with its many different shades of gold, caught the morning light, creating an aura that glowed and swirled around her like an ethereal crown. How was it, with all the years behind them, Jane was even more beautiful than she was at twenty-one? Maybe it was the years that made her so luminous. The inner wise woman was proving to be more attractive than any ingénue he'd ever dated. That was the moment that Danny realized he had it bad.

He'd always had it bad for her.

"If you have some time today, I'd love to talk to you

about my book. I'd really like your opinion about my story idea."

"Really?" Jane smiled. "I'd be happy to. We can chat over lunch."

"Perfect."

With a nod, Jane stepped inside and let the door shut behind her. Danny kept his eyes on the entry, even after she moved out of view.

What the hell was he going to do?

Danny directed his gaze back to the street and let himself drift back to the way she felt when he held her the night before. There was something so right and natural about it, and for the first time in ages, the idea that he didn't have to spend his life as a confirmed bachelor crossed his mind. Who would have thought at fifty-one he would finally grow up?

Convincing Jane that they should see where things could go might be tougher. He didn't have a great history to fall back on. She was tied to the town, and he never saw himself here for the long term. At least, *he never had.* Past tense.

Now he wasn't so sure. There was an appeal to settling down in a place where he could blend in and be part of something steady and safe.

Holding the mug in both hands the heat softened his edge, just like Jane. Holding her in the light November snow had brought him a sense of calm, when Dan was never calm. He looked up at the sound of footfalls on the porch steps and was greeted by the smiling face of a woman, about his age, with a shoulder-length strawberry blond bob. He got the distinct feeling he should know who she was.

"Hey there, Danny Gallo." She smiled, her pale blue eyes

twinkling in the morning sun. "I almost didn't recognize you without your notebooks and computer."

How did he know her? She'd called him Danny, so they went way back, but he was drawing a blank. "Wow. Hey! It's nice to see you."

Narrowing her eyes, she shook her head slightly. "You have no clue who I am, do you?"

He was the worst liar. How he made stuff up for a living, he'd never know. "I—" This was not going to work. "I'm so sorry. I know I should."

"We went to high school together. I'm Tracy Kelly. I was Tracy Neilsen in school. Jane and I were, still are actually, good friends."

Of course. She and Jane were very close, but she looked different. Then again, thirty years could do that to a person. "There's no excuse. Of course I should know you. You were the best backseat driver I ever had."

"Ha! You do remember me!" Tracy laughed at his description, so he could relax about not remembering her right away.

"I really am sorry. I should have recognized you. Here to see Jane?"

"Actually—" she shrugged "—I work here."

"Wait. What?" That blew him away. Was he completely oblivious?

"Yep. Full time."

"Now I feel dumb." Why hadn't he noticed her? "I've been here pretty consistently…"

"You've been a *little* busy. Jane filled me in. I figured I'd leave you alone. Once I get talking…" He remembered.

Tracy could talk. And talk.

"I am sorry, though. I totally zone out when I write. I'm like a zombie."

"I could see that. It's kind of cool to watch. It's like a cross between laser focus and obsession."

He chuckled at her spot-on assessment. There was something kind and decent about this woman. Dan remembered how she and Jane were like sisters in high school. It was nice to see friendships that lasted over the long haul. "That's accurate."

"Can you give me a hint about the next book?" Tracy giggled. "I'm a total fan."

"You might be disappointed then. I'm not writing a thriller."

Her face froze. This was how his fans were going to react. "No? *Wow.* I feel like I have the scoop of the century."

"I don't know how it's going to be received. That's all."

"Pssht. Your fans will follow. Good for you for trying something new. That's so exciting. I'll read anything you write."

"That's good to know. I'm a little worried that not everyone will react like you do."

"Some won't like it, but you'll reach other readers who haven't read your thrillers. There's no downside to it. You just have to give it your best."

"You sound like a mom."

"Three kids, all grown up. I consider the fact that they survived to adulthood a major accomplishment."

Danny laughed. "I'm staying with my sister and her family while I'm in town. That is a huge accomplishment."

"Damn right!" she exclaimed. "Well, it was awesome chatting, but I'm going inside before I freeze my buns off. Let me know if you need anything." Tracy folded her arms across her body to ward off a stiff breeze that bit into them. "Ack, it's cold. Lately it's like I have no blood. But I mean it, just ask. Anything you need."

He couldn't help smiling. "Thanks, Tracy. I appreciate it."

She smiled, and it was as welcoming as every day he'd spent in Angel Harbor. People were just nice here. It wasn't perfect, not by any stretch—the town had its issues. There was some petty bickering going on between town officials. One of the longtime store owners didn't like all the changes being implemented around the holidays, and he stopped into the bookstore almost daily to grumble at Jane. But overall, it was a peaceful place, and he'd acclimated far more easily than he thought he would.

He'd scribbled pages and pages of dialog over the past few days and now that he'd fleshed out a plan, he was ready to start building his early chapters. His process was convoluted, but for the first time in a while, Dan felt comfortable with it. Over the years he'd been tweaking and changing how he wrote based on his publisher's needs, his editor's advice, or his agent's prodding. From plotting every little twist and turn, dictating, using different methods to build characters—he listened to all the outside voices, and each time his books got further away from who he was.

It was like he told Tara the night he found her agonizing over her story; it was about the passion the writer brought to the work. An author owed the reader his truth.

His new book was going to do just that, and he was more certain than ever that Jane was going to help him find his way there.

THE BOOKSTORE ALWAYS put up two Christmas trees. One in the main area of the store, near the café and one in the children's room. The tree in the children's room was traditionally decorated on the Saturday after Thanksgiving when any child visiting the store was invited to make an ornament to hang on the tree. They served hot chocolate, cider, and cookies, and the space would be buzzing all day. It was one of her favorite days of the year, not because they sold a lot of books, but because the good will and holiday cheer permeated the shop. It all led up to the Harbor Lights festival that night. She was at her desk, ordering the supplies she would need for the ornament stations when a small knock made her look up. It was Tracy.

"Is everything okay?" Jane asked.

"Running like clockwork. I checked all the lights for the big tree—we're good there—and I grabbed the outdoor lights while I was in the basement and brought them up. We can get going on that project as soon as your uncle and the guy you hired get here."

Uncle Joe was going to put up the lights a week ago, but it had been too cold, so Jane finally hired a landscaper who was doing decorating during the off-season to do the actual light installation. Her uncle could supervise from the ground. "Thanks. I just ordered a gross of markers, stick-on stars, and glitter glue. The pinecones were ordered last week."

"It's going to be so much fun. I love watching the kids work. Will we have enough help?"

"Yes. The English Honor Society from the high school will be here. They're doing shifts to help the kids who come in. They're also doing a wrapping table. Free gift wrap on all in-store purchases, but people can donate what they want for the service."

"Awesome. I think we're ahead of schedule."

"We're getting there. Oh, can you help me set up the mailbox tomorrow? I expect we'll be seeing some Santa letters very soon." She knew there would be at least three coming in the near future.

"I'll put it on my list. Is that it?"

"I, ah, I think so."

Tracy narrowed her eyes for a second, before she pulled up a small chair and sat down with a plop. "Okay, girlfriend. Give it up. I've known you for too long not to have noticed that you are not yourself, even after having a hot date last night. What's going on? Is everyone okay? Are YOU okay?"

Of course she was okay. Everyone in her family was healthy and happy. Her business was doing well. She had good friends. But Tracy knew her better than almost anyone, so she'd obviously picked up on Jane's uneasiness.

"I'm fine, and I wouldn't exactly call it a hot date." Now she was lying. Never a good look on her. There might not have been a lot of sizzle between her and Danny, but there was definitely heat.

"Oh, for Pete's sake. Something isn't right, Jane. Is it

Tara? Your mom?"

"Everyone is fine!"

"Right." Tracy leaned back in her chair, frustrated. "I'm not clueless. I was going to come in here and harass you about Mr. Gorgeous Author out there, but you're preoccupied. What's going on?"

Did she tell her? There was no concrete reason for Jane to be worried. It was pure speculation.

"I guess I'm thinking too much about next year. Tara and Mom will be off on their respective adventures, and...I don't know, something has been bothering me for the last month."

"What? A disturbance in the Force? You could just be distracted by Danny."

"No, that's not it." She took a deep breath. "It's probably nothing, but I haven't received my new lease yet. Normally, I'd have it. It's been eating at me and I don't know why. Danny said not to worry..."

"*Danny* said?" Tracy's eyebrow shot up as a grin teased the corner of her mouth. "What did Danny say?"

"Stop it." Tracy's playful tone actually made Jane shiver a bit as she remembered the walk she took with him in perfect detail. "He said not to worry. There's plenty of time, and there are a thousand reasons it could be held up."

"But?"

"I dunno. It's not right." No matter how many times she reassured herself, Jane couldn't shake the feeling that something bad was brewing. "I'm acting crazy right?"

"Your woo-woo is usually pretty tuned in to the universe. Do you want me to talk to Elena Martin? If anything is going on with the real estate in this town, she'd know. She hears about changes in the market, offerings—whatever—before anyone. I don't know how she does it."

That was true. Elena did know everyone and everything that was happening within a ten-mile radius of Angel Harbor. "Sure. That might be a good idea. We're going to be so busy over the next two months, I don't need this weighing me down."

The bell over the door tinkled, and they both watched as Danny came inside. Jane's heart fluttered a little, just like a schoolgirl's. It was ridiculous, but it still felt wonderful. Like something was coming back to life, blooming inside her. Before making his way back to the table, he handed the china mug to the barista at the coffee bar, and sent a sweet smile in their direction.

"Wow," Tracy said, fanning herself. "Is it getting warm in here?"

Watching him go back to the table, Jane couldn't deny the man was a powerful presence. "It sure is."

WHEN DANNY GOT back to his cottage, he dropped on the couch, content for the first time in a year. He'd made real progress today, and he'd forgotten how satisfying that could be.

Jane had talked through some setting points with him over lunch, giving him some insight on "modern" small-town life, but mostly they caught up on what they'd been doing over the years. In some ways she was still the girl he knew in high school. She was whip smart, a little nerdy and awkward, but now she possessed a spine of steel, and a contagious calm. Dan was bottled nervous energy, always under extreme pressure, but being in Jane's presence had started to change that.

Sure, coming home, being with his family had been great, but there was something magical about her, something so centered it was seeping into him. Even as she faced huge changes in her own life, she found a way to focus on others. He wondered who worried about her. Dan was an intense individual. He didn't do calm, but for the first time since he'd left home all those years ago, he wasn't on edge.

It was nice. He could definitely get used to it. He could get used to her.

The woman was all heart and Dan wanted a piece of it for himself. It had only taken him thirty years to work up the nerve to be worthy of her.

He was brought out of his own thoughts by a small knock.

"Uncle Danny? Are you busy?" The little voice outside belonged to his niece, Jamie. Only eight years old, she acted like a toughie, but the kid had a heart of gold.

"Come on in, Jamie Girl." He watched as she poked her head in the door like she didn't know what she was going to see. "Hey!" he said. "Long time no see."

Not exactly true, since he'd seen her at breakfast, but she didn't react to his joke, letting him know there was something on her mind.

"Have you been at the bookstore all day?" she asked.

"I have. I've been working there. They have that big

round table and a comfortable chair. And coffee and cookies. It's a nice space to write."

"Better than the cottage?" She wasn't looking at him, and there was a tiny bit of fear in her voice.

"It's different. Not better or worse. Sometimes a writer has to stay with what's working." He patted the sofa cushion next to him, encouraging her to sit down. "Sweetie, what's this all about?"

After a second she seemed to screw up her courage. "We want to know if you're going to leave when you finish your book."

"We?"

"Me and Ella and Gavin."

At least they were talking again. When he heard about last night's row, he had his doubts. Not sure what he should say, he thought about her question. If she had asked him that a week ago, he probably would have said yes, because initially, he'd come home to change his mindset, to feel the vibe of the small town, and the East Coast. He still had a house in Hawaii and he did love it there, but his time back here had started to shift his perspective. His house was in a secluded area, and unlike New York or California, he didn't have a lot of friends living in the islands. If he spent an hour walking in Manhattan, he'd probably meet at least three people whom he knew. But even in the middle of the city, he could disappear if he wanted to.

In Angel Harbor it was different. For the first time he wanted the connection it provided, and that meant his answer to Jamie wasn't such a clear thing.

"You know, I think I might stick around for a while. As

long as Mom and Dad don't boot me out."

Jamie rolled her eyes. There was the attitude. Her mood must be passing.

"I don't think that's a problem." She grinned. "Are you going to eat with us tonight?"

He hadn't been in for a meal since he started on his writing tear earlier in the week. Watching Jamie's eyes bloom hopefully, he had no intention of saying no. "What's for dinner?"

"Homemade pizza. You can help if you want."

Standing, Dan reached out his hand and Jamie took it, her smile broad and happy. The feel of her small hand in his made him think about what he'd missed not having kids of his own.

It might be too late to be a dad, but he could be a better uncle, a better brother and brother-in-law. He could have been a better son, and paid more attention to his parents when they were still alive.

Dan always thought regret was a pointless emotion, but he was learning it had a purpose. It could serve as a catalyst for change, and he was all for that.

Chapter Eight

JANE LOOKED AT the blanket pattern for her next step and dug through her yarn bag for the right shade of blue. She'd just found out one of the young moms who came into the store regularly with her twin girls, was having another baby. She was due in only a few months and was both thrilled and overwhelmed. She and her husband had given up hope of having another baby, but after years of trying, Caitlyn was finally pregnant.

A baby was such a joy. Jane decided that since the new little bundle—a boy—would probably be one of her favorite customers, she could make him a baby blanket to welcome him to the world. She would add a couple of favorite children's books to the gift, because what kind of book pusher would she be if she didn't?

Caitlyn was the type of customer Jane loved best. She didn't spend a lot of money, but she was there often, using the store as a respite, a place to bring her girls when she needed a break in the routine. It was less structured than the library, and Jane was happy to offer the young mother, who had no family in the area, some friendship.

She wasn't the only one, either. There was a group of retired teachers who came twice a month to have coffee and catch up. She'd had her book clubs, and the writers' group that utilized the meeting room every month. There were so many people who had become friends, and she valued those connections more than she ever thought she would.

Nights like this were exactly what she needed when her brain was filled with too much stuff. Turning her attention back to her work, Jane transitioned to the new color. It was tricky, but Jane loved the calm, repetitive hand motion crocheting provided her. It was perfect for a quiet night at the store, and tonight was certainly that.

She'd had one customer come in for a book they'd put on order, but other than that the place was dead. She was sorry her part-timer was sick, but she wouldn't have had anything to do if she had come in.

That gave Jane some cherished time to think. No people, just her, some soft music, tea and her yarn.

She was trying to focus on the good things coming up. Thanksgiving was less than a week away, Tara would be hearing from her early decision school very soon, and her mother would be home from her trip. Then Christmas would go into overdrive, and she wouldn't have time to think about anything until after New Year's Day.

Shaking off the negative thread that wound through her brain, Jane focused on her stitches. Her fingers worked, pulling the soft gray-blue yarn through a series of twists and loops. It was predictable, and the pretty Celtic weave was coming out better than she expected.

The bell over the door jingled, pulling Jane out of her work. As soon as she looked up, she saw Danny coming toward her. Her heart, the dirty traitor, skipped a beat as his smile bloomed. Lord, that smile was everything.

"Are you by yourself?" he asked, looking toward the back room. "Where's Chloe?"

How could she not be affected by a man who loved her dog? "I am. Tracy took Chloe home around dinnertime, and my clerk didn't come in tonight. She's sick. It's probably just as well. Not that she's sick, but it's been pretty quiet, especially for a Friday night. I might actually close early."

"Yeah?" He unzipped his jacket. "Do you do that often?"

"Close early? Rarely, but I'm tired and town is dead except for the theater." Noticing his bag, she backtracked. "I can stay, though, if you want to work."

"Not necessary." He leaned over and looked at what she was doing, grazing his fingers over the blanket. "This is nice. Soft."

"Thank you. It's for a…for a friend. She's having a baby boy."

Danny tucked his thumb under the strap on his shoulder, giving it a tug into place. "Look," he said, "I should tell you, um, I didn't come in to work."

"No?" A little shudder raced through her. Jane knew what she wanted him to say, but she didn't dare hope. "Then why are you here?"

There was a moment's hesitation, just a second before he spoke. His eyes sparked, giving her a look at the depth of what he was feeling and this time, instead of his hand brushing the soft yarn of the blanket she was making, it landed on hers.

Warmth tickled through her, fluid and comforting. With just that single, intimate touch, Jane was lost.

"I came to see you."

"Ohhh." Her breath caught in her chest, while her heart patted rapidly along. "I…um…you did?"

"Yes." He looked away, and then back. "I feel like a kid. I mean, I thought you would be busy, and I was going to pretend to write. Is that stupid? I sound like a stalker."

Jane shook her head. How many times when she was a smitten teen had she stayed late with her dad just to be close to Danny? Should she tell him? "You're not a stalker," was all she could muster.

"I like being around you. You…" With a pained look he glanced up at the ceiling, then back at her. "This is going to sound strange, because I don't exactly understand it, but you settle me."

"I don't think it's strange. We gravitate to those who have something we need. Maybe—"

He cut her off, jumping on what she said. "Maybe you're what I need, Jane."

His words burned through her, allowing a long-protected part of her heart to crack open a little bit. In that tiny space, hope bloomed, and Jane thought maybe second chances weren't just for everyone else. His hand still covered hers, and Jane, feeling brave for the first time in ages, turned hers over, allowing her fingers to tangle with his. Danny stared at their joined hands, his thumb moving back and forth over her knuckles.

There was a bond between them that went beyond the old feelings and crushes. These emotions were mature, deep. They were the kind of emotions that could change lives forever. Feeling the heat rise in her face, Jane was determined not to miss another chance.

"You know what? I do think I'm going to close the store. Would you like to, I don't know, hang out?" She laughed at herself. "Is that the correct terminology?"

With a grin, he nodded. "I'd love to hang out with you."

"Okay. Let me start wrapping things up."

With a sense of purpose, Danny took off his jacket. "How can I help?"

ONCE SHE LOCKED the front door and set the alarm, Danny realized they were going on their second date, and without meaning to, she had asked him. This day was getting better and better.

"So," she said, turning to him, "what do you want to do?"

"I don't know." He really didn't care. Just having the opportunity to spend time with her was enough. "I saw the bakery was open—do you want to go there?"

Jane tilted her head and thought for a second. "Oooh. Good idea. I love Viti's chocolate mousse, and she makes an amazing apple tart."

"You won't get any argument from me."

"No? How's your blood sugar?" It was a joke, but not.

"I'm fine. It's why I run every day. Keeps all those numbers in check."

"I do my thirty on the elliptical. It's not as hardcore as the running, but it gets the job done. I'm careful because of what happened with my father."

"The maintenance is getting harder, isn't it?" He was only half joking. Jane's statement about her father was a good reality check.

"Yeah, but it's not bad. I'm actually in pretty good shape." Jane smiled and raised her arm in a mock flexing of her biceps.

He wanted to tell her she was in great shape. From where he was standing, she was pretty perfect. Jane had been rail thin when she was a teen. He'd seen her eat, that wasn't the problem, but she seemed to have the metabolism of a jackrabbit on speed. It got her teased pretty badly in junior high school, especially when combined with her braces and big glasses. No one could see past the big brain to the even bigger heart. But he did. He always knew what was inside. What made her special.

By the time she hit senior year, Jane had finally started to grow into herself. There was more confidence, a sense of adventure, but overcoming that shyness would be her challenge. When she left for college in DC, the braces were long gone, and she'd lost the glasses for contacts. She was pretty, smart, and ambitious. And she had big dreams.

Danny remembered visiting her once when he and a couple of his frat brothers stopped in DC on their way south for spring break. They waited for her in the student commons, a big open space in one of the newer buildings on the campus, which was a stone's throw from the National Mall.

He and his friends were picking through some fast food, when he heard her. That voice, clear and sweet, traveled over the din of the crowd around him and evoked a hundred memories.

"Danny!" she'd called.

When he looked up from his soggy fries, and saw her coming toward him, Danny's heart stopped in his chest. No longer skinny, but long and lean, Jane looked like she should be walking down a runway in a gown, not wearing a sweatshirt with a picture of the Rosetta Stone screened on the front. Her hair fell in soft waves to her shoulders, and when her smile bloomed and her dimples popped, the world pretty much stopped.

His friends had lost all powers of speech as she stood there chattering endlessly in that way she had. Charming. Adorable. Happy.

They hadn't seen each other in months, and sitting there Dan realized two things. The first was that he had missed her. He missed her so much the ache from it came roaring from the shadows. The second was that he couldn't do anything about how he felt. They were both too focused on school and the future to get wrapped up in a long-distance relationship. It was best for him to keep quiet and suffer in silence.

And he did. Mostly. They stayed safely in the friend zone until they graduated college and spent the following summer inseparable. Those months changed everything, and he wasn't man enough to admit it.

Janie was brave, though. She'd told him how she felt, but that didn't stop him from making the biggest mistake of his life.

Dan rationalized that Jane's work couldn't be fixed in one place. Back then, being on the move was the only way she would thrive. She wanted to make a difference in the world. And while she wasn't making all those great discoveries she'd dreamed of, by running a bookstore she put positive energy into the universe every single day.

Without any conversation, they left the confines of the porch and turned right onto the brick sidewalk that wound through town. Each passing day brought more holiday spirit to the streets. Wreaths and garlands adorned the outsides of stores, and twinkling lights made all of Main Street sparkle like it was dipped in crystals and jewels.

"It's not as cold tonight as it's been. I'm a little surprised."

Jane shrugged. "It's so unpredictable lately. I want it to get cold and stay cold for the season. This up and down stuff messes with my head."

"I get it."

"Are you having a hard time adjusting to the northeast after spending a year in Hawaii?"

"It's getting better, but I'm with you. Cold isn't a bad thing. It allows the environment to reset. I like the seasons."

He'd thought that all through November and December last year while he was skimming shells on his beach in Hawaii. Tiki huts decorated with garland and tinsel, barbeques and a surfing Santa just didn't feel right to him. Dan had turned his back on his life because he no longer wanted to inhabit the world of psychopaths and murderers. Unfortunately, he'd created another type of prison; this one just had a beach.

It had taken a long time for him to pull himself out of the pit he'd fallen into. But the climb out started on the day he opened his computer and put in a simple search. "Angel Harbor."

He hadn't been home in years. When his mom died, he flew his family to her favorite beach in Florida so they could reminisce and say their goodbyes. It was appropriate, and odd, and it kept him from setting foot in the town. He was sure with enough therapy someone could tell him why he'd avoided coming home. Guilt was probably one part of it. Fear was another, but after a full year of being alone 99 percent of the time, he'd had enough.

The search yielded an excess of results. He saw the renovated waterfront. A list of restaurants that would make any foodie happy. There were quirky new businesses as well as the ones that had been there for years. And finally, in one picture he saw Jane, standing on the front porch of the bookstore, her eyes shining and her smile wide and welcoming.

For the first time since he got the news about the murder that had been committed using one of his books as a blueprint, Dan felt like there was light pushing through the darkness. He'd fallen into a pitch-black hole and even surrounding himself with endless sunshine hadn't pulled him out. Seeing Jane was like having a bucket of ice water poured over his head. It was a shock, a catalyst, a summons. The universe had sent him a wake-up call.

His new book, his time in Angel Harbor, and Jane, were all part of Dan's epiphany. Especially Jane.

They were close, their arms brushing as they made their way up the street to Sweet Chemistry. Dan loved the name of the place, and he'd stopped in there when he first came back to town when the smell coming from the inside was too much to resist.

The business had an amazing story to boot. The brainchild of a former industrial chemist, Viti Prasad found she liked mixing butter, sugar, eggs, and chocolate more than messing with acids and bases. The shop created the most amazing pastries, donuts, hand-poured chocolates, cakes, and desserts from here to the Hamptons, and based on what he'd seen, Jane was addicted. She kept a stock of Viti's cookies and croissants in the treat case at the bookshop and there was rarely a day that she had anything left over.

With polished black and white tile floors, sparkling stainless steel, gleaming wood and brass accents for a vintage touch, Sweet Chemistry looked like a cross between an old-fashioned ice cream parlor and a lab.

As he should have expected, the shop was packed when they arrived. The crowd, which skewed older, was happily chatting and laughing while sipping coffee and eating Viti's goodies. There wasn't a seat to be had—even the window seat was taken.

"Wow. I guess you know where everyone who is normally in the bookstore is hanging out."

"It must be the theater crowd. Viti keeps the café open on nights the theater has events. I think tonight was a string quartet."

"That's great for her business, but bad for us."

"No. We can just take our desserts to go."

"Back to the bookstore, then?" He wouldn't mind that. As long as he was with her, he didn't care where they were.

"I was thinking my kitchen is probably more comfortable. And as much as Viti makes great food, I make better coffee."

Her house. She was inviting him to her house. "That sounds perfect."

Her smile, sweet and soft, affected him on the most visceral level. This woman, with her twists and turns, her history and her worries was becoming more important to him than she was before.

When they stepped inside, the warm air mingling with the scent of sugar, cinnamon, and butter brought him back to his family kitchen when he would come home from school before Christmas, and his mother had spent the day baking. Jars and containers were filled with different kinds of cookies and sweets, and the memory of Christmas, and his mother and home, made him nostalgic.

He knew scent was a powerful trigger. Between the heady aromas in the shop and the soft woman next to him, Dan was falling into an abyss of memories.

He'd become so wrapped up in the life he'd made as an author, that he'd forgotten where he'd started. Forgotten who had given him the time and the confidence to pursue his dream. Sure, he'd worked hard, and honed his craft, but it was this wonderful woman, and the girl she'd been, who gave him the courage to try in the first place.

"What are you thinking?" she asked him. Jane was bent slightly at the waist, her eyes surveying the contents of the case that held a dizzying array of goods.

"The apple tart looks good. But look at *that.*" Dan pointed at a gorgeous dessert of layered pastry, berries, and cream. "I had that once when I was in Europe. It would go right to my gut, but I'm tempted."

"*Mille-feuille.* Mmm. I haven't had it in years. There was

a little French patisserie in London that I loved. When I lived there, I'd go at least once a week. They made it like no one else. Between that and the Pot de Crème, I put on ten pounds."

"When did you live in London?"

"Long time ago. I had just finished my first year of grad school, and I had a short fellowship at the British Museum."

"That must have been cool. What was your specialty?" He ordered the pastry and some macarons, while Jane ordered the chocolate mousse.

"I ended up focusing on Celtic history and folklore. Ireland, Wales, and Scotland were particular areas of interest for me. I was also doing a little research on Nordic raiders."

"Wow. That's intense. So when Ella wanted the *Camelot Academy* book…"

"God, I love that series," she sighed. "It's as magical as it should be. The author did great research. The premise is as grand as the twelfth-century legend, with a little of the darker fifth century sprinkled in. Kids just love it. I'm going to have a book discussion about the newest title over Christmas break, a lunch and learn, so the kids have something to do. Tell Ella, okay?"

"I will." He loved listening to her talk. There was such affection and passion not just for the legends and history, but for books and children, as well. The depth of her love and understanding for all creatures, human and otherwise, made Dan feel honored to know this woman a little better than he did before. "Do you want to go back? To the UK?"

"I'd love to. I had such a good time living there. I had an adorable little flat in Covent Garden. It was a fourth-floor walkup, with an amazing view. So beautiful. I walked to work every day. You would have loved it. So many stories." Her eyes looked distant, like she'd slipped away for a little bit. "Anyway, after that I had a few semesters back in New York, and then I was off to Scotland on that dig—"

The dig that never was, he thought. She was on her way home before it ever really got started. Her studies, and her career, were derailed with one horrible phone call. But in spite of the setback, Jane had made an amazing life for herself in Angel Harbor. She made an impact every single day, even if it wasn't obvious.

They left the bakery and were standing on the street, neither of them focused on where they were going. Jane seemed to realize she was rambling.

"I guess we should head to my house. I think I promised you coffee."

"You did. I'm parked right next to your store. Let's go." This time, instead of taking his arm, Jane reached down and clasped his hand. Lacing his fingers with hers was so incredibly easy, comfortable—it felt too good to be true.

Could they have a shot at something more than this odd, but special friendship? Did Dan have the nerve?

He had no idea. What he did know was that this woman changed the way he saw himself, and what he valued. Dan didn't know if there was any way to turn back.

OF ALL THE things Jane never expected this evening, the one she expected the least was that she would be sitting in a car next to Danny Gallo on the way to her house.

She'd walked to work that day, knowing the weather would be cooperative. Evening walks home were quick, and sometimes chilly, but she relished the quiet time to unwind from her day. Riding in a low-slung sports car, with French desserts in her lap, was definitely an interesting turn of events.

She couldn't complain, though, because he was absolutely delicious. And Jane had to admit, she loved being with him, maybe even more now than she did when she was a silly teen.

He was easygoing and funny. His needs were simple, but his goals were still lofty. Dan was a man who took nothing for granted, and while she could sense this in him, it felt like it was new, and he was coming to grips with it himself. He still hadn't filled her in on everything that had brought about his career pivot, and kept the details to what she already knew.

When he parked in her driveway, the outside lights came on and brought her home into focus. It was the home of her childhood, and her adulthood, and while both eras had their memories, the second act was not what she'd expected.

Maybe it was her own immaturity that had led to her being blindsided by the course correction. Sure, she'd weathered the grief and sadness over her father's death and the loss of a career that she was passionate about, but was she happy now? Content?

She was. After all this time, Jane could honestly say that while her life wasn't what she expected, she had no regrets. There was too much to be thankful for to ever be sorry.

Danny was leaning against the steering wheel, looking at the house through the windshield. He was quiet, his eyes unblinking as he took in the details.

"This is a really beautiful house. The changes you've made are subtle, and the character of the place…it suits you."

"Thank you. It's not large, but it's perfect for us. Having a good-size piece of property so close to town is a big plus. Chloe appreciates that."

He glanced over and that enchanting grin made an appearance. "It's you. Charming, and elegant, but welcoming."

"Elegant? I don't know about that."

"Sure it is. Look at the lines, at the way the room out the back extends without any jerky angles. The gardens are well proportioned, and I imagine bursts of color bring that rich gray to life in the spring and summer. It's a perfect coastal cottage. Everything fits."

"Wow," she said, feeling the flush rise in her cheeks. "You're great with words. Are you a writer or something?"

"Or something," he replied. Yep. There was that grin again.

He pulled the door handle and exited the car leaving Jane in a puddle of her own thoughts. While she gathered her things, including the pastry box on her lap, Danny came around and opened the door. He took the box from her with one hand then extended the other to help her out, allowing her to relish the warmth of his touch. It was such a gentlemanly thing to do, and she so appreciated all the little courtesies.

She rarely dated, and if she did, Jane found the men lacking in so many ways. Not showing up on time, being attached to their devices, canceling at the last minute, or just general rudeness, seemed to be the order of the day. There was an abundance of self-importance, and a serious lack of gentility. Age wasn't a factor either, as some people had suggested. Since she only dated men close to her own age, she often wondered if maybe she was too picky, that she had unrealistic expectations, but it had become more and more apparent that Jane was just a loser magnet. There was no other explanation.

The way Danny behaved, like being with her was more important to him than anything else, was a change she could get used to very quickly.

As they walked down the driveway toward the side door, he looked at the large double window when he heard Chloe's bark of alarm. Her long nose had pushed aside the sheer curtains and she was smiling in anticipation.

"She knows we're here," he said. "That's a happy dog."

"I swear, she hears my car a block away." The dog was going to go crazy when they walked in, and Jane hoped Danny was ready for all sixty-five pounds of wiggling fur that was going to hurtle in his direction. The dog absolutely loved him, and Jane was beginning to understand why.

He stopped suddenly and fixed his eyes on the end of the driveway. "Now *that* is a garage. It's huge!"

Ah, testosterone. Her garage was the envy of almost every man in Angel Harbor. It was, as he declared, huge. "That it is. My dad built it after I left for college. It might have only slightly less square footage than my house."

The bottom of the garage had three bays and was extra

deep so there was plenty of room for a workbench and tool storage. Shingled in the same blue gray as the house, there was a little covered stoop on the side, which led to a set of stairs. The building had a full second story, which already had heat and plumbing roughed in. She hadn't yet done anything with it, but often thought it would be a good office, guest suite, or even a space for Tara if she wanted a little more distance when she was at home during school breaks.

Writers needed space, didn't they? Jane thought.

"It's twice the size of my sister's cottage, and that's more than comfortable. How did I not notice it when we went to dinner the other night?"

"If you didn't have the cottage at your sister's, I'd suggest getting a place in town so you could, you know…" She hesitated. "Ah, visit more. I know a good realtor."

"Hmm. Something to think about. But I wouldn't be able to make trouble with the kids as easily if I wasn't right there."

Jane laughed. "Noted."

He stood back while she unlocked the door, and they both braced for Chloe's greeting.

Dan set the pastries down on the washing machine just inside the back door and went down on one knee. The dog's entire back end flew from side to side, not because Jane was home after a long day, but because Chloe's new best friend had come for a visit.

Jane admired her dog's taste in humans. It was, indeed, exceptional.

Chapter Nine

"I DON'T KNOW how you can say *Die Hard* is a Christmas movie." Jane took the plate from in front of him and walked to the sink. The man had eaten his weight in baked goods and was still picking at one of the macarons that was left in the box.

"Sorry. I'm not budging on this," he said before licking a bit of chocolate cream off his index finger.

"It's set at Christmas, but it's NOT in the genre." This was a ridiculous argument. Why was it even a thing?

"You're a holiday movie snob," he teased. "It's a Christmas movie. There are Christmas carols is in it. Christmas lights."

"Are you serious?"

Danny laughed. "Christmas is mentioned in the script eighteen times!"

Jane shook her head. Now he was just messing with her. "Eighteen times? I'm sorry. Why do you actually know that?"

"I'm a lawyer. It's how I win arguments."

He was going to pull the lawyer card? He had no idea who he was dealing with.

She was a scientist; facts were her wheelhouse. "Was it the intent of the studio and the filmmaker to market it as a

Christmas movie, counselor?" Jane turned to face him and reached back to place her hands on the edge of the cool granite countertop.

"What did you say? Intent? I'm not going to dither over intent."

Rising, he picked up both coffee mugs and moved to where she was standing, setting the mugs in the sink before turning to her with a smile. "You're not going to win this, Janie."

She narrowed her eyes. That silly man. "Intent doesn't matter?"

"No."

"Hmm. Attempted murder, robbery, assault. That sounds to me like intent matters. Attempt to defraud? Intent."

"Those are crimes. It's not the same thing." His eyes narrowed, however, and she could see that her argument had hit home.

"Calling a movie about a murderous gang of bank robbers a Christmas movie is a crime."

"Come on." He folded his arms, digging in.

"No. It was released in July. It was never marketed with any Christmas theme. The tag line focused on the adventure aspect. Not. A. Christmas. Movie. Santa wasn't even in the movie, not once."

Danny chuckled and moved a little closer. His scent was subtle, but made her oh-so-aware of his proximity. *Bergamot, cedar, spice. Just like the other night.*

"We're going to have to agree to disagree then."

"Fine." Jane folded her arms and looked away. She

couldn't keep up with the zing of desire pulsing through her. The man was lethal. "You'll still be wrong," she muttered.

When she glanced over, she saw his smile, while his blue eyes flashed with humor. And heat. Intense heat that traveled through her body on a wave.

Jane remembered these feelings all too well. She'd hoped she'd be immune to him after all this time, but it appeared the years and the maturity only made him more attractive. But Danny wasn't staying in Angel Harbor. He had come home with a specific goal, and a relationship with a small-town shopkeeper wasn't it.

For so long, Jane had kept her emotions wrapped up tight. Now she was on the cusp of letting go of all that control because of the wonderful boy who was now an amazing man.

She shuddered when he reached out and took her hand. He was so close, she could feel the heat coming off of his big body.

He filled the space, six feet tall, broad and muscled. Danny's proximity caused the warmth to bubble and churn in her belly. When his other hand came up and tucked a loose strand of hair behind her ear, Jane was undone.

"You're still the same, you know?"

"The same?" Jane looked up and nearly drowned in the blue of his eyes. "How so?"

"Sweet. Kind. Always thinking about others."

The words floated around her, dredging up the old feelings even more. She remembered the little wisps of hurt in her heart every time she heard news of a new book, or movie, or saw photos of his glamorous author life.

She wasn't enough for him. She knew it then, and it was still true now.

What she needed was a little distance, and the car door slamming outside gave her the perfect excuse to step back.

"That's Tara." Jane could barely hear her own voice over the pounding of her heart. It took a second for her words to register, but when they did, he dropped his hands.

"Right." The disappointment cast a shadow in his eyes, and it forced her consider what might be going on in his head. Did he want more? Was he feeling the same pull she felt, something that went beyond just a fling?

"What's wrong, Jane? Tell me."

Was something wrong, or was Jane just a realist? Sometimes the truth hurt.

"Nothing. Don't worry about it." Jane felt the flush rising in her cheeks. *Fabulous.*

He was about to speak when Chloe hopped off her bed, ran to the side door, and started barking. In seconds she heard Tara greeting the dog.

"Mom!" her daughter said, excited and breathless. "It didn't suck! I was really worried, but—" Tara stopped short when she walked into the kitchen and saw Danny leaning against the counter right next to her very red-faced mother. "Oh, hi."

His hand came up in a little wave.

"So, it went well?" Jane asked. "No missed cues? No set disasters?"

Tara shifted her gaze back to Jane and nodded. "It was perfect. Everyone loved it. I can't wait for you to see it tomorrow. Aunt Tracy is going to pee herself."

Danny looked away, grinning at that little bit of information.

"About that. She called. She can't make it."

"Oh no! So you're flying solo?"

Jane went out by herself all the time. Tracy had a wonderful husband, and she wasn't always available to be Jane's wingman. She'd checked with Viti and Claire, and both of them were busy as well. "It's fine. I'll run into someone I know."

"I'll go with you." Danny had moved to one of the stools at the kitchen island, looking casual and completely at ease with the suggestion. He was obviously out of his mind. He shrugged while Jane stood there, stunned silent. "What?" he asked indignantly. "Got a hot date?"

"No. But, um, I guess I don't understand. There will be a lot of people there. You don't have to come with me."

"That's actually perfect," Tara said clapping her hands together. "Have you been back to school since you graduated?"

"I have not," Danny said.

"Then I'll have to give you a tour of the new theater complex. It was renovated two years ago. The entire auditorium, and music hall. It cost a fortune. Five million dollars, all donated."

"Wow," he said with a raised eyebrow. "Someone has deep pockets."

Jane watched the exchange and something about his reaction to the information about the theater renovation was…off. *Interesting.* She dismissed the idea before it took hold, but she wondered what was behind his response.

"I'm happy to go with you, Janie."

Realizing she was beaten, Jane nodded. What was his game, she wondered? "The show is at seven-thirty."

"Dinner first? Or after?" he asked. Now he wanted to go to dinner too? The man was not making this easy for her. How was she supposed to resist him?

"Um, after!" Tara said. "The directors could always use some extra adults at the diner. Why don't you come there after the show?"

Who was this child? Jane mused. "Wait. Are you inviting us out with the cast and crew? This is your fourth show, and I've always been banned from such activities."

Tara rolled her eyes. "Mom, stop. It's my senior year. Why not?"

Danny had dropped his head, trying to hide the laugh, understanding this was going to be a lot more than either of them bargained for. He was being a good sport about it, but for someone who was laying low, this was a pretty public outing. "Dozens of loud teenagers? Sounds like a great time."

"You don't have to…" This was getting worse and worse. She didn't know if she should try to save him from the mayhem, or toss him right in the middle of it.

"Nah. I'm in."

Tara smiled wide, and Jane felt like she'd been double-teamed. "Fine. I'll meet you there at…"

"I'll pick you up. Six-thirty? Seven?"

She didn't even bother to put up a fight. There was no point. "Six-thirty. It's going to be crowded."

"Great." Popping off the stool, he nodded to Tara. "I'm going to take off."

"See you tomorrow," her daughter said brightly. What a turncoat.

This was getting more and more bizarre. He was flirting openly, in front of her daughter. It was like he'd been issued a challenge and Jane was the prize.

She stood in the doorway between the kitchen and the mudroom, watching him as he put on his coat. The dark wool fabric spanned his broad shoulders and back. It was such a simple thing, so unremarkable, but it was so incredibly sexy. He was too damn gorgeous for his own good, or for hers.

"What are you up to, Danny Gallo?" she whispered.

"Me?" he grinned. "Nothing. Third time, Janie. Third time." With that he kissed her on the cheek, lingering just a little above the corner of her mouth. He winked and let himself out.

Jane was left speechless, once again.

Tara, on the other hand, was kinetic, running to the window with the dog, and dashing back to her. She was darting around like The Flash.

Jane still hadn't moved. *Third time,* he'd said. As in *third time's a charm?*

"Mom! Oh my God!" Tara grabbed her hand and yanked her back into the kitchen. "He's totally into you."

"What? No! Don't be ridiculous."

"*Janie?* He calls you Janie? It's adorable."

It was adorable, and it made her insides quiver like a plucked bow. Everything about him was dangerous to her very vulnerable heart. He was charming, smart, and so funny. He was a talented man with a deep emotional well, and even though he hadn't mentioned it, he was hurting.

Tara was chattering away about the play and her friends, and how cool it was that Dan was going to come to the performance. She reached into the sea green bakery box on the table and pulled out one of the macarons. "These are so good."

"Nothing from Viti's shop is ever less than bliss-inducing."

"Amen to that." Tara finished the last bite and leaned in, curiosity swirling in her eyes. "You like him."

Always, she thought. In fact it was probably more than just liking him. She was halfway in love with him already, and that was halfway too far because it was beyond any hope to think there could be more between them. He was leaving, and Jane didn't think she was equipped to handle what Danny Gallo could do to her tender heart.

TARA FALLON WAS impressive. The thought was on an endless loop in his head the more she talked about the renovation. She'd found him and Jane as soon as they'd walked into the school, and once she walked them to their reserved front-row seats, she took him on the tour she'd promised.

He'd lied about not being back to the school since graduation; he'd actually come in after hours a few weeks ago. Matt Hennings, the theater director, had given him a look at the upgraded facility. Matt grew up next door to Dan's family and he'd spent more than a few nights babysitting

Matt and his little brother. When Mel told him the district was running short on funds to bring the theater program to the next level, Dan knew he had the power to make it happen. It wasn't for the five million that Tara had quoted, but the amount was in the seven figures, and Dan had no problem sending them the money.

His agent and his business manager thought he was crazy, but why did he have all that money if he couldn't do some good with it? The arts were important, and they were consistently shortchanged. He had his business manager write the biggest donation check of his life and send it off. Nothing had felt that good in a long time.

Dan had been a jock in school, playing football and lacrosse, but in his heart he had always been a writer. He believed in words, in paintings and photographs, in sculpture, and in film. He knew math and science were important, but the arts spoke to the soul.

Jane got this. She might have been a scientist by training, but her appreciation for what past civilizations left behind was grounded in the arts. The beautiful things humans created told a powerful story, and unearthing those stories had been Jane's passion.

Like her mother, Tara's enthusiasm was contagious as she walked him through the tech booth and then the changes made to the stage. This was her domain. As the stage manager, Tara made sure the production ran smoothly. She coordinated the actors, stage crew, costume and prop departments. The modifications to the stage wings made controlling the flow of people and scenery so much easier.

"The drop-down prop table has been a game changer. It

was one of those little additions that made a huge impact. Also, the expansion into the classroom next door gave us rooms for quick changes. The actors have privacy and we have space to store costumes."

"This is amazing, Tara." Every inch of the stage was well thought out and functional. "I appreciate the tour. I was never a theater guy, but there were more than a few times I brought your mom something to eat when she was here for long days, painting sets."

"You did that?" Tara's eyes went dewy at his admission. "That's so sweet!"

"Eh, that's what friends do for each other."

"I guess." Tara gave him a sly grin and the side-eye. "Sounds like you were a *very* good friend to her."

Sure. Until he'd graduated. Then he wasn't just a lousy friend, he'd hurt her. He wasn't proud of the way he'd acted and was trying to do better.

"I have to get to work." She smiled, anticipating their closing night. "Can you find your way back?"

"I can manage. Thank you for the tour. Break a leg."

He'd barely gotten the words out when she dashed off with a wave. Dan could feel the energy ricocheting around the space. It was electric, even more charged than a locker room before a big game. He envied Tara. She had so much ahead of her, and if she embraced every opportunity, she'd never have to live with regret.

As he made his way into the auditorium, he passed Matt Hennings, who gave him a quick hug and thanked him again. Dan tried to brush off the thanks, but seeing how much the renovation meant to the kids, he was glad he'd made the gift.

It was one of those small things that made a big impact.

The crowd in the auditorium was growing, and he found the sense of community another reason to love Angel Harbor. It felt like the whole town had come out to see the high school production of *A Christmas Carol.* Whether the people were there to get in the holiday spirit or support someone they knew, the attendance was something to behold. This was what friends did for each other. They showed up.

He saw Jane leafing through the program, running her hand over the full-page ad for the bookstore. Dan stood for a moment, watching her; he started when she caught him staring. His heart actually skipped a beat.

"How was your tour?" she asked, moving her purse from the seat next to her so he could sit.

"Oh. Ah. Great! They've made a lot of changes since you were a theater rat."

"They have. The kids and the teachers deserve this. So does the town." Warmth seeped through him as she took his hand in hers. "You did an amazing thing."

Her words, soft so only he could hear, sent a shockwave through him. Where did that come from? Did someone tell her? Dan had made it clear that the donation was to remain anonymous. He didn't want accolades or anything named after him; he just wanted the money to go to the kids.

"I don't know what you mean," he said. That was stupid.

"Stop it."

Jane nailed him with that all-knowing gaze, and he gave up the ruse. He couldn't fool her. He never could. "How did you find out?"

She shrugged. "Just a feeling." Her hand squeezed his. "I can't wrap my head around it. It's so incredibly generous."

"It's only money, Jane. The results of the investment are so much more important."

"It was kind."

"And the least I could do."

She leaned into him, closing the space so their arms and shoulders touched. It was subtle, almost imperceptible, but he could feel her gratitude, her respect, and her affection. Maybe there was even a little bit of forgiveness. It meant more to him than any award, or bestseller list. Her respect was all he craved. He hadn't led an exemplary life, but with that simple gesture, Dan felt like he'd been given his second chance.

THE SHOW WAS so well done. Heartwarming and funny in spots, it had hit every note a holiday play should hit. During the curtain call the cast had the whole audience singing Christmas carols, and the after party at the diner was noisy and fun. The kids had developed such an incredible bond. He patted himself on the back for giving them a new playground where they could shine.

He'd meant what he'd said earlier—it was *only* money. The time and effort put in by the students and their teachers, and by their parents, was what needed to be celebrated.

The ride back to her house had been quiet, with Jane looking out the window, lost in her thoughts. He'd loved watching her at the diner, joking with the kids, and chatting with other adults. He wished he had her gift, the ability to read people even when they said almost nothing. She could make the most introverted person feel comfortable and welcome. Dan knew Jane was important to the town and all the people in it, but he was especially moved by Tara, whose pride in her mom spoke volumes.

Mother and daughter had shared an affectionate hug right after the curtain came down, and again when they were at the after party. The two of them, to use a cliché, were two sides of the same coin, with one exuding excitement at the future and the other sending out her understanding into the universe. Their vibe encircled the room, and Dan was lucky to be part of it.

"You'll come to our house for Thanksgiving." Her words, which were a statement, not a request, broke the thick silence in the car.

"I…uh…okay?"

Stopped at a light, he looked over and found her smiling sweetly. "Tara overheard you telling Matt Hennings your sister is going out of town to her in-laws. She…insists."

He did tell him that, unaware that Tara had been in earshot. *Those Fallon women.* Always finding out people's secrets. He could have declined the invitation and said he was going to spend the time on his own to write, but the idea of being at a family gathering in her comfortable home was far more appealing than heating up a frozen pizza.

"Thank you," he said. "If you're sure it's not an imposition, I'd love to be there." Just as he said it, the light turned green, and he made the turn onto Bay Avenue, fully aware their evening was close to being over, and wishing he could make it go on forever.

"You're not going to argue with me?" She chuckled. "Not even a little?"

"Nah. No point. Resistance is futile where you're concerned." That was the truth. Dan was such a goner.

"I'm glad you finally understand."

He understood it long before then. It was probably one of the reasons he didn't come home, why he didn't call, why he didn't make any attempt to see her. Dan knew that Jane was his siren song. He couldn't defy the pull she had on him. Tonight was proof.

The outside lights turned on when he pulled in to the driveway, illuminating the familiar scene. The home she'd created was imbued with her kindheartedness and goodness.

"There's the welcoming committee." Chloe was smiling at the car from the big window, her tail swishing behind her.

Jane leaned over to take a look. "She's not barking. I guess she's used to you already."

If only. He wanted to be part of her life, her family, more than he ever thought possible.

"I had fun. Thanks for putting up with me," he said, wishing he had come up with something else.

"Putting up with you? Are you kidding?"

"Hey, I can be a pain in the ass."

"I'm aware." Jane didn't wait for him this time, opening her door and climbing out of the car. He did the same and met her as she rounded the hood.

They stood close, and Jane surprised him, stepping into his space, closing any distance between them. Heat surged through him, a reaction to the swirling emotions he felt just being near her. Their hands brushed, fingers lacing together as they stood without a breath of space between them.

He examined her face, still as beautiful as when she was a girl, but now her eyes possessed a wisdom and a calm Dan desperately needed.

"I wish you could see yourself as I see you," she said. "You're such a good man. I know you have all these ingrained ideas about who you are, but you need to let those go."

With a shake of his head, he dropped his forehead to hers. "I should have done better, with everything. Everyone. I—"

He was surprised by the soft pressure of her mouth. A gentle touch that shocked him into awareness.

"Shush," she said. "Stop. I won't have you talking badly about my friend."

"He's lucky to have you—you know that right?"

"I'm lucky to have him too. I've missed him." Jane's eyes glittered with unshed tears and Dan lost his whole heart. This time, when she kissed him, everything spun and crashed; the only thing he was aware of was the lush feel of her lips on his. The gentle sips and sweet taste, like vanilla and whipped cream, surrounded him. He reached up and cupped her face in his hands, angling her mouth so he could go a little deeper, get a little closer. There was no way he wanted to stop.

He didn't know how long they kissed before they were snapped out of the trance by Chloe's plaintive bark. The awareness of the woman pressed into him, of his response to her, swamped him. The rush of emotions had his brain, his heart, and his soul screaming at him not to be an idiot this time. God knew, he had the potential.

"I think she's jealous," she joked.

"I love your dog, but I don't want to kiss her."

"Good to know." She stepped back and he was aware of her absence immediately. He missed the feel of her body, of her mouth. Dan realized he'd been craving that kiss for a very long time.

"I'll see you tomorrow?" she asked, hopeful enthusiasm dancing in her eyes.

"Bright and early." After tonight, he didn't know how he would stay away.

Chapter Ten

TEN PEOPLE. SHE should be able to seat ten people at the table without overthinking. Yet here she was, turning the task into a major project. It wasn't brain surgery.

From the amount of mental drama they were causing her, the cards in her hand could have weighed a thousand pounds. Somehow, adding one new person to the table was a heavier problem than it should have been. How had this particular person become so important to her again, so quickly? Was she channeling her inner seventeen-year-old self? Was she desperate? Or was he hitting an emotional note—was he that elusive soul mate?

She hadn't seen him for a couple of days. He'd taken the kids into the city for a play yesterday before they headed to their grandparents upstate this morning.

Sunday morning, after their kiss, he showed up at the bookstore right at nine while she was getting ready for the day. She had come in early to get more decorating done and check her inventory for Small Business Saturday, but he knocked on her door bearing egg sandwiches from one of the best gourmet delis around. Their cheese biscuits were to die for, and Jane had no problem taking a break to have breakfast with him.

It should have been awkward considering what had happened the night before, but it wasn't. If anything, Jane was hyper aware. Danny was such a presence. While youth certainly had its appeal, a strong, mature, somewhat complicated man who knew his mind was all she was interested in.

Their kiss—sweet, almost chaste—set loose a cascade of feelings. Things she remembered so clearly from her youth but didn't fully appreciate were now beginning to take shape again, and checking off so many boxes.

There was only one thing—his leaving—that left her wondering if she was making a huge mistake letting him get close again.

Jane was on tenterhooks, and as she stood by the table, she thought about all the people who would be with her. Blood relatives or not, the people coming today knew her better than she knew herself. There was a closeness that belied distance and time. Especially time.

"Penny for your thoughts?" Her mother, who had arrived home on Sunday, glided over, like a skater on the ice. Jane felt a little guilty for not telling her what had been going on with Danny, but her concern was twofold. First she liked having something just for herself. Whatever Tara thought she knew, she didn't really know that much. Hell, Jane wasn't sure. What would she tell people?

Second, what were Danny's plans? That was the million dollar question.

"The table looks lovely, as always," her mother said. It really was pretty. The deep autumn-themed table runner was a brown, burnt orange, gold, and deep red plaid, with traces of ivory. The round, deep brown placemats were set with her beautiful dimple-etched cream stoneware, autumn-colored napkins, and her good flatware. She'd finished the place settings with wine and water glasses as well as adorning the table with gourds grouped at each end.

A pretty table was something Jane took pride in. Naturally, she wanted to serve a delicious meal, but the table, where everyone gathered, had to reflect the love and affection of the season. Perhaps it was unnecessary, but a pretty table said that she cared.

"Thanks, just trying to seat everyone."

"Hmmm. Who do we have? Tara, you, and me. Uncle Joe and Aunt Nancy. Jasper and his wife." Her cousin and his new bride were last-minute additions. He could be a little abrasive, but he was family and there was always room at the table for family, and his new wife was lovely. Anna definitely mellowed him some, and it was lovely to see. "Tracy and Greg, no kids?"

"No, they're all off in different directions. Tracy was willing to take one for the team and not have the kids home for Thanksgiving, so they would all come to town for Christmas."

"Got it. Hmmm. Dan Gallo. He's an interesting addition."

"He's by himself for the weekend. There's always room at the table." Jane didn't like how defensive she felt, but as much as she loved her mother, she was careful not to share too much.

It was the age-old push and pull between mothers and daughters, and she expected at some point that she and Tara would experience the same thing.

"I agree. I think it's lovely you invited him."

"It was Tara's idea, actually."

"Yep. It was."

Her daughter walked into the room like she was managing a large cast production. Ever the stage manager, she plucked the place cards from Jane's hand and stepped to the table, eyeing the configuration and arranging the seating.

Maybe it was her creativity, her ability to think outside the box, that gave Tara an innate sense of how to fit the pieces together. She went from one area to another, taking the cards and putting them in the little turkey holders Jane had placed on the table. She moved a few chairs, swapping one for another, and within a few minutes everyone had a place and there was more useable space.

Thankful the decision was out of her hands, Jane could go back to her cooking. There was still a lot of prep to do, and she had guests coming in a few hours.

Along with Christmas—which was just magical—Thanksgiving was Jane's other favorite holiday. It was all about spending time with those you love, sharing a meal, sharing stories, and being together. There were no gifts other than the gift of time.

She supposed that made her lucky. Whatever the future brought her way, Jane had a lot of wonderful people in her life. She'd never be alone. Even though Tara and her mother were heading off on their own paths, this would always be home for them. And she had her store.

She hoped she did, anyway. She still hadn't heard from her landlord, and now she wasn't the only one who was concerned; her lawyer was as well.

Jane didn't want to waste her energy on what-ifs, but

there was a vibe in the universe that was telling her something bad was swirling around, and the shop didn't feel safe. If she had a clue what she was dealing with, she could take action. Without information, she was frozen in place.

As she measured and mixed her special cornbread, Jane tried to put the troubles at the store out of her head. There wasn't anything she could do about it. But the baking helped. As did all the other prep. She could focus on simple tasks like measuring and mixing. Anything to keep her mind off her worries.

Tara and her mother were sitting at the island chopping vegetables, which would go in a myriad of dishes, including her corn and clam chowder. Always a favorite, she tweaked the recipe from time to time either out of boredom, or a guest's dietary needs. This year, there wouldn't be any variations, just her tried and true favorites made with lots of love. She smiled at the two of them, and reveled in how much she loved them both. In spite of her troubles, she was a lucky woman. Jane couldn't forget that, even though sometimes it was hard to block out the static that made her feel otherwise.

Chloe's head popped up and she let out a little woof. It was recognition rather than alarm. A familiar-sounding car could have been coming down the street and Chloe just wanted her to know. "What is it, girl?" Jane asked.

"Maybe Aunt Tracy is here." Tara shrugged. "She said she would be over early to help."

"I hope she wore her pajamas," Mom said, wiggling her behind. It was true, they were all still in their pajamas, and Jane was rocking her special Thanksgiving pair, complete with her turkey slippers. Chloe jumped up, barking her way into the mudroom. Jane heard the back door open, and then the ticking and squeaking from the dog's excitement.

"We're in the kitchen, Trace." Jane was surprised her friend was here so early. She was not a morning person.

"I'm not Tracy, but I come bearing breakfast." The smooth baritone triggered a combination of excitement and panic. She was split between, a sighing *"Oh, he's here,"* to a nervous *"Why is he here?"*

When he crossed the threshold into the kitchen, Jane's hormones, what was left of them anyway, went south. Dressed in tight jogging pants and a fitted athletic shirt that emphasized every muscle in his broad chest, Danny had obviously been out for a run. He was holding out two paper shopping bags—one from the bakery and the other from the bagel store.

"Good morning, ladies." He tilted his head to her mom and Tara. Her mother smiled in response, and Tara sprung off her stool like a jackrabbit.

"Ohhh! Yes! Bagels!" Tara dashed over to take the bags. "You are amazing. I'm starved."

Jane looked at the plate on the counter near the stove and raised her hands. "I made cinnamon rolls this morning. You ate two!"

Smiling Tara pulled bagels from the bag, drawing in the aroma. "Mmmm. These smell delish. Oh, cream cheese and lox? You brought lox?"

Jane never bought the salty cured salmon to go with bagels; as far as she knew, no one else liked it but her. "Since when do you eat lox?"

"When I went to visit Callie at NYU in September, we went to this great deli on Carmine Street in the West Village," Tara said, as she gathered plates and utensils. "Got myself a fully loaded bagel when I was there. Why did you deprive me of this delicacy? Definitely a Mom Fail."

Jane squeezed her eyes shut and processed the reprimand. A Mom Fail. Wow. "I am chastened."

Danny turned away and put his focus on petting the dog who hadn't left his side since he'd walked in. She could see, based on the way his shoulders were shaking, that he was laughing. Hard. This was becoming a regular occurrence.

"I'm so glad you're amused by this."

He drew a breath and turned around, his face as red as a beet. Jane couldn't even muster the tiniest bit of annoyance because, while she should be mortified that he'd dropped in with all of them in their pajamas, she wasn't. She liked him here, in her kitchen…hell, she liked him in her life. His presence had added a little more fun to their morning, and all he'd done was show up with bagels and fixings.

And, she almost forgot, a bag from the bakery.

"What's in there?" she asked, pointing to the Sweet Chemistry bag.

"Oh, this?" he held it up, teasing. "Nothing."

"What's in there?" She took a step toward him, and then another. Danny was grinning at her adorably, and Jane's insides shook again in a way that was becoming all too familiar. Why did he have this effect on her? And how was she going to get through dinner without becoming as sloppy as a bowl of cranberry jelly?

He held out the bag, letting it dangle on one finger. He

was such a tease. Jane reached out to take it and in response, he raised the bag over her head. Was that how this was going to go? "Give me the bag, please?"

He lowered it just a little, then pulled it up when she went for it a second time. "Ha," he teased.

"Are you kidding me?" Now Jane was annoyed. "Give it." She still couldn't do much more than touch the bottom of the bag when she went up on her toes, so she jumped. It was just a little hop, ridiculous at that, but it didn't stop her from trying again. If she needed proof that she wasn't any more coordinated than she used to be, Jane stumbled when she came down from her pathetic attempt to overcome their height differences.

Michael Jordan, she was not.

If Danny's arm hadn't come around her at just the right moment, she would have landed on her ass. Instead, she was pulled against his solid chest, where she was able to feel his steadiness, his heat, and his delicious maleness.

"You're twelve," he whispered in her ear. "You do know that, right?"

He was big, just the right size to tuck her against him, and he smelled of the chilly salt air and of sweat. Clean, but musky, it was there, pressed into him that she could appreciate how well she fit. How much she didn't want to move away.

Her body melted into his and she tried not to react to the little tremor of awareness. She wanted to cling to him, and to sink into his strength. She knew Danny was temporary in her life, but at this moment she didn't care.

He looked down at her, amusement spreading across his

face. "Nice pajamas."

"Thank you. I like to keep things festive. You're welcome to wear yours later."

Narrowing his eyes, he considered her proposal, before shaking his head. "I don't think so."

"No? Not your style?" Her blithe tone was meant to keep him off guard, but it wasn't working. He was still grinning at her like he could read her mind.

It was very possible he could. Jane had determined she had no guile.

He didn't seem too keen on letting her go, but once he came to his senses and realized they weren't alone, he released his hold and stepped back.

He passed her the bag, never losing eye contact. "I brought dessert for later. The bakery is only open until noon, so I thought I'd pick it up early and bring it by. Apple tarts, a selection of pastries, including the pumpkin pie squares, and a chocolate mousse pie."

"Ohh. I love the chocolate mousse pie," Jane said, folding her hands as if in prayer.

"I heard that someplace," he said as he leaned in to kiss her cheek. When Jane looked up, a grin just barely ticked up the corner of his mouth, but his eyes were bright and filled with emotion. Doing this for her made him happy, and if her heart wasn't already lost to him, that would have done it. This was who he was, open and kind, not the dark enigma the spin doctors sold to the masses. He was such a good man, and Jane wished he could see it.

With a nod to Tara and her mother, they locked eyes and Danny leaned in just a little bit. She thought he might kiss her right on the lips, which, other than having an audience, she wouldn't mind at all. In fact, she kind of hoped he would.

He didn't; instead her grasped her hand and gave it a gentle squeeze.

As he left the house, Jane glanced at the clock. Only four hours until he returned. Maybe she could steal that kiss then.

DAN DIDN'T KNOW what was motivating him, but he was obviously going crazy. Bringing breakfast to Jane's house that morning had been pure impulse. One second he was picking up the items he'd ordered for his contribution to the festivities, the next he was in the bagel shop across the street, ordering a dozen bagels with all the fixings. He couldn't wait to see her, not even a few more hours. It had already been a few days, and it killed him how much he missed her. The time he spent with Jane had become as important as breathing. It scared the hell out of him, but not for the reasons he would have thought.

Taking an early run was a good way to clear all the cobwebs from his head, especially since he'd been up all night writing. He must have knocked out close to sixty pages. Unable to sleep, he opened his computer at eleven o'clock last night, and before he knew what had happened, the sky was turning gray.

He hadn't pulled a legit all-nighter in years, ever since he started writing full time. He'd stay up late, or find himself crawling out of bed when an idea hit before the sun came up, but nothing like last night. Inspiration had come hard, and he wasn't able to contain it. Every thought in his head flooded out in a great rush, and half the time, Danny didn't know what he had written until he read it back. Some of it needed work, but other parts were brilliant. Earth-shaking and brilliant. He didn't have a lot of those moments. He'd usually put down a crappy first draft, and then spend months revising and rewriting. But last night, his vision for the story became crystal clear, and it was the mother of all moments. The story flowed. The people, the plot, the nuance were all there—all he had to do was polish it.

His characters weren't just talking to him, they were battering the inside of his brain, begging to get out and say their piece.

The emotion, the humor, it was a thrill he'd never experienced. He couldn't tell if what was happening with Jane was controlling his narrative, but his heart was vibrating with excitement for the first time in ages.

Dan always felt an adrenaline rush when writing his crime thrillers. That was the nature of the genre. If he didn't feel it, his readers wouldn't. But this love story was about the thrill of being connected, deeply, to someone else. The stories might have been different, but the excitement was the same.

Jane inspired him to be who he needed to be, as a writer—but even more—as a man.

The water from the shower was therapeutic, pounding down, and washing away not only the sweat from his run, but also the fuzziness in his brain.

He was adrift, off-balance, and it was the most energized

he'd felt since he'd been a kid who didn't know what was coming next. He felt that way now—with his career, with Jane—everything was new. His return home was triggering a massive shift in his life, but this time, instead of trying to control every facet of his existence, Dan was going to let things unfold, and see what happened.

It had been just a couple of weeks since he'd walked back into the bookstore, and what he'd always felt for her was rising to the surface, like some long-buried treasure. How was he going to handle it? He never intended to stay in Angel Harbor, believing his life was elsewhere. But now, Dan was fairly sure no place would feel like home if Jane wasn't there.

He'd never been reckless or inclined to sentimentality. Danny was methodical. Focused. He determined where he wanted to go and figured out how to get there. That single-mindedness had pushed him to rationalize Jane right out of his life when he'd left for law school.

He wasn't going to make the same mistake again.

He wondered if she would ever consider leaving Angel Harbor. Jane had always dreamed of traveling, and Danny could take her anywhere she wanted to go. He could write any place, and Jane could finally see the world.

Who was he kidding? She'd hate it. That store was almost as important to her as her family. He couldn't take her away from here. She was the heart of Angel Harbor.

Jane with her calm, steady presence, her insight and intuition, her gentleness, was special in ways Dan couldn't fully articulate. Her friends and family were so used to her strength he wondered if perhaps they took it for granted. But once again he was learning the power of it, and he didn't want to lose it.

THERE WAS SOMETHING very Zen about doing the dishes. Jane let the feel of the running water and the scent of the soap penetrate her senses as her mind wandered. It was soothing. The steady warmth and pressure of the water allowed her to relax into the monotony of the moment. The task required no thinking, which was definitely a welcome change from her usual frenetic existence.

It had been such a lovely day. Currently her house was filled with people she cared about. Her family and friends, her connection to all that was right in her world, were congregated in the living room engaged in a spirited game of Monopoly. Tara was accusing her grandmother of cheating, which Jane's mother vigorously denied, but the accusation was probably accurate. Her mother was a ruthless Monopoly player and everyone was always on alert for her real estate shenanigans. The day was everything Jane had hoped for, perfect in so many ways, and it was ending just as it had begun, with a shiver of awareness.

On her back, she felt the weight of Danny's hand settle, as he stepped up next to her.

"No Monopoly?" she asked, continuing with the dishes.

"Nah. I'm bankrupt already." He chuckled when he shook his head. "Your mother cheats."

Jane chuckled. His presence was not just welcome, but comforting. It made her think about the growing attachment between them, and what would happen when he finished his book.

He wasn't staying, and that was the only thing keeping Jane from fully letting him inside her heart.

They were friends, good friends, but that was all they could be. His life wasn't in Angel Harbor, and hers was. It wasn't what she'd planned, but it was her home.

"You look like a woman with something on her mind," he said, picking up the dish towel that was folded on the countertop. He took the porcelain casserole dish that had held the cornbread dressing from the drain and started drying it.

"I don't know," she began. "I was just thinking about how nice today was. I love Thanksgiving."

"It was a great day. And the food. God. Everything was delicious. I should have packed a pair of sweatpants." He patted his belly.

"I told you to wear pajamas." Jane smiled. She'd changed after dinner into a pair of plaid flannel pants and a hideously ugly Christmas sweater to kick off the season.

"Thank you for including me," he said quietly. Jane could see on his face that he was genuinely touched. "Being here was much better than being on my own."

"I wouldn't have let that happen."

He raised an eyebrow and grabbed the large stainless steel soup pot from her hands. "Glad to hear it."

There was a hint of skepticism in his voice, and she wondered why. "*Maybe because the thought of having him here makes you nervous as a cat in a kennel,*" a little voice in her head reminded her, but still, she challenged him. "You don't believe me?"

He hesitated and looked down, concentrating on the droplets of water sparkling off the metal surface. "I wasn't sure. When you mentioned it, you looked a little…unnerved by it. You did say it was Tara's idea."

She had been, but not for the reasons he thought. Jane was fully aware of everything that was brewing between them. The attraction was off the chart. She was already at risk of losing her heart to him because of all the old feelings that never really went away, but this new, bubbling awareness had the potential to leave her completely wrecked. She wasn't seventeen anymore, with a lifetime of adventure ahead of her. Now, her heart wouldn't just be broken, but shattered.

"Maybe a little? You do keep me on my toes, but I'm glad you're here. I am. I love…"

Stop! Ugh. Not that word. Not the "L" word. Jane looked out the window over the sink, seeing the large bare maple that stood on the opposite side of her driveway. How did she express this without it sounding pitiable?

"Jane?"

"Shh. Let me think, okay?"

"Okay." Danny picked up another serving piece and dried it, the motion of his hands steady and rhythmic.

"I do love that you're here," she finally muttered. "You confuse the hell out of me, but I'm happy you're back home. Happy you're in my life again. Like I said the other night, I've missed you."

"I know. I was a lousy friend. I'm so sorry. I should have been here for you, especially after your dad died."

"It was so long ago and your life was elsewhere." She shrugged, not feeling bitter and angry although she probably should. "I wasn't even a blip on the screen."

"That doesn't make me feel better," he said, with a tone of disgust in his voice. "You were my closest friend. You were…everything, and I just walked away. I thought I was giving us room to breathe, but I think I was just a coward. It's possible I still am."

Jane turned off the faucet, keeping her eyes focused on the gray dishwater spinning down the drain. She was everything? Everything? What did he mean by that? When he kissed her after their dinner the other night, there was so much energy radiating off of him, she couldn't untangle the feelings. The tenderness was unmistakable, but was there also loss and regret? If she did mean that much to him, cutting her off completely made little sense. Danny didn't shy away from challenges; his life was proof of that. So, what was he afraid of?

"I think you're too tough on yourself." She took the dishtowel from his hands and dried her own. "It's life. Things happen."

"No. That's an excuse. I have to own the fact that I screwed up. With my family, and you. My sister has been so welcoming. I don't deserve it." He turned, his body tight as he shifted his hip against the counter, facing her.

"You're here now. Moving forward you can make different choices."

He stared at her, his gaze intense and dark. He looked edgy, hard, almost a little dangerous, like he had a mission and nothing would deter him. His hand came up, and his fingers left a soft trail of heat and electricity on her skin. "Can I?"

Jane squeezed her eyes shut, the heat between them wrapping her up in a fantasy she dared not have. *What if* wasn't a productive way to live. The tiny phrase was littered with heartbreak and disappointment.

"I think that's up to you. Do what feels right." As soon as she said it, Jane realized it sounded like an invitation, and maybe it was. Danny inched a little closer, settling a hand on her hip while the other cupped her cheek. His lips landed right at the corner of her mouth, leaving a barely there sizzle of electricity. Every nerve ending lit up like the Christmas lights strung all over town. The power in the kiss was in the tenderness of it, with his gentle, sweet ministrations making her dizzy. His touch was like a drug, his kiss a balm for her soul.

Never, even when she was married, did a simple kiss have the power to undo her. Something about Danny changed that. He applied gentle, but steady pressure, moving and teasing, drawing her essence into his own mouth. Jane felt breathless, dreamy. Without a doubt, her heart was losing its battle to keep him at a distance.

How had she gotten to be this age, a middle-aged woman, without knowing the joy of bonding with someone like this? Had she deliberately avoided this kind of emotional connection? Or had she just been waiting for Danny to come back to her?

It was clear, whatever the case, that Jane's heart was in major trouble. The most surprising part was that she didn't care.

Chapter Eleven

"MISS JANE? IS this a good snowman?" Austin Trebour was as cute a little boy as Jane had ever seen, with his big green eyes shining at her, but he worried way too much for a five-year-old. He waved the snowman ornament he'd been working on for the last forty-five minutes over his head, effectively spraying glitter all over the table, the floor, and himself. With his red hair now dusted with silver and gold sparkles, he looked like a little Christmas elf.

It was the Saturday after Thanksgiving, and the shopping season had officially kicked off in Angel Harbor. The day was all about the community, with activities for kids, sales for the adults, and the big Christmas kick-off on Main Street once the sun went down. Jane hosted arts and crafts in the children's room, and later there would be a holiday story time. In all, it was good fun, and the small businesses all chipped in to make the day enjoyable for everyone in town.

"Austin, that is a pretty spectacular snowman." Jane sat in the child-size chair next to the boy, examining his work. "You definitely made him sparkle."

"I like the sparkles. I think snow sparkles, so that's why I used a lot." He reached for the shaker of silver glitter, to add more, but just in time, his mother stepped up to the table and crouched down next to her son. Lindsey Trebour was a teacher at the local elementary school and had three kids ages five, four, and two. When people heard about her three very young kids and her having a full-time job, they wondered how she managed while keeping a smile on her face. Jane figured she was some kind of magical creature—there was no other explanation.

"Austin, I think you've used enough glitter. That snowman is going to melt under the weight of it," she said. "And you need to leave glitter for other children."

Jane never ran out of glitter, but Lindsey was right. Austin had layered it on pretty thick. "Why don't you give your snowman to Miss Tracy and she'll put it in the back room to dry?"

When Jane nodded toward the workroom door, the boy agreed, taking his creation and leaving a trail of glitter on his way to Tracy.

"I feel like I should help you clean up," Lindsey said. "You're going to be vacuuming this up until Valentine's Day!"

"Oh, what's Christmas without bling? Come on, Lindsey, if I remember, you liked your sparkles too. And you were a teenager."

Lindsey laughed and dropped to the floor, moving into a perfect lotus position. "That is true. I still do." Watching her other kids do a coloring project with Tara and the English Honor Society students, Lindsey relaxed for a minute. "This is such a fun day. The merchants go above and beyond for everyone."

"It's our pleasure." Jane said sincerely.

"How was your Thanksgiving?"

"It was lovely, thank you for asking. We had a relaxing day. Everyone pitched in, there was no stress. The food was awesome, if I do say so myself, and the company even better."

"That sounds wonderful. The grapevine has been chattering about your resident artist."

The grapevine should learn to mind its own business, she thought. "Has it?"

"Come on, Jane. You've had a man writing in the back of your shop for the last few weeks, and apparently, you two have been out together a few times."

"He's an old friend. We went to high school together."

"Did you? And he just dropped back into town and made himself comfortable in the bookstore?"

"He did."

Both Jane and Lindsey were startled to see Danny smiling down at them.

"And he's been lucky Jane didn't toss him out on his ass. You know those writer types. Very surly."

Did her heart just pitter-pat? Jane believed it did. That smile of his was going to end her. "Hi!" She stood. "I didn't know you were coming in."

"I have the kids. Mel and Peter went shopping, so I volunteered to take them to lunch. I'm also going to help them get presents for their folks."

"That sounds like fun."

Danny extended his hand to Lindsey, who was also standing. "I'm Dan Gallo."

"Hi, I'm—" It was right then that Jane saw awareness flash across Lindsey's face. Her smile went from bright to awestruck. "Wait. *The* Dan Gallo? The writer?"

"That would be me." Jane watched his eyes drop modestly. He was so humble, so unimpressed with himself. Where did the obnoxious, self-absorbed Dan Gallo he kept telling her about actually reside? Because it wasn't with the guy she'd been seeing.

"I am SUCH a fan. Oh my God." Lindsey took his hand and shook it with both of hers. She was having a total fangirl moment. "I've been reading your books since I was a teenager."

"Not that long, then?" His charm just oozed, and Lindsey giggled like a twelve-year-old.

"Oh, wow. Longer than you'd think." The woman blushed. She was a mother of three and an accomplished professional, and the man made her weak at the knees. Thinking about it, Jane could relate.

"So, you've been writing here?" Lindsey asked. "What are you working on? Can you share? Oh, I bet it's a secret. Still, could you tell me?"

"Do you always talk so fast?" he joked, extracting his hand without her realizing it.

"Oh, gosh. I'm sorry. Yes. I have three kids and I teach third grade. I'm always working at double speed."

"No wonder." He smiled and Jane waited to see how he answered her questions. She wondered when he would be ready to share information about his book. He hadn't even told her very much. "I can tell you it's different from anything I've done before, but that's it."

Lindsey folded her arms and tried to be cool. She was still vibrating with excitement, but she did make a good effort. “That’s so exciting. I can’t wait.”

“When I’m ready to reveal the details, I hope Jane will let me do something here. I think it would be fun to have a discussion with readers, don’t you?”

This was the first Jane was hearing about his plan. Would she let him do something here, at her bookstore? Was he kidding? The publicity would be insane, and her store would be packed.

“It’s a great idea.” Jane replied. “We’ll have to talk about it.”

“I think that’s amazing,” Lindsey gushed. “I will be in the front row. Wow. Does that make me sound like a stalker? I mean, I’m not, but I would be here.” She took a breath. “I’ll stop talking now.”

Danny laughed out loud at her babbling. “Lindsey, it was a pleasure. I’m going to steal Jane for a bit, if that’s okay?”

“No problem. Jane, I’m going to round up the kids. Thanks for all this—you rock. We’ll be back for story time later.”

Jane waved as Lindsey trotted off to find her offspring. “Well, you sure impressed her.”

Danny grabbed her hand and leaned in for a quick kiss. “She’s a kinetic wave, but it seems her life requires it.”

“She is, but she’s great. A wonderful mom and the kids in her class love her.”

“I bet. Do you have a second?” His eyes appeared a deeper blue today. Dark, almost stormy.

“I do. Where are the kids you’re supposedly in charge of?”

“I think they were taken by fairies.” With what felt like

the whole world watching, he pulled her into her office and closed the door. His mouth came down on hers without even a moment's pause. "I've missed you," he said after stealing her breath with a long, teasing kiss.

"I saw you yesterday." Jane grazed her fingers across his cheek, so touched by his need to see her. "Seriously, where are the kids?"

"They're with your mom. She's helping them pick out gifts for their parents."

"I thought you were doing that?" Taking advantage of their closeness, Jane slipped her arms around his waist.

"What? I have no clue how to pick out presents. I'm just paying. Kathleen will do a much better job than I would."

"I'm sure you'd do fine." He loved his family, and whatever he chose would come from the heart.

"I love that you have so much faith in me. Even about the little things."

Joy bubbled up, filling Jane with a bottomless happiness as she rested her head on his broad chest. When his arms came around her, she felt peace. This was what she'd been waiting for, this bone-deep contentment. She'd missed him without even knowing it.

"Hey," Danny said pulling her close. "Is everything okay?"

"Perfect," Jane responded. "Everything is perfect."

ONCE THE KIDS were back with Mel and Peter, Dan's original plan was to go back to the cottage to work a little more, but instead he spent some time browsing through the different stores in Angel Harbor. He was amazed to find he was feeling the Christmas spirit for the first time in a long while. He attributed it to a sweet, brainy woman who had changed the way he saw life.

Just as he got into his car, his phone buzzed in his pocket. On the screen he saw it was his business manager. He'd made the call yesterday, not expecting to hear from him so soon. Zach Gordon was a shark of an attorney who had a lot of high-profile clients. He took care of their business interests and helped solve problems when needed. Not the kind of guy to be labeled a fixer, Zach was still the one person you wanted in your corner if you needed something done.

He'd reached out to see if he could help Jane get some answers about her lease. He had the feeling her lawyer was jerking her around, so he dropped the problem in Zach's lap. The guy had connections that went deep, so when Zach said "he had a guy," he really did have a guy.

"Hey," Dan answered. "That was quick."

"Ask and you shall receive. It only took a few phone calls, but I don't think you're going to like what I have to tell you."

Danny had been trying to ease Jane's mind about the lease, but just this morning when he was out for a jog, he saw a woman with a clipboard outside the store. She was taking notes and examining every area around the old house. Naturally, he stopped to ask what she was doing, and she said she was "assessing the property for her clients."

"Assessing the property" was not something he wanted to hear.

Assessment to him meant "sale." And if the building were on the market, that would explain why Jane's lease was held up.

"Is it what I thought?" *Please say no…*

"The building is up for sale. It's being kept very quiet. There's no formal listing."

"What the hell does that mean? No listing?"

"It could mean a lot of things. I'm guessing the landlord had someone approach them about the location. Or he had a business contact. Whatever it was, no one is making the usual noise." That made sense. It didn't make him feel better, but it made sense.

"Shit."

"Why the interest in a small-town bookstore? I mean, I get the bookstore connection," Zach said. "But what's going on?"

"A friend of mine owns the store. It's been in her family for generations, and means a lot to the town. I can't get my head around Angel Harbor Books fading from existence."

"Ah. Gotcha. I mean you could give her a heads-up, but I don't think there's anything she can do other than throw a wad of cash at the landlord."

"Do you know what they want for the building?" The question popped out of his mouth and he had no idea why. Okay, that was a lie. He'd buy that building in a heartbeat if it would help Jane.

"I don't, but I guess I could find out. Why?"

"Just find out for me, okay?"

"Are you going to do something crazy? I thought donating all that money to your old high school was nuts, but buying a building for some woman…"

The snarl in Zach's voice came right through the phone, and Danny didn't like it one bit. "Watch it. She's not just *some woman.*"

"My job is to manage your money and your affairs. Buying a building for some small-town bookstore owner doesn't sound like a good investment."

"Just find out."

He closed the call before Zach could ask any other questions.

AN HOUR LATER, while he was sitting in the cottage, Dan got his answer. He picked up on the first ring. "Talk."

"I can't believe your girlfriend doesn't know her building is being sold."

Dan never referred to Jane as his girlfriend, but he wasn't going to argue it. "Zach, get to the point."

"It's being bought by a big restaurant conglomerate. They have catering venues, restaurants, and cafés all over New York. They're paying a fortune for her property and the one right next door. I guess your hometown will have a new place to eat if the sale goes through."

"How much?" If he helped, maybe Jane could figure out a way to buy it herself. Even if she couldn't, he could afford it. For her, he'd do anything. He doubted the landlords cared very much who bought the building, as long as they had the cash at the end of the deal.

"One point two million."

Dan felt like he'd been punched in the gut. The building wasn't that big, but it was in a prime downtown area with lots of foot traffic. There were probably other solutions, but he didn't know what they were right now. "Go after it. I don't care how much, but I want you to counter their offer."

"I don't think it's wise..." Zach's voice took on the tone of a person trying to talk a jumper off a ledge.

Slumping back on the couch in the living room, he groaned. "I know you don't, but I need you to try."

"Dan, I've known you for over fifteen years. You've always trusted me, but I have to be honest, I'm getting worried. What's going on? I know you haven't talked to your agent or your editor in weeks. They've called me asking if I've heard from you. They think you're out of your mind. Did you really reject an eight-figure contract?"

He had rejected the contract, but that wasn't part of this discussion. "What did you tell them?"

"I lied. I told them it's been radio silence."

"Thanks." He paused to gather his thoughts. "Look, I know you don't agree with me. But I need you to look into buying the building. I wouldn't be where I am today without that bookstore, or Jane, the woman who owns it. This is about a lot more than a building."

There was a long silence on the other end of the line. Zach could be pushy and in your face, but he was a good man. Dan trusted him. "All right, Danny Boy, I'll look into it. You'll have to tell me about the woman over a beer sometime."

"Absolutely. Keep me posted."

They ended the call and Dan felt like he now had a giant

time bomb sitting in his lap. He had to tell Jane. She had a right to know what might be coming, even if it hurt. He'd do his best to keep it from happening, but right now, he wasn't hopeful.

Chapter Twelve

WHAT A DAY.

Jane flipped off the lights in the front of the store after a day of shopping the likes of which she'd never seen. As she fell into her desk chair, Tara and Tracy walked in looking as shell-shocked as Jane felt.

"Oh my God," Tara said. "That was insane. Our daily total is ridiculous."

Jane looked up. "How ridiculous?"

Stepping forward, Tracy dropped a hand on her shoulder. "As good as the entire week, starting with Black Friday, last year. We're going to have a great season."

This had been one of their best-attended festivals. Town was buzzing all day, merchants were busy, and kids found fun activities in almost every shop. Restaurants offered special treats and there was an incredible sense of closeness and community. People chatted with neighbors, had a meal at a large communal table, or shared a hot drink and a cookie by the harbor.

Tonight, Gina, the owner of the local candy shop, capped off the day with the lighting of the leg lamp. Just like in the classic movie *A Christmas Story* the lamp would watch over Main Street in all its smutty glory for the entire season.

It was fun and silly, and the entire street filled up with

friends and visitors, the high school band, and the dance team. People dressed up, wore ugly holiday sweaters, shared cookies and other treats with their neighbors. The tradition dated back years now, and it just kept getting better. Then, all down Main Street, merchants turned on their store holiday displays. There was no official competition, but there was definitely a sense of pride in having people talk about a proprietor's effort. And there were rivalries, some pretty heated.

Jane had kept the bookstore décor simple and classic with garland draped over the porch rails, white lights outlining the windows and roofline, and wreaths adorning the door and the windows. Inside, there were two trees, garlands, flameless candles, Santas, and snowmen.

The lighting of Harbor Park culminated with the multicolored lights decorating the giant spruce, the pathways, the dock, and the two gazebos. It turned their little slice of waterfront into a magical Christmas scene.

"It's amazing, Mom. You might be able to do some of the renovations you were talking about."

Jane could only nod. "Let's get through the holidays before we make plans. We have plenty on our plates."

Unlike years past when she'd always be thinking about her next move, Jane was hesitant to talk about anything beyond the immediate future. Tracy had talked to Elena, and she hadn't heard a peep about the building. There was no logical reason for her not to jump at a new idea. But she was going to play it safe. Once the new lease was signed, then she could think about changes.

Jane heard a shocked intake of breath come from Tara.

She was staring at her phone, eyes wide, her face blanched white. Jane's blood ran cold thinking about what could have triggered the reaction.

"What? What is it?" Jane jumped from her chair and went to her daughter, her adrenaline surging as she wondered whom she might have to hurt.

"I got in." Tara looked up, tears filling her blue eyes. "I mean, it looks like it, anyway."

"You shouldn't be hearing anything from your early action schools for another week, at least. Got in where?"

"Trinity." Tara's voice cracked, coming out on an emotional breath.

There was a Trinity in Connecticut, and a Trinity in Washington, DC, but somehow, she knew those weren't the schools Tara was talking about. "In Dublin? Ireland? I didn't...didn't know you'd applied."

Jane swallowed hard. *Get the whole story,* she told herself. *Don't freak out, get the story.* "How, um...how did this happen?"

"So, you know how I love Ireland. And I've wanted to go back since you took me there. The college has an amazing English Literature major, and I can pair it with two years at Columbia."

Sitting, Jane took another breath. The last thing she wanted to do was squash her daughter's dreams, but Ireland? That wasn't a quick weekend visit. It wouldn't be easy to come home for the holidays. Jane's heart was pounding. "Go on. You're not sure?"

"Remember that essay contest I entered last summer. The one about Irish heritage? Well, one of the judges is a professor at Trinity. She encouraged me to apply. She said I had a 'singular gift.'"

There had been so many contests, but Jane remembered that one in particular because Tara was so excited with the response. "I see. You left the application part out when you told me about the feedback."

"I didn't think I had a shot. But the professor just emailed me and said I should be getting my offer in a week. Oh my God, Mom. I could be going to Ireland for college!" Tara threw her arms around Jane's neck and squeezed. "This is amazing."

Tracy was silent, which was good because Jane didn't want to fall apart until Tara couldn't see.

There was a light tapping coming from the front of the store, and both Tara and Tracy rolled their eyes at the interruption. Jane, however, looked up and remembered the lost cell phone she'd found near one of the big armchairs.

"Could you get that, Tee? It could be the owner of that phone."

"Sure. Of course."

Tara left the room and without looking over, she could feel Tracy staring at her. Those bright blue eyes had a knack for zeroing in on deception, as Jane well knew from their years of friendship. The woman had a built-in bullshit detector.

"Are you okay?"

"No! I'm not okay. Ireland? I was just getting used to the idea of her going to Vermont!"

"I know. Try to breathe. It's new and she's very excited—"

"Look who I found." Tara popped back into the office with Danny trailing behind. Her daughter grinned, teasing her old mom with a wiggle of her eyebrows. Jane really hoped she was putting up a good front. The last thing she wanted to do was destroy Tara's moment.

Good front or not, Danny stopped short, his face going from relaxed to concerned in a split second. Could he read her that well already?

His hand went up in a little wave and she'd never been more relieved to see anyone.

"What's going on?" He inched closer, his eyes intense and concerned.

Tara jumped toward him like she was on springs. "I'm going to college!"

"I think that was a given," he said calmly. Without a word, he seemed to know what to do, taking Jane's hand instinctively.

"No! Look!" Her daughter was so excited. How could Jane be anything but happy for her? Obviously, she was a terrible mother. Danny read through the email on Tara's phone.

"Tara, that's incredible. I had no idea you wanted to study abroad."

"Isn't it amazing? I mean I still have other schools to hear from, but oh my God."

It was time to change the subject. Jane's heart was near breaking.

"So, what brings you out?" she finally asked him.

"I wanted to see how your day was. I didn't get to talk to you for long after Gina lit the leg lamp." He chuckled, taking her cue to shift away from the college conversation. "*That* was a fun time."

"We were just saying we had one of our best days ever," Tracy piped in while Tara had started furiously texting someone. Her thumbs were moving at light speed.

"I was hoping you'd let me take you for a late dinner," he said.

Anything to get her out of there would be good, because she was inches from falling apart. Tara was so happy, but Jane wanted to curl up into a little ball. The problem was there was still a lot to do. "I have work. I don't know…"

"Don't be silly," Tracy said quickly. "You've been here since eight o'clock this morning. We've got this."

Tara nodded furiously. "Yes. Mom. Go. Aunt Tracy and I can close up."

Sweet relief flooded through her. Not because she didn't want to do the work, but because she didn't know how she was going to hold it together. "Are you sure?"

Tara rolled her eyes so hard it gave Jane a headache. "Mom. Come on, we got this. Go. Oh, and remember I'm staying over at Rosa's house later."

She shrugged, nodded, and then turned to Danny. "Sure. It looks like I'm not needed."

"If you're too tired, I understand," he said.

She was tired. But she needed to be with him more.

It should scare her senseless. Everything about this relationship was a risk, and Jane didn't know if she could cope with the personal fallout. But right now, he offered her escape. That was all she needed.

"I'm not that hungry, but I could handle a bowl of soup

or something. What I really need is some fresh air. It's been a long day."

Tara and Tracy stepped out of the room, giving them some much needed privacy. Jane didn't hesitate and stepped right into Danny's waiting arms.

"Are you okay?" he asked, dropping a soft kiss on her head.

She shook her head in response. "But can we not talk about it for a little while? I need to wrap my head around what just happened."

"Whatever you need." His arms tightened ever so slightly, and Jane melted into him. His heartbeat was strong and steady, but a little hitch in his breath made her look up.

There was a shadow in his eyes. Something was wrong.

"What's going on with you? You could have called if you wanted me to meet you."

He had the look of a man who had been found out. "I could have, but I've been out walking for a couple of hours. I had to leave the house to clear my head."

His bearing changed, or maybe she just hadn't noticed it when he first came in, but he seemed tense, distracted.

"Are *you* okay?" she asked, stepping away. His features went tight suddenly, with his mouth narrowing into a firm line. He wasn't angry, at least not with her, but he was agitated about something. He didn't speak, letting her gather her things and pull on her coat before he finally broke the silence between them.

"My agent found me. When I got back from the Harbor Lights festival, he was waiting at my sister's house."

"Just waiting there? Your sister, and her family were here

with you. The three of you had to drag the kids out." That wasn't a lie; Dan had to carry a very unhappy Gavin over his shoulder.

"I know. He was parked in the driveway, waiting in the car."

"That's kind of creepy." One of the reasons he was in Angel Harbor was so he could avoid the stress of dealing with his agent or his editor, but his reasons were still pretty vague. He was the writer; there must have been some reason for the secrecy surrounding his location and the book.

"Yep. It felt like an ambush."

Considering the very long driveway, with the house set way back on a hill, his agent waiting for him like that was an invasion of privacy as far as Jane was concerned.

"So, just tell him to buzz off." Jane waved her hand around like she was swatting at a bug. "Seriously, that's pretty nervy."

"Tell me about it." He moved in and dropped a hand on her shoulder. "If you don't want to eat, how about a walk?"

"A walk?" That sounded like a perfect plan. They could both use the time to blow off a little steam. Jane took his hand, giving it a gentle squeeze. "Yeah. Let's go."

JANE CLOSED THE door of the shop, leaving behind her friend and her daughter to close out the day. They thought they were playing matchmaker, but this wasn't about romance, even though they'd gotten a good start in that department too. No, she wanted to help him talk out whatever was bothering him. It felt right to lend a shoulder and an ear, to help him get a handle on his roiling emotions. It would also distract her from the news Tara had dropped a few minutes ago.

Since he'd been working in the shop, he'd only shared a few tidbits about his new book, and Jane had a sense Danny's tension was bound up in the project even more than in his agent's visit. Fame and money weren't the endgame anymore. He wanted to create something that would last.

He'd always been that way, eager to discover new things. Jane would dig into the past, and Danny was all about the future.

She admired that he was trying to change direction, but Jane was worried about the guilt that haunted him. Letting go of his demons was the only way he'd stop running from himself, and everyone else.

His hands were jammed securely in the pockets of his navy blue parka while Jane linked her arm with his in a move that was becoming comfortably familiar. She liked the feel of him next to her. It felt normal, like something they had done every day for years even though their history had ended decades ago.

Or had it? Maybe this was their time.

He'd slipped into her life so easily, Jane knew she'd miss him when he resumed his life and left Angel Harbor, maybe even more than before. It wasn't just about the sweet kisses; it was him. His intelligence and his creativity. The kindness he showed to people. How he always wanted to help. His generous spirit. Danny was a good man, and Jane understood that good men had feelings, often deep, and often guarded.

"Your agent really got under your skin, didn't he?"

"He did. Mostly because he didn't respect that I need him to back off."

From the bookstore, they'd turned onto Main Street, heading away from the harbor. Jane followed his lead because it was obvious he really needed to talk.

"I mean, how hard to understand is 'Leave me alone?'" The man's anger was etched in his strong features.

"Not very. I was wondering though…" She didn't know if what she was going to say would piss him off more or trigger some kind of awareness. "He does work for *you*, right?"

Danny looked over, his eyes full of the turbulence that churned though him. "Eh. I've never seen it that way. It's more a partnership. I have talent and product, but without him it gets nowhere."

"Um. No. As Tara said when she discovered your identity, you're *'Dan-Freaking-Gallo.'* And she's right about that. You are."

Danny grumbled in that way she'd come to really love. He still wasn't completely comfortable with his fame, and he didn't want anyone to talk about it. He was exceedingly polite with Lindsey today, but he was uncomfortable with the gushing praise. She wondered how much success someone needed to chase away doubt.

"Yeah, well, you need to teach that kid of yours not to be so easily impressed," he snarled.

That made Jane laugh. "Wow. You are grouchy."

She didn't need to talk if he didn't want to. Especially if

it was only going to make him more brusque.

Settling into silence, they passed by the gray clapboard Episcopal church, its red doors adorned with big beautiful wreaths; the old drug store, which was a lot more than a pharmacy, fully stocked with souvenirs and gifts; the theater, which was advertising its annual holiday production; and just at the edge of the retail district, one of the largest houses in the village. Sitting lonely on a large piece of property was an old Victorian that had seen much better days. With a huge porch and gingerbread trim, Jane wondered what kinds of stories the house would tell if it could talk. Named *Sail House*, it was originally the home of one of the most prosperous sailboat builders in the east. It was empty now, sadly, and it had been for years. A FOR SALE sign sat outside, prompting Jane to wonder if anyone would ever occupy the old building, or if it would just be a relic, a reminder of the town's history on the waterfront.

"I love this house," Jane said. "It's one of those places where you'd want the walls to do the talking."

"That sounds like a series of ghost stories. Maybe you should write it. Stories from the Sail House…"

"I'm not a writer. I wouldn't know where to start!" Jane couldn't possibly consider writing.

"No worries, I know a guy who can help you. He's kind of a writer."

She laughed at the reference to his first meeting with Tara. "I heard about that guy. Does he have any talent?"

"Depends on who you talk to."

Jane leaned her head on his shoulder. "What happened with your agent?"

Finally, Danny exhaled a long breath. "I just want to write my book in peace. I've been making good progress on it, but tonight, he messed with my head. What if this is a huge mistake?"

"I doubt it is, but it would help if I knew more. We talked a little in the beginning, but you haven't told me anything about what you have planned. I've been told I have excellent taste and a good sense of the market."

"I'm sure you do, but I'm not ready to talk about it yet." Danny was very protective of the story. It made her wonder what he'd gotten himself into.

The thought seemed to put him on edge. She could feel him tense, like a big cat ready to spring at a threat. What the devil was the man writing about?

"I can tell you it's very personal to me."

"Okay."

Danny stopped walking, forcing her to turn, and Jane's hand slid down to his. "*Okay?* You're not going to try and get it out of me? No probing questions."

She could feel the laugh bubble in her chest. "Do you want me to?"

His eyes focused on hers, and she thought for a second he might tell her what he was writing, and more, why it was so important to him. Instead, Danny shook his head and pulled her arm back through his. "Your opinion matters to me. But no, I'm not ready to tell you yet."

"That's fine." Jane leaned her head on his shoulder as they walked on. It was incredibly comforting to be so close and so at ease with him. It was nice to let her worries slip away.

"You could beg a little, you know," he said. "It would be good for my ego."

That tickled her. She knew he was kidding, but she loved the teasing between them.

"I think Lindsey doled out enough hero worship for you today. You'll be fine without any more from me."

She could feel his body unwind as they talked. The walk had relaxed her, and she was so grateful for the pretty night. Jane was also grateful for him.

They crossed the street, heading back toward the harbor. On the way they came upon a shop that specialized in blankets and textiles from the UK and Ireland. The small shop was filled with beautiful handmade crafts and home goods. Jane had bought Tracy a throw from there just last week. "I love this store. It reminds me of a shop in Ireland, in Kinsale, that had the most beautiful blankets."

"I've never been," he said. "To Ireland."

"No? I took Tara when she was ten. Obviously, it made an impact on her." The wonderful memories now collided with Jane's scary reality. "We went to Dublin to see the Book of Kells and the Long Room at Trinity College, and spent some time touring the countryside. My father's family is from County Galway, near Kinvara, and I swear, it's God's country. So gorgeous. But Kinsale, in County Cork, is all charm. That's where my mother's people are from. I bought us blankets there at a place called Granny's Bottom Drawer, to remember the trip. We still use them." She felt the coziness of the memory wash over her. That trip was one of the best times of her life. "Harbor Knits reminds me of that. Claire, who owns the shop, is Irish, and she has a full stock of textiles—blankets, linens, and yarn. *Lots* of yarn."

"You speak of it with such reverence," he chuckled.

"Yarn is serious, like a religious experience."

The window of the yarn shop was decorated with lights and a Christmas tree made from knitting needles and crochet hooks, woven together in an intricate pattern. There were baskets of yarn, blankets, stuffed toys, and hand-knitted items on shelves and racks. Christmas ornaments made from balls of yarn hung from a glittering curtain rod suspended from the ceiling. It was creative, festive, and inviting.

Just like her sweet friend, the shop radiated all the love Claire brought to their town.

A light breeze circled around them just as Jane felt a tickle of cold and wetness on her cheek. Then again. And again. She looked up. "Oh," she sighed, catching her breath. "Snow."

Just like that, the sky was filled with magic. Angel Harbor didn't often have a white Christmas, but sometimes the maritime climate cooperated and dusted their waterfront village with what looked like a perfect coating of powdered sugar. It wasn't that they didn't get winter, they did. February, and sometimes March, could be especially brutal with huge snowfalls, ice storms, and winds that whipped up the bays, the harbors, and Long Island Sound.

When the storms came, they all hunkered down and watched out for one another. But these December snows were usually gentle and pretty, and Jane felt like she'd been given a gift from the heavens.

This night was turning into something unexpected. A mixture of sadness and resignation, with a sprinkle of happiness. Jane wondered what kind of magic Dan Gallo could bring to her life.

"Where's the best place you've ever traveled?" she asked him.

"It's hard to say. If I'm on tour, I don't stay long enough in any one place to enjoy it. I'm there for a day and then I'm off."

"Where have you spent time?"

"I love Italy. Lake Como is probably one of the few perfect places on earth. Malta is beautiful and so is Sardinia. But my favorite place is probably Norway."

"Norway? Really?"

"I cruised the fjords once. Just took off last minute on my own and traveled for a week. The country is beautiful. Imposing. I decided to go back a few months later."

Their arms were now entwined and Danny gripped her hand. "Did you go in the winter?"

He smiled down at her. "I did. Last January. I made reservations at a hotel above the Arctic Circle. The rooms, which were actually apartments, had walls of glass. The sun never really came up but hovered over the horizon for a few hours every day, and the lights in the sky took my breath away."

He looked up, like he was searching for the lights here. "But it was more. The small community we visited? The people have completely adapted to the harsh environment. They love the dark, the cold. There's joy in the season. The stark landscape should have felt desolate, but it didn't. I learned so much, mostly about myself."

Jane had dreamed of seeing the Aurora Borealis. Not only had Dan done it, but he had gone so far north he was likely surrounded by it. These were the kinds of things she'd missed, immersive adventures that consumed a person's body and mind. In her heart, she could live with it—she'd had her daughter and nothing in the world would ever be better. But now that she was faced with Tara leaving, really leaving, she didn't know what her next adventure would be, if any. It was something to consider.

"You have an amazing life," she whispered.

"I've been lucky. I don't think you've done badly," he reminded her. "You have a beautiful daughter, great friends, a business…" Danny stopped abruptly and kissed the top of her head. "You matter to the people here. They care about you, and your daughter adores you. Nothing can ever take that away."

"I hope so. Tonight was hard, though. Dublin is awfully far away."

They were standing across the street from her store. The lights sparkled, trimming the building with an otherworldly magic. From this distance, the scene looked almost too perfect, like a Christmas card come to life.

"I feel at loose ends. I have so many things to be grateful for, but I kept thinking I'd be ready for her to grow up, and I'm not."

"I'm sure there are a lot of parents who feel the same way."

"I'm sure. Tracy embraced the changes. As she says, 'Each milestone is proof I didn't screw up.'"

He chuckled. "I like that. It's good advice."

"But Ireland? She didn't even tell me she'd applied. I

should be excited for her, that she's brave and determined and following her dreams, but my heart is breaking at the thought. And what if she's not ready? What if I've messed up and she's not ready?"

He let go of her hand and looped his arm around her shoulder, pulling her close. "You are still so tough on yourself. Whatever she decides it's going to be great. She's a bright, talented young woman, and you are an amazing mom."

Was she hard on herself? Probably. That was her default setting. "I wish I had your confidence. I just don't know how."

They continued their walk and entered the miracle that was Angel Harbor Park. There had to be a hundred thousand lights strung in the trees, on the gazebo, and on the pier jutting out into the water. Like a mirror, the harbor reflected the lights, casting a spray of stars across the earth. Boats in the marina were decorated for Christmas, and Jane felt her heart sing and cry, so moved by the beauty of it all.

He stood behind her, hands on her shoulders, and to her surprise, Jane felt safe. If nothing else—in this insanity—she had that.

"Every light is a reason for you to believe. To keep going. I know you're sad, but look at what you've done here." He waved his hand around at the park and the marina, and smiled down at her. "She's ready and so are you. This is your chance to have adventures of your own. I have faith in you. And I don't have faith in anything, so that should tell you something."

Jane wished she could share his belief, his willingness to

see options and possibilities. Right now she felt lost, adrift in a storm over which she had no control. Tara's news pushed her brain into overdrive. There wasn't just one thing racing around now; every problem, every worry was confusing her. Jane still didn't know what was happening with her store, and she had to admit, that had her more anxious than anything. But more than a few people, smart people, had told her there was nothing to be concerned about.

Unfortunately, her gut wasn't listening.

Danny had been trying to ease her mind by mentioning all the good things she had in her life. He wasn't wrong; however, the shadow following her around was a lot harder to shake. God, she would miss her girl if she went to school across the pond, but Jane couldn't help thinking there was something else coming. Something life-changing. It forced her to remember that day in Scotland when she was called to the phone in her makeshift office to find out her father had died. Her dad was her cheerleader, her support system. Her world shattered into a million pieces that day, and it had taken a long time to put it back together. She didn't know how she would handle something like that again.

"I hope you're right. I really hope you're right."

Chapter Thirteen

EVERY WORD DRIPPED with sadness, and all he wanted to do was make it better. Dan knew Jane was a smart, capable businesswoman, but she was going to be crushed under the weight of the news that the building housing her store was in the process of being sold.

He honestly didn't know if he should tell her, especially after hearing Tara's news about Dublin.

Jane's family was changing. Her house was going from a home that had the energy of three people to a house for one. He guessed Jane didn't know where she fit in the world. When she spoke about Tara going to college, her pain was so visceral, he could almost feel it himself. Of course she was proud of her daughter, and excited, but it left Jane without the role she'd had for the past seventeen years.

She was looking at the lights in the park with a wistfulness that revealed just how much she cared for her town and the people. Responding the only way that felt right, he dropped his hands from her shoulders and wrapped his arms around her. Rather than stiffen or pull away from the sudden intimacy, she let him comfort her, leaning back against him, allowing him to absorb her weight and her troubles.

The flash of protectiveness was overpowering. Acknowledging that she triggered every protective instinct was the first step into new and frightening territory. At the same time, her wisdom and her calm, her goodness brought him peace. She was why he was writing again.

Dan wasn't ready to share it yet, but the story he was working on was Janie's book. It was the story he wanted the two of them to write together. It was about finding love and belonging after a life of loss and detachment. Resting his chin on her head, he faced glaring reality. He was in love with her, and if he was truthful, he always had been. She was never far from his thoughts. His feelings for her were likely why he'd never married, never really settled down. It was why he kept relationships at arm's length. All these years, his heart, his soul, belonged to Jane.

The realization over the last few weeks was more epiphany than anything else. He had no heart-fluttering awareness other than the deep, abiding peace he felt when he touched her, held her, kissed her.

His heart was hers. All he wanted was to make her happy. To make it so she had nothing to worry about ever again.

Which was why this wasn't the right moment to tell her what he'd learned about the sale of her store.

He would break the news to her, but considering how upset she was, this wasn't the time. It was her business, and she had a right to know, but the news about Tara had pushed her to her breaking point. Granted it was good news, but Jane was crushed at the idea of her daughter being so far away. She had so many other things on her mind, did she really need the stress about her store right now?

He'd tell her, just not tonight.

Gently, he turned her toward him, taking her face in his

hands. Her eyes, bright with tears, reflected the jeweled lights that were strung in every tree.

"I wish I could help." Once again he squashed the little voice screaming at him to tell her what he'd found out. He could fix it.

"That's sweet, but unless you're going to help me keep her prisoner, I don't know what can be done."

"Uh..." The thought of it actually made him smile. "I haven't known Tara long, but I doubt she'd be a particularly cooperative prisoner."

"You would be correct."

"Everything will work out."

"You don't know that," she said. "What if she goes and she hates it? What if—"

"Shhh. Stop torturing yourself." Dan could feel the tension in her body rachet up. "If she hates it, she'll come home. And you'll be there for her just like always."

"Will I? I'm still wondering if I'll even have a business. My attorney is worried. I can feel it."

Keeping the information about the store from her wasn't going to be easy. The Fallon woo-woo was legend in town. He should know better than to mess with it. Still, he wanted to reassure her. "The bookstore is an institution in Angel Harbor. It's as important as Old First Church or Village Hall. I doubt the town would let anything happen."

He knew damn well that if the building was being used legally and there was proper zoning, there wasn't much the town could do.

"Now you're trying to placate me. You know there's nothing the town can do. I've even thought of moving. If something happens, I guess I could…"

"Jane, try not to get ahead of yourself. You don't know what's going to happen."

She stared at him, her eyes piercing through the darkness like a pair of cat's eyes. "That's true, but I don't know how to just shut it off. That must be some special gift and I don't have it."

"I wish I could help."

"How can I be feeling like this?"

"Like what?" he asked.

"I feel like I've lost control of everything. It's Christmas and I want it to be wonderful, but knowing this is the last time I'll have Tara home full time, I want it to be special. That email tonight from Dublin just drove home that she's not going to be around, and she could be thousands of miles away. Everything is happening so fast. I want her to have good memories, to know I'm proud of her."

"She knows, honey. She knows."

Jane was on a precipice, the cusp of great change, and watching her fight against the fear and self-doubt, holding it together for everyone around her, was the most extraordinary thing. This woman was remarkable. If he was in possession of just a fraction of her bravery and her nerve, he'd be able to face all the changes he wanted to make. The life-altering kind that, with luck, included Jane for the rest of his days.

She was, without any doubt, the best person he knew. There was never a moment that went by that Jane's light didn't affect someone. He only wished she could see that brightness herself.

"Can we talk about something else?" She gazed up at

him, and he fell deep into the misty depths.

That simple request, right there, ended any deliberation he was having with himself. He'd figure out a time to tell her about the store, but tonight she needed some peace.

"Tell me about the lights," he said, tucking her head under his chin. "The town didn't always go all-out like this for the holidays."

"No. The decorations have been growing over the past ten years. It went in stages. The gazebo was always lit, even when we were kids, as was the tree."

"I remember."

"But we added the pier, and the walkway, and then the other trees..." Light and color danced around the snow-dusted park, making it look like it was covered with glitter just like the floor in the children's room earlier.

"We? Tell me about the we." He knew what her answer would be before he even asked the question.

"It's a committee. We're a family here, and we want to share our town. Especially at the holidays. I mean, look how pretty this is. How could anyone not feel happy?" They were gazing at the scene in the park, and Danny had to admit, he'd never seen anything so magical, except when he saw it through Jane's eyes.

"I don't know. I think you could tell me that."

She turned her head, catching his gaze, her sparkling eyes reflecting her own sadness and confusion.

"I'm sorry," he said. "Out of line?"

"No. You just call me on the lies I tell. I guess that's what friends do, right?"

He laughed softly. "If you say so." Pulling her closer and

reveling in the connection they were sharing, even if it was only for a few minutes, Dan didn't know how he was going to walk away from all he'd gained over the past month. The town and his family, and Jane, meant everything to him. How could he leave it all?

"It's going to be okay, Janie. I promise."

The thought of going back to his solitary existence, of keeping people at bay, had lost its appeal. For the first time since he'd left town for what he thought was forever, Dan felt like his life had meaning—as corny as that sounded. The pace had slowed, and he'd found each day brought something new to celebrate and enjoy. That he'd been given a second chance with Jane, was the most unexpected, and remarkable, development.

Maybe, leaving Angel Harbor *was* a choice to be made, just like it had been before. He could go, or he could stay.

The choice was all his.

THIS FELT WAY too good. Being here with him, looking at the lights, feeling the chill in the air, triggered memories of a lifetime ago. She wanted to put all her trust in him, so very much, but with so much on her mind, could she take a risk on him as well?

She felt, whether she had reason or not, that her life was imploding, and Jane worried that Danny would only make things more complicated. Jane wasn't the type to be distant. Her very nature craved closeness. She'd tried to keep him at arm's length, but the pull was just too strong. There was no way for her heart not to be involved.

"What do you want to do? Dinner? Movie?" Danny's deep voice drifted over her.

"I wish I knew. I'm usually so good at making decisions. This isn't like me."

"You're facing huge changes, and that's not easy. Try to focus on something else." It was good advice and he certainly knew what he was talking about, but he was proactively making a change, while Jane couldn't stop thinking that life was going to change around her no matter what.

"Work is crazy busy, and my mind flits from one thing to another." On top of her melancholy over pretty much everything, Danny was in there causing more distractions than she wanted to admit. "Christmas is just a few weeks away, and I don't even have a tree."

He tilted her face to his, the snow falling lightly around them. Jane should be charmed by the scene. She was with a handsome man who cared about her, the lights were magical, and it was snowing. She couldn't have written a Christmas movie with a better setup. Internally, however, she fought against the warring sides. On one side, she wanted to put on a good face and do what everyone expected. Jane was the strong one, the person everyone depended on. The other part of her wanted to lean on him, to depend on someone else.

"No tree? Even I have a tree."

"I haven't had time."

Danny leaned in and kissed the top of her head. "Come on." He took her hand and pulled her along the path.

"Where are we going?" She followed, barely keeping pace because her boots slipped a little. But he held her up, not letting her fall.

"Where are you parked? Next to the bookstore?"

"Yes. What are you doing?" she protested.

"We're going to get a tree."

"A Christmas tree?" His pace slowed and she settled in next to him, but he kept her hand firmly in his. "It's not necessary. I can go another day."

"When?" His question, simple and to the point, drove home the reality of her next few weeks. She'd been so preoccupied by the store, the Harbor Lights festival, her family, Thanksgiving, she'd forgotten about her own Christmas preparations. She loved Christmas.

"I have no idea. Like I said, I'm not myself."

"Come on. Let's go. There's a tree farm on the way to Compass Cove. It's open late. We can get you a tree and I can help you put it in the stand."

The idea was appealing, no doubt, but her inner independent, the one who didn't want to need him for so many reasons, balked at the idea. He sensed that too.

"Give yourself a break, just this once. Let me help. It will be fun, and God knows, you could use some fun."

"What's that supposed to mean?" Was she so unfun that she needed an intervention? "I have fun."

"Not nearly enough." He dropped a gentle kiss on her lips. "What time are you opening tomorrow?"

"We open at noon on Sundays, but I'm off tomorrow."

"That works. Now I don't have to worry about keeping you out too late on a school night. Let's go find some fancy coffee or hot chocolate and get you a Christmas tree. We have decorating to do."

Chapter Fourteen

AFTER A PIT stop at the store to pick up her SUV, she and Danny headed out of town to find her Christmas tree. Like some kind of fairy tale, it was a cold night, there was light snow, and a gorgeous man was trying to make things better. She'd let him drive mostly because she was worn out from the day, but also because she could spend her time watching him. And he was addicting to watch. She'd spent entirely too much time sneaking peeks at him in the bookstore. It was so middle school, but she did love when he caught her looking.

It amazed her how her feelings for him were as strong, if not stronger, as when they were younger. There was something settled now, mature. She never expected it, but it was there, surrounding her, comforting her from the inside out. Her doubt made little sense, and she wondered, was she doubting him, or herself?

The shadow of a beard covered his jaw, and not knowing what made her do it, she reached out when they were waiting at a light, and gently touched his face. His skin was warm, rough with heat, much like his gaze. His eyes stayed on her as he leaned into her hand. The intimacy of the touch, the connection, took her breath away.

The truth of what they meant to each other hit her like

water from a dam burst. It was hard and fast, a tsunami of realization. Jane was in love with him. Now, then…it had always been Danny.

They roamed the tree lot first, but none of the precut trees looked right.

"Are you seeing anything? They all seem too big or too small for your living room."

"No, but I can always go smaller. That's not the end of the world."

Danny didn't seem satisfied with that option, based on the way he examined one very large tree.

"That one is too big," she said. "Later I'll tell you about the time my Uncle Joe took Tara out to cut down a tree, and he got one that was so big it filled half the living room. And bent over at the top. It was enormous."

"Your uncle is a character. He didn't notice it was gigantic?"

"Well, according to Tara, who was around eight at the time, 'It didn't look that big next to the sky.'"

Danny blinked twice, staring at her with an expression she couldn't read. "Well, there you go," he said. "I guess it wouldn't."

"I said the same thing."

"So, a cautionary tale." He looked up at the very large spruce next to him and made a decision. "Hmm. Hang on." She watched him walk over to the little hut where everyone who worked at the lot was gathered. One of the older men stepped into the little wooden shack and came out with a saw. Danny returned to her quickly, his long stride covering a lot of ground quickly. "Okay, let's go."

"Go where?"

"Well, I don't usually carry around a bow saw," he said holding up the tool. "Let's go find a tree."

There were at least a hundred uncut trees to pick from, but it didn't take long to narrow their search. Knowing she wanted one that was about seven feet tall for her front room, they came upon a group of trees that appeared to be just the right size.

"These look perfect," she said. The small cluster must have been planted at the same time as they were all similarly sized. Some were more dense, some fatter, others more conical in shape. Jane zeroed in on one tree at edge of the small grove. She almost missed it.

"This one." Looking up, she ran her gloved hand over the needles, and almost none fell off. It was full, but not so dense they'd have trouble stringing lights and hanging the ornaments. "How tall do you think this one is?"

"Based on the sky, or for real?" He smiled, and the little inside joke, that tidbit of familiarity, brought them that much closer.

"For real."

Extending his arm, he tilted his head. "This one is about seven and a half feet tall. Give or take a couple of inches. How tall is your ceiling?"

"Nine feet."

"You're golden. You sure about this one? Last chance to change your mind."

"I'm sure."

While he got down on the ground to cut the tree, Jane held the trunk, letting the smell of pine and snow seep into her senses. Just being outside, being with him, helped her feel better.

The thought of Tara missing the build-up to Christmas next year caused a bit of an ache in her chest, but that would happen whether she was in Ireland or Vermont. Jane had to accept that her life was changing, but looking at Danny as he cut down her Christmas tree reminded her that all change wasn't bad.

The two of them managed to carry the tree back to the main part of the lot, and without much help, Dan hoisted the Fraser fir onto the roof of her car. Jane noticed that he had an easier time securing the tree than the much younger helper employed by the farm. It almost didn't seem fair.

What was it about men and aging? Why did it always go so well for them? Glancing at the tree on her roof and then at the man who'd made it happen, Jane felt herself smile. At least that was something.

DANNY PULLED INTO the driveway and cut the engine. It was comfortable, like they'd done this particular routine a thousand times. If her tales of woe earlier that evening had brought him down, she couldn't tell. He was smiling and humming along with the Christmas music on the radio. He seemed happy and at ease, and Jane wished she could hold on to some holiday spirit for more than five minutes.

Her phone buzzed in her bag, and when she pulled it out, she saw a few text messages had come in. One was from her mother, one was from Tracy, and one was from Gary, her lawyer. Her lawyer? It was eleven-thirty at night, over a holiday weekend. What the devil was he thinking?

It didn't say much, which was getting to be the norm, but hearing from him was definitely progress. Until she read the message, which indicated anything but. *No word,* it said. Nothing else.

It put her back up, and she typed furiously back into her phone. *I need answers.*

"He probably thought I was asleep," she mumbled.

"What?" Danny had no idea what she was talking about. "Who thinks you're asleep?"

"Gary. My lawyer. He just sent me a text. '*No word.*' That's all it said."

Danny gripped the steering wheel with both hands, tension evident in his fingers. Jane wondered if he was angry that she couldn't let go of the issues with the bookstore for one night. They'd been having such a good time. Had she ruined it?

"His timing was impeccable." Danny was very still, and obviously annoyed.

"Tell me about it. I'm sorry." With trembling hands, she fished her keys from her bag. Her life was never-ending whiplash, with her feelings being yanked around from one side to another, all while she tried to maintain her calm.

She didn't know if she was feeling off because of Danny, or her business. Maybe it was a little of both. Him *and* her business. Both disasters waiting to happen. Why was she opening herself up to this kind of heartache? Especially when she had no idea how to be in a relationship.

It was fine. She could regain control of the situation.

He'd help her get the tree in the stand, and then he could go, with her thanks. Jane could put on her pajamas and eat all the chocolate mousse pie that was left over from Thanksgiving.

But therein lay the rub. Jane didn't want him to go. She loved being with him, and the thought of the night ending made her desperately unhappy.

She was crazy. That was it, she was plain old crazy. She didn't know how to manage her business or her life, and it was going to be a glorious crash when it all went down.

He'd obviously regrouped, much more resilient than she was. "Come on. Since you don't have to work tomorrow, we can put on the lights too."

"That's not necessary," she said quietly.

"It's no problem. It will be fun." He seemed intent on getting her to have a good time, which should be endearing, but Jane was too exhausted.

Why didn't he listen? There must have been something in the male genetic makeup that made them selectively deaf.

"You don't have to do this, Danny. I'm not your project." Jane got out of the car, and closed the door. Keys in her hand, she started toward the back door, but she froze when she heard him close the driver's side door.

"Janie, come on." He didn't sound angry. In fact, he sounded annoyingly rational. Jane looked up at a sky that was crystal clear and a deep midnight blue. Now that the storm had blown out to sea, the stars twinkled and blinked, and Jane would wish on every one of them if she could.

She'd wish for answers. And wisdom. Lots and lots of wisdom.

The excuse that a relationship with him was out of the question was wearing a little thin because it was patently untrue. It was time for Jane to admit that she didn't just want him, she needed him.

But that ran contrary to the person she'd always been. She didn't ask for help. *Ever.* Jane was the helper. If she'd learned anything about herself, it was that feeling dependent on anyone made her uncomfortable. She'd been let down before, and it was just safer to keep her trust circle very small. She had her people and they should be enough.

Standing with her at the bottom of the stoop, he rested his hands on her shoulders with gentle patience.

"Talk to me." He seemed honestly confused, and why wouldn't he be? He'd done everything right. He was kind and helpful. He listened. He kissed like a dream. He wasn't staying, but that didn't stop her heart from going all in. She'd tried, hadn't she?

Staring into his ocean blue eyes, Jane drowned in the knowledge that it was already too late. That genie was out of the bottle. For good.

"I'm sorry. I'm just not used to someone else taking charge of my life."

"Taking charge? I thought I was being a friend." His eyes narrowed, not buying her excuse. "Why don't you tell me why you really sniped at me just now? And for the record, I don't consider you a project."

He wanted a confession? Yeah. That was the perfect way to feel festive. His eyes were locked on hers, intense and unwavering as he waited for her to answer.

"Let's go inside," he suggested.

"Okay. Did you grab the soup?"

He held up a small brown paper handle bag. "Right here."

They'd picked up two bowls of chowder at a local pub that had a particularly good late-night menu. Jane didn't have much of an appetite after snapping Danny's head off, and ruminating about everything that could go wrong wasn't helping, but she wasn't going to admit to any of that either.

There wasn't much they could talk about if she kept pulling things off the table.

The house was quiet. Her mother was upstairs in bed, and Tara was staying at a friend's house. The only one there to meet them was Chloe, and her girl conveyed to her that she definitely was not happy about being on her own today. That was until she saw Danny, and her pooch's mood picked right up.

It seemed her dog was as gone over him as she was.

They settled in without speaking. He took her coat and hung it in the mudroom and then let the dog out while she put the soup in mugs and gave each one a shot in the microwave. She found some crusty rolls in the bread box, and poured them both a glass of wine.

He gave an occasional glance outside, watching for the dog quietly, and there was something so sweet about it. He was ridiculously handsome, rugged and rumpled; he looked like he belonged in this house, in this town. But he also had a refinement, a sensitivity that you generally only found in a man who was secure with who he was. Rough patches and all, Danny knew himself, and that was, without a doubt, the most attractive thing about him.

By the time Danny let the dog in, Jane had them set up at the island for a cozy late supper. It was like they'd been doing this forever. An intimate night in, wine, a Christmas tree, two people who had known each other forever, all combined to make the scenario perfectly romantic, or perfectly ordinary. Whatever it was, the comfort of it all scared her to death.

Dan sat down and took a sip of his wine, nodding approval. "I'm not usually a white wine guy, but this is good."

"It's one of my favorites to have with seafood."

"Ah. I like it." He took a spoonful of soup. "Mmm. That's really good. I'll bring the tree in after we finish."

"Thank you. I do appreciate your help."

"Okay." He grinned, and dabbed at the corner of his mouth with the napkin she'd put out. "I think we should talk about your lease."

"Ugh. No. I'm sorry I snapped. It's not your fault." Being called out made her uncomfortable, but she deserved it. He was only trying to help, and she'd been mean.

"I know. But I want to tell you something…"

Jane cut him off. "No. I've been totally irrational about it. I don't want to ruin our evening. You've been wonderful, and the project comment, well, it wasn't fair. I'm just not used to…"

"Being handled?" She started to object, but Danny waved it off. He put the spoon in the soup mug and leaned back in his chair. "You have a point. I can be overbearing sometimes. I forget that my way of managing something isn't your way. I'm a fixer. It can be a problem. Ask my sister."

"No. It's not your fault. Like you said, you're trying to

help, but I'm not good at accepting it. You obviously didn't get the memo that I'm the one who does the helping."

"I wouldn't have known." He bit his lower lip to hide his smile.

"Go ahead. Make fun."

"Later." He reached out and took her hand. "We have to talk about the elephant in the room. Your lawyer…"

"Stop. I don't want to talk about it." Jane folded her arms almost defiantly, but she couldn't hold the pose when Chloe decided to goose her backside. "Jeez, dog!"

A short burst of laughter came flying out of Danny as he watched Jane pop out of her seat. He sobered quickly, however, and squeezed her hand again. "Okay. No real estate talk tonight."

"Good," she said.

"We're a pair, aren't we?" The amused rumble from his core was low and sexy.

"It's true, though. I'm not good at asking for help," she said. "I'm just not. It annoys everyone. I'm stubborn."

He nailed her with his eyes. "You don't say?"

She ignored the note of sarcasm in his voice and plowed on. "I've been let down by people, so I'm cautious. I have a very small circle and I find it's a lot less complicated if I…I don't know…lower my expectations."

"That is one way to avoid disappointment."

"Exactly. No expectations, no disappointment."

It was a philosophy that didn't sit well with her. In her heart she hoped people wanted to do for her as she did for them. Jane always gave her whole heart. Sometimes, she got hurt as a result.

"You don't trust people."

"I'm *cautious*," she said again.

"You don't trust me?"

"I trust you." More than she should, considering. "You're a good person, kind and generous. I have no doubt about that, but I don't want to..."

"What?" he asked. Waiting for her to finish.

Want you? Need you? Fall in love with you? she thought. Nope, none of those would do. She couldn't bare her soul like that.

"Get used to you," she finally said, settling on a phrase as innocuous as she could muster. She put her spoon down and folded her hands in her lap. Jane didn't want to put up a wall, but she felt like she had to. "I guess I'm worried about how *close* we're getting. You're a risk."

"Because I let you down?"

He'd done more than let her down. As much as Jane had put the past behind her, she wouldn't forget how much it hurt when Danny never looked back after leaving for law school. The feeling of abandonment, the knowledge that he didn't care about her lingered, and she couldn't deny that it made her hesitant, regardless of what her heart was telling her.

"You're not staying," she whispered. There it was. Every bit of the past and present, all the love, all the hurt, was laid out with that statement. Not able to face him, she took her half-empty bowl to the sink and stood there, her back to him while she tried to gather her thoughts. Jane hadn't planned on dropping that little bit of vulnerability out there, but there was no taking it back now.

"AW, JANIE." DAN went to her as soon as the words sank in. "Come here." Talk about opening a raw wound. He pulled her into his arms and held on tight, hoping he could convey to her how much he cared. He didn't dare tell her what he wanted to. That she was everything to him. He didn't want to flip back a response that was predictable and trite. Jane might see it as a way to win points, but the truth of it was that he wanted nothing more than to stay here with her and make a life.

With her head pressed into his chest, she slipped her arms around his waist and held on. "I lost you once," she said, her voice filled with sadness. "I don't know if I could deal with that again. Especially now."

"You won't lose me. Even if I'm on the other side of the world, that's not going to happen."

He didn't know how to reassure her. He meant every word, and more, but convincing her would be the challenge. How do you prove your love to someone who is so afraid, she might not want to accept it? That's where Danny was right now. He was so in love with Jane, it consumed him. They were right for each other, of that there was no doubt. But she didn't trust him, no matter what she said.

"I was at one of your signings once. Did you know that?"

He leaned back and took in her beautiful face. Her eyes were overly bright, on the verge of tears. "You were? When?"

"Four years ago. I went to the signing and book talk you had at The Strand. It was packed."

He nodded, remembering the event. It was chaos, mostly

because the book was also made into a movie and that brought out even more people. He hated when that happened. Often the book and the movie had little in common, and he didn't have anything to do with the production other than to show up and collect his checks.

"Why didn't you say something? I had no idea you were there."

"I tried. The books were sold out already, so I was just going to say hello. But security didn't buy my story that we grew up in the same town. I left you a note. I guess you didn't get it. They shuffled me out pretty quickly."

"Shit." Her experience wasn't his doing, but it was a testament to the kind of insular life he'd been leading. Security, handlers, he was a writer and he had a damn entourage. It was so bad she couldn't even say hello. "God, I'm sorry."

"It wasn't your fault. I mean you didn't know I was there. We hadn't kept in touch."

"I was the one who didn't keep in touch. I should have known." With a finger under her chin, he tilted her face to his and kissed her softly. "I will not let you go again. I promise. You're stuck with me now."

"Don't make promises you can't keep. Your life isn't here."

"How do you know that?" Well, now he'd stepped in it. There was no turning back. "I can write anywhere, and Angel Harbor has been good for me."

Her eyes locked on his, and in them he saw his future. "What are you saying? You want to live here?"

"No." As soon as he said it, he saw her face drop and realized what he was trying to convey wasn't translating well.

"I'm saying I want to make a *life* here. I don't like being so disconnected from my family, and I think we owe ourselves a chance, don't you?"

He could see that what he'd just proposed, a simple chance, sparked a tiny bit of joy in her dusty green eyes. He'd take it. He would do anything for her, including saving her store.

Jane threw her arms around his neck and buried her face in his shoulder. He was going to guess that was a yes. He splayed his hands across her back and pulled her as close as he could, reveling in her weight, in her curves. She fit him perfectly. Dan couldn't believe how long it had taken him to get to this place. Finally.

"You're sure you want to do that? Take on the small-town life? The gossip and the politics and the nonsense? It can be pretty overwhelming."

Those were all good questions, and good reasons to go back to his peaceful existence. But the thought of being without Jane canceled out all of them. "Yeah. I'm ready, as long as you're there to guide me through."

AT THREE O'CLOCK in the morning, Jane and Danny sat on the sofa in her living room and stared at the Christmas tree they had just finished decorating. Jane sipped on a hot chocolate she'd spiked with Irish cream liqueur, and Danny was in the midst of inhaling a plate of chocolate chip cookies and a big glass of milk.

"It looks good. We did a great job," he said between

bites.

“It does. You’re excellent at stringing lights.” She glanced over, loving how in that moment, he was nothing more than an older version of his teenage self.

“Thanks. Considering I haven’t put so much as an ornament on a tree in ten years, I think I did all right.”

“That’s a long time. Not into Christmas?”

“It’s not that. I was always either alone or out of town for the holidays. I can’t remember the last time I had a tree where I lived.”

Jane found that incredibly sad. For everything he had, the simple joy of a Christmas tree wasn’t part of his life. Maybe this would start a new tradition.

He was still enjoying his cookies. So much, in fact, he had eaten almost half a dozen.

“How can you eat so many of those cookies? Where do they go?”

“Are you insinuating I can’t hold my cookies?” he said, taking a swig of milk.

Jane laughed out loud, forgetting how late it was and that her mother was asleep upstairs.

“No, but I know what I put in there. You still eat like you’re a teenager.”

“You say that like it’s a bad thing. I’ll run them off tomorrow. Want to come with me?”

“Running? No. If you see me running, it’s because there’s a zombie apocalypse. You have fun though.”

Jane started to stand, but the spiked hot chocolate had done its job—she wobbled and dropped back onto her big camel-colored sofa. “Ohhh. Well, that was unexpected.”

Now it was Danny's turn to laugh. "Little too much booze in your chocolate?"

She leaned into him, taking advantage of his solid frame. This was nice. She was wonderfully tipsy, and he was big and gorgeous and sweet, and he cared about her enough to stay.

The tree was so pretty and lit up the room with flicks and spots of colored light. She was normally a clear light kind of girl, but the colored lights definitely won the day. "Oh!" She popped up from the couch and stuck her arms out when the room spun. "Whoa."

Danny grabbed her hand to steady her. "What's the matter?"

"Nothing. I forgot something. For the tree."

"Can you walk?" He thought he was making a joke, but it was a good question. Jane wasn't so sure. Taking a tentative step, she waved him off. There's was only one way to find out.

"I'm good." She took another step and didn't face-plant. This was progress. "I'll be right back."

She headed down the short hallway to the smallest bedroom, the one she used as her office. On the shelf, in a red velvet box, was a beautiful angel ornament from her father. Dad bought it in Ireland for the child he would have one day, and it looked almost identical to the one in her office at work. This one, however, was just a tiny bit smaller, and was meant for her tree. The word *"faith"* was etched into one wing. The handblown crystal reflected the light in bursts and would make the entire tree look like it was touched by a host of angels.

When she brought it out to the living room, Danny was

standing next to the tree, adjusting a light strand that was sagging a bit. "What did you forget?"

"This." She held up the ornament for him to see. "My dad gave it to me the day I was born. It's always the last ornament to go on the tree."

Jane reached up and felt a rush of awareness when Danny took hold of her waist to steady her. With a stretch, she was able to hang the ornament near the top, where it would have its chance to sparkle and shine.

Coming off her tiptoes, Jane stared up, and she shivered when Danny's arms wrapped around her. They stood there, quiet and close, taking in their handiwork.

"It's beautiful," he said. "The angel was the perfect finish."

"The angel brings my dad back, even if it's just for a little while."

"He'd be proud of you."

Jane shrugged. "I hope so. I did my best."

There were moments when Jane thought her dad was doing his best to help, sending signs that everything would be okay. "There was a cardinal sitting on the bookstore porch rail the other day. Whenever I see one, I feel like my dad is with me. That he's trying to help me figure things out."

"I think he's always with you. You were his pride and joy—he'll never be far." Danny's arms tightened around her waist while she grasped his arms and pulled him closer. She felt safe with him. Maybe it was foolish considering his track record, but right now, in this moment, she was safe.

"Thank you," she said, tears welling in her eyes. Not sure

what brought about the torrent of emotion, she considered that possibly the alcohol she'd had was making her sloppy and sentimental. But after everything that had happened between them, she didn't think so. No, Jane was overwhelmed by the depth of her feelings for this man. "Thank you for helping me get out of my own head for a while."

Turning her in his arms, Danny gazed down at her with such tenderness, the tears that had been threatening spilled over. Not exactly happy tears—Jane was swamped by the love she felt in that moment. With a gentle brush of his thumb across her cheek, he wiped them away. "Don't cry, Janie. I'm not going anywhere. I promise."

Chapter Fifteen

"WHAT DO YOU mean it's been sold?" Over two weeks had passed since he'd told Zach to make an offer on the property. Like an idiot, he'd never told Jane, and now he was in deep trouble.

He heard a long exhalation from his business manager on the other end of the line. He'd never thought it was a good idea, and Zach was probably relieved. "I just got off the phone with the seller's attorney, and she said she'd let me know if the deal falls through, but they have a solid offer on the property. It's in escrow."

He swore under his breath, hating that his Hail Mary pass to save Jane's store had failed.

"Up the offer. See if they'll break the deal with the other buyer. Money talks, right?"

"Not if they've gone to contract. This is a big, stable company. It's money in the bank."

"I'm a big, stable company."

"Are you?" Zach shot back. "You've made some dumbass moves lately." Danny wasn't going to argue with him because on paper that looked to be the case.

Frustrated, he paced. Danny wanted so badly to do this for her. There was nothing more important than taking away the worry he saw in her eyes. Tara's college acceptances had started rolling in, and while none of them were as far away as Dublin, each little celebration was laced with a hint of sadness.

Now he'd have to tell her about the building sale, and that he'd tried to save the day without asking her. Jane didn't need a white knight, but he'd wanted to try.

"She said if anything changed, I was her first phone call."

"Thanks, Zach. I appreciate it."

"Look, if you want to invest in real estate, there are some great properties in the Hamptons that would be perfect for you. Spend your summers partying with the rich and famous. I hear there's even a big charity book fair out there in the summer."

He'd already done too much partying. He'd spent the last fifteen years in that life, and where had it gotten him? Life was easier here in Angel Harbor and Danny wasn't interested in messing with what was working. He was finally feeling like a real person again. Over the past week and a half he'd written another thirty thousand words. And he was in love.

The story was flowing like a river after a rainstorm. The words were coming like never before, and he was happier than he'd been in a long time.

When the call came in, letting him know his offer had been rejected, he was already on his way to the store. It never occurred to him that it wouldn't work out.

Now that his plan had fallen apart he had to think about how he was going to tell Jane she'd been right all along.

Heading down the hill into town, he tried to think of alternatives to Jane closing up shop. He'd had his business manager check for retail spaces Jane might have missed, buildings he could buy in other towns that weren't too far away from Angel Harbor.

So far, he'd come up empty.

Repositioning his messenger bag onto his right shoulder, Dan didn't know why he hung on to the old leather satchel. It was a battered mess of chestnut brown leather, which had been repaired three separate times. He'd always claimed he wasn't a sentimental guy, but more and more that was being called into question.

He wasn't fooling anyone. Even hanging on to the old bag was his way of hanging on to some of his history. He'd bought it when he started his first job out of law school. The bag, which looked every bit its age, had served him well, transporting briefs, journals, case studies, manuscripts, and his laptop. It had witnessed his life in all its forms. Now it would see one more change.

Walking down Main Street, he passed by the old Sail House and reflected on how much this town meant to him. As he'd gotten to know the businesspeople of Angel Harbor, his neighbors, and spent time with his own family, he realized just how much he'd gained since coming here. Finding the love of his life was a bonus he never expected.

Dan had become a fixture at the store and he and Jane were, by all appearances, a couple. The last few weeks had sealed it. Ella had even asked him if Miss Jane was his girlfriend. They'd been doing everything together from Christmas shopping, to eating meals, to spending time watching movies and wrapping gifts. There was nothing extraordinary about what they did, except that they were doing it together.

Dan had been alone for so long; that was how he saw the world—as a solitary existence, peppered with people he didn't particularly care about. His friends were nice enough. Publishing people fawned over him, but he didn't consider them friends. If he took a good look, his close circle had been whittled down to almost no one. Now he had his sister, his brother-in-law, the kids, Jane and her family, as well as an expanding group of people in Angel Harbor.

In little more than a month, he went from going days without talking to anyone to a rich, full life, with a cadre of people he could depend on. He walked past Sweet Chemistry and saw Viti put something fresh into the case, and decided to see what she had concocted that morning.

Her donuts, which were dense and delicious, were dipped right in front of you. Jane loved the chocolate frosted, but Dan had become addicted to Viti's apple cider donuts. They tasted like the holidays. With the subtle flavors of apple, allspice, and cinnamon, he was reminded of the mulled cider he'd had at Jane's house on Thanksgiving. Another wonderful memory made since he'd returned home.

The bakery was in its mid-morning lull, so why not stop? He liked Viti. She was quick, with a sharp tongue, and he enjoyed talking to her. Like him, she'd returned to Angel Harbor after leaving for college and her corporate life.

His identity wasn't a secret anymore, but to most of the good folks in town, he was just a kid who had come home. Other than the small circle of regulars he saw at the bookstore, Viti was the only person who talked to him about his books and why he'd come back. It turned out she'd seen him speak years ago, and didn't it figure, when she mentioned the event, he couldn't even remember it.

Dan's life had been a blur, and that was going to stop.

His senses were assaulted as soon as he walked into the store. The mix of smells alone made his mouth water, and the bright smile he received from Viti just added to the experience. He found her work history as a corporate-level chemist in the biotech industry fascinating. How she'd come to love baking so much was another great story. In her words, *"Everything is chemistry. Why not make delicious fresh food using those principles?"*

"Hey there!" she said. "How goes the book?"

"Not bad. I'm almost done." Dan surveyed the bakery case under the watchful eye of the proprietor. "What's good today?" he asked.

"Duh. Everything." Viti was not the least bit shy about her skills. In her late forties and divorced, it seemed to him the woman worked twenty-four hours straight five days a week. She had big brown eyes, and dark hair that she always wore pinned up and under a green Sweet Chemistry ball cap.

"I have apple cider donuts if you're interested."

"Always," he responded. "I'll take four."

"Four? Bad day in the authoring business?"

"Why would you think that?" That was unnerving. Was the woman a psychic? He was beginning to think the whole town had the gift. He wasn't able to get anything by these people.

"Your books may take people on a wild goose chase, but you're pretty predictable. You're either feeling creative, or cranky. Which is it?"

He wanted to tell her it was a little of both. Knowing the bookstore was already in escrow definitely put him more in the cranky column. Like he told Jane, Dan considered himself a problem solver. Whether it was years ago trying a case or recently working out a plot issue, he was all about focusing on the cause and the outcome of a particular problem. His solution to the building problem was to buy it himself. Jane wouldn't have to close, problem solved.

He was frustrated because now he didn't know what to do. And if he was honest with himself, he knew she was going to be angry, and probably hurt. He'd been sitting on the information about the store for two weeks. He should have told her.

"Viti, add two chocolate frosted for Jane and a couple of glazed."

"Not enough goodies at the bookstore?"

"I haven't been there yet, but I know Jane loves the chocolate icing."

"There you are!" A booming voice that sounded like it came straight from Brooklyn broke the sweet quiet of the bakery.

Viti's eyes widened at the imposing form of Brian Webb, Esquire, his agent. A little younger than Danny, Brian had taken over the agency from his father, Jerry Webb, a legend in the business, who'd taken a chance on Dan when he was a total unknown. Brian was a big, tough-looking guy, with the build of a linebacker and a New York attitude. He'd also graduated first in his class from Stanford Law. He was very good at his job.

Danny turned around when Brian's meat hook of a hand

dropped on his shoulder. "I was about to go looking for you in the bookstore, but I saw your sorry ass walk in here." Brian looked around at the bakery with its retro fittings and old-time coffee shop vibe, and uttered a single word. "Cool."

"What are you doing in town again, Bri? If you're going to try to talk me out of finishing my book, forget it."

"Absolutely not! I didn't think it was possible, but there are two publishers ready to go to war over it, and I don't even know what it's about. I'll have to pitch it to a few more. Then it could get interesting."

"Are you serious?"

"I know, right? I never woulda thought it, but it's gonna be a hot property. Get it done, and you're looking at a major advance. Probably another movie."

"Wow. Okay. I have another ten thousand words or so to write. Then I'll give it an edit."

Brian was bent over at the waist examining the cakes and pastries in the glass case. "I think I've gained ten pounds lookin' at this stuff. Are you the baker?"

Viti grinned. "I am. Viti Prasad. Welcome. Can I get you anything?"

"That apple thing looks good," he said, pointing at the personal apple tart.

"Put it on my tab, Viti." She gave a nod before Dan turned toward him. "You didn't come all the way from the city to tell me that, though. You could have called. Why are you here? I told you not to come back out."

"Because Zach told me you wanted to buy some old building out here? So you can keep the bookstore from being evicted? I wanted to make sure you hadn't been abducted by aliens or anything."

Holy hell. The idiot just blurted that out right in front of Viti. This was bad.

"I beg your pardon?" Viti cut in, her expression frozen and serious. "Evicted?"

"Zach told you that?" This could not have been worse.

"He said to make sure you get a good deal on your next book because you're acting crazy with your money, donating it to the school, buying an old house…"

"Stop talking." Dan was so angry he could see red. His head hurt from the rush of blood to his brain.

"What?" Brian threw up his hands. "I'm not supposed to tell you what I think? That's my job."

Viti had come around the counter and was all kinds of mad. "You can tell me what's going on. Right now," she demanded.

Without taking a breath, Brian snapped at Viti. "Mind your business, honey."

"You did not just say that to me in my store." Viti snarled at him with an attitude that matched Brian's, and raised him.

His friend took a step back, obviously not expecting the pint-size baker to come at him for his obnoxious remark.

"I'm sorry, Viti." Danny wasn't just mortified by Brian's rude behavior, he was so angry he couldn't see straight. On top of that, he was screwed. He'd lost every chance to tell Jane in his own way.

"You're not going anywhere until you tell me what he's talking about. If my friend is in trouble, I want to know about it. I wouldn't have been able to stay in business if not for Jane. She helped me so much, I can't possibly repay her, but if she needs me, I will damn well try."

"I can't say much."

"Why not? This person knows. He's a stranger to us."

"Yeah, but Jane doesn't."

"What? She doesn't know? How is that possible?"

Brian started to say something but stopped short when Viti shot him a look that was like death.

"Say nothing. Go eat your food." She sounded like every mother he ever knew.

Brian nodded and wisely took a step back. "I'll wait outside."

"Good. Now you." Viti turned her eyes on Danny. "Tell me everything."

JANE UNPACKED BOXES of children's books in the stockroom, loving every story. This was the kind of job that often took way longer than it should because she spent so much time flipping through the old beloved titles that they always had in stock. Today's shipment brought copies of *Chicka Chicka Boom Boom*, *The Velveteen Rabbit* and *The Snowy Day*. Jane remembered reading *The Snowy Day* to Tara every day for three months when she was four years old.

She flipped through a few other favorites, remembering her father reading to the kids who gathered in the store on rainy Saturday afternoons. It wasn't something that was ever announced. There was no registration, but everyone in town knew if the weather was bad, Mr. Mike would be reading stories at the bookstore at two o'clock. The place was always packed.

Jane continued the tradition, but in this day and age, with phones and video games, turnout was a lot lighter. However, there were still people who had a long history in town, who wandered in and waited for that story on a rainy Saturday. It reminded Jane of where she came from, and a vast appreciation for the gifts she'd been given washed through her.

"Jane?"

The voice belonged to her mother, and rather than its usual lilt, it was solemn and serious, almost like someone had died. "Hey, Mom. What's up?"

"Can you come out here please?"

Putting down the copy of *How the Grinch Stole Christmas*, Jane stepped out of the workroom and followed her mother to the front of the store. There, with his briefcase in his hand, was her attorney. Standing next to him was a tall woman with a jet-black bob who had been in last week. She didn't look quite the same as she did when she'd bought a couple of Christmas gifts, but it was definitely her.

Today, instead of jeans and a chunky sweater, Jane could see a tailored suit under her very expensive coat, and heels that were too high for a cold December day.

"What's this all about? Gary? To what do I owe the pleasure?"

Jane felt like she was in a nightmare going in slow motion, and there was no way to get out of it.

"Jane, this is Mariel Consuelas. She's with The Homestyle Group."

Was this supposed to mean something to her? "Hello. You were here last week, weren't you?"

"Yes. It's a charming place. Thank you for all your help." Mariel smiled in that way people do when they're trying to be friendly, but they're going to deliver really bad news. For all her polish the woman appeared uncomfortable.

"What's going on?" Jane insisted again.

Behind her, the door opened and closed, and she could hear Danny's breathing close in behind her. "Janie…"

Jane held up her hand and waited for Gary to tell her what she didn't want to know.

"Jane," Gary began, "I know you've been frustrated about your lease, but I've just been informed that Van Velt Realty is in the process of selling the building. Mariel is here from the company that's buying the property."

She felt herself wobble a little, and Danny's hands landed on her shoulders. "I see. I doubt I need a committee to tell me I have a new landlord."

The silence was thick, ominous. Gary looked down, Mariel looked up, but no one was speaking.

"Tell me," she demanded firmly.

Mariel took one step forward and drew a deep breath. Jane was curious about her. Was she the woman shopping for Christmas gifts, or the one who was trying to look like she owned the world? "Ms. Fallon. The Homestyle Group will be taking control of the property, and we aren't going to renew your lease. I'm very sorry. Since this is unexpected, the company will work with your attorney to compensate you for any loss of business while you relocate. We want to be good neighbors."

"Relocate? There's no place to relocate."

Viti was there now, and so were Gina and Tracy.

"Good neighbors?" Gina whispered. "Are you kidding?"

Tracy was pacing she was so angry. "This is outrageous. How can you do this to her? To the town?"

"It's not personal," Mariel said with a glance around the room. "We're putting in a beautiful restaurant, and we will help you make the transition. The property is perfect for what we have in mind. We're going to combine it with the building next door."

"It's been perfect for the bookstore and has been for eighty-five years." Jane's voice shook and she fought the tears that were building in response to her anger. "Why here?"

"I don't know what went into making the choice, but the property is in escrow. We will be closing on it by Christmas."

Jane felt a huge weight settle on her chest.

"This is tragic," Gina said, her voice cracking as she spoke. "The bookstore is the town's anchor. Jane is the anchor. This is unconscionable."

From the expression on her face, Mariel wasn't expecting this kind of backlash. "I'm sorry. Like I said, we will help you. I can write you a check today. Maybe this is an opportunity to downsize. I mean, who goes to bookstores anymore?"

"How can you be so tone deaf?" Viti retorted. "You don't know anything about us."

Jane leaned into the desk. Closing her eyes, she wanted to drown out the noise in her head, but all she could hear was the noise of people talking around her. The outrage from

Viti, Gina, and Tracy pulsed through her, but it was her mother's gentle hand dropping down on hers that brought her back. Opening her eyes, Jane saw wisdom and strength in her mother's eyes. "You're made of strong stuff, Jane Mara Fallon. Don't let this beat you. You have always controlled your story—don't stop now."

"I don't know what to do." The words caught in her throat, choking her.

"You don't have to know." Danny, who was standing behind her, leaned in. "Let them sweat a little. Give yourself time to think."

It was good advice. She didn't want to be pressured to make a decision when she felt so blindsided.

"Stand up tall," Mom said. "Show everyone what you're made of." Kathleen Fallon was a force to behold, whether she was in the classroom or tending to her family. Jane needed to remember that she had as much of Kathleen in her as Mike.

Straightening her back, Jane surveyed the scene. Elisa, the owner of the local pub and the president of the Chamber of Commerce came rushing through the door, and Viti and Gina intercepted her. There was too much going on. Too much chaos.

"Everyone stop!" Jane never raised her voice, so when she did, it got people's attention. "Gary, Ms. Consuelas, you need to leave."

Mariel looked distressed. It seemed she was starting to understand this wasn't going to give her company the great optics they were hoping for. "Can we talk privately? We will work with you."

"Yes, you will. But I'm not discussing this now."

Gary, who'd dropped the ball in a hundred ways, nodded. "I'll call you later, Jane."

"No. You won't. I'll be hiring someone else to negotiate with Homestyle. We will not be in touch about this, or anything else."

"You can't be serious. You're firing me?"

"Do I look like I'm not serious? Get out." Jane walked to the door and pushed it open. "Mariel, leave your card. Someone will reach out in due course."

Doing her best to exit gracefully, Mariel did what Jane asked, leaving her card before making her exit. Gary was a little slower, but he also made his way out.

Jane was wrung out. How had she been so blind? Signs had been thrown at her left and right, and she'd ignored them. The wobble in her legs finally dropped her into the big chair by the front window. Bending slightly, Jane hugged her dog, who had faithfully come by her mama's feet, exactly where she was needed. Her Chloe. Her sweet Chloe, who didn't offer any advice, leaned in quietly while Jane clutched her fur and wept.

ONCE GARY AND Mariel left, Jane lost it, and Dan went to her immediately. He'd tried everything to spare her this pain, and he'd failed. He couldn't protect her.

"God, Janie, I'm sorry. I'm so sorry."

Her eyes, red and puffy from crying, focused on his. "I told you something was wrong. I knew it."

"Well, so did he," Viti snorted. He had to admire Viti's

loyalty, but her timing sucked.

"What?" Jane rubbed her eyes with the heels of her hands. "He who? What are you talking about?"

"Viti, please..." Dan said, hoping she would let him ease Jane into what had happened. But he had no such luck.

"Your boyfriend. He knew the building was for sale. How long have you known?" she asked him. "Weeks?"

Jane's face froze. "I'm sorry. You knew and you didn't tell me?"

Dan didn't even have the chance to answer. Viti kept going.

"He was at the bakery this morning with his agent. The agent guy was talking about this one's new book, and when he was going back to Hawaii, you know, agent–author stuff. But then he started getting on Dan's case about how he tried to buy this house so you wouldn't go out of business. Dan knew when the bigmouth said something in front of me, it was a problem. I didn't let him leave until he told me the whole story."

"You tried to buy the house without telling me?" Jane was listening to Viti, but she was looking at him.

"Yes. But I was too late."

"How long have you known?"

This was what was going to finish him off, but he couldn't lie to her anymore. "Since the Harbor Lights festival."

"So, two and a half weeks. Two and a half weeks, almost THREE, that I could have been working to save my store." Rising, she shook her head. "I should have trusted my instincts. I shouldn't have let anyone tell me it was going to be fine. It's not fine, is it?"

Sadly, Dan knew that question wasn't just for him. Her mother and Viti had said the same things he had. Kathleen had laughed off Jane's worries more than once.

Tracy went to her longtime friend and wrapped Jane in a hug. "How did this happen? I just got off the phone with Elena, and she was shocked. There was no listing."

"It wasn't listed," Dan said. "It was a private contract and sale. Flew right under the radar. I guess the Van Velts had a connection with Homestyle."

"*But you knew.* And instead of telling me, you tried to play the hero." Jane's expression was flat, completely without expression.

"I wanted to help. You were going through so much with Tara's colleges and your mom retiring, I didn't want you to have to deal with this too. That's all."

"We could have done something if we'd known," Tracy looked right at him. "Protested, brought it to the zoning board…something."

Jane held up her hand. "It's my fault. I had my head in the sand for weeks."

"We can go to village hall right now," Viti offered.

"No. I don't think so," Jane responded quietly.

"But Jane…" Tracy was ripping mad, but it didn't matter. Nothing did. "You have to fight."

"No, I don't." Pressing her fingers into her temples, she finally. "I can't do this right now. I just can't." Her tone was sharp, wounded.

That hurt Danny was hearing in her voice? It was his fault. All his.

"It was bad enough I-I—" she stuttered. "I can't do this. I'm sorry if you think we should storm the village hall, but you're going to have to do it without me."

After heading into her office, Jane emerged with her coat and bag. "I'm out. Keep the store open, close it, whatever you want. I need to get out of here."

"I'll take you home," Dan said. It was the only thing he could think to do. He didn't want her to be alone.

"No. I'm going to take a walk." She clipped on Chloe's leash and went to the door. "I need some time to think."

Jane pushed her way out of the shop and turned toward the harbor. He wanted to follow her, but he knew it wouldn't help, and it might just make it worse.

He'd made a colossal mess of the situation, and no good intentions were going to fix it. The only thing he could do now was to give her some space and hope she forgave him.

TWO HOURS LATER, feeling so drained she couldn't move, Jane sat on the couch in her living room, beneath a warm throw, nursing a cup of tea. Her mother and her friends who had witnessed her epic meltdown had only checked in to make sure she was safe, but otherwise, she'd been left to think.

The Christmas tree stood in the window, a symbol of joy—of love—but at that moment, all she could feel was loss. Loss of hope. Loss of faith. Loss of trust.

It was the loss of trust that hurt the most. Danny had been calling and calling. Each time she let him go to voicemail. Part of her wanted so desperately to see him, but the other part couldn't face it. Not now. He'd betrayed her confidence and brought down a world of pain. She'd been careless—blind—and because of that, Jane was responsible for destroying something precious. In a few hours she would have to tell Tara. That was going to hurt most of all.

Chloe, who hadn't left her side, nuzzled Jane's hand. The dog's fur was so soft, and petting her was the only calm she could find in this horrible storm. Without warning, the dog lifted her head. She didn't move or make a sound, but she was definitely on high alert.

The side door opened and closed.

"Jane?" *Danny.* She didn't answer. "Janie?" His voice was thick and unsteady.

She should have figured he'd come. He wasn't the type to let voicemail stop him. "What do you want, Danny?"

Once he rounded the corner to the living room, she could see on his face the moment he saw her. His expression grew sad, with a thousand regrets running through his eyes. "Oh, Jane."

He dropped to his knees next to her and took her hands. Too tired to fight she just looked away. "I asked you to leave me alone for a while."

"I know, but I couldn't stay away. I'm sorry. I'm so sorry. About everything."

He was still holding her hands, and when she finally turned toward him, she saw a man who looked sad and scared. It was the scared that surprised her.

"You tried to buy the building? What were you thinking?"

"I wanted to help."

"How is that helping? Telling me the truth would have helped."

"I thought I was protecting you."

"I don't need protection, Danny. I need honesty. I need you to trust that I know how to run my life."

"I don't think for one second you can't run your own life."

"You tried to handle me. Manage what I knew and what I didn't. Not following up and trusting my gut is my own fault. I've let everyone down. The whole town. But you lied to me."

Danny's mouth dropped into a deep frown. "I was going to tell you, but…I don't know." His voice cracked with nervousness. "So much was happening, I thought I could spare you. I was wrong, and I'm sorry."

"Yes, you were wrong."

"I'm sorry. Truly sorry."

But was he? Jane's faith was so shaken, it was hard to know what she should believe. "Apparently, you're going back to Hawaii? Viti said she talked to your agent, and he mentioned that you had already booked your flight."

"Jane, please listen," he implored. Now she sensed panic. "*Of course* I have a return ticket. I have to pack up my house. I was going to ask you to come with me."

"Really? First I'm hearing of it."

Everything hurt. It was like one nerve ending was triggering another, and it was enough to make her shiver with cold. Danny reached for another blanket and draped it over her. His eyes, weary and resigned, searched hers for an answer.

"Please don't give up on us."

"I don't know what you want from me, but I don't have anything left right now. Maybe we can talk later, but I need some time to process all of this."

"I don't know what you heard, but I need you to hear this: I love you."

The words, the ones she'd been desperate to hear him say since they were teenagers, went straight to her heart. She loved him right back, but that didn't make any of this easier.

"Jane, I just want us to have a chance." He waited for her answer, keeping hold of her hand. "Please."

"I gave you a chance. You broke my trust, and my heart. Just like you did before."

Chapter Sixteen

"WHAT ARE YOU still doing here?" Jane looked up from the old photos of the store spread in front of her and found Tracy and Viti standing in the doorway of her office. Both of them were bundled up in big warm coats, and had snow covering their hats and the shoulders of their jackets. She hadn't looked outside in hours, forgetting that a big storm was rolling in.

With everything on her mind, there wasn't room for details about the weather. "What time is it?" Jane wondered.

Tracy crouched down next to her and laid a hand on her arm. "After eleven, and it's snowing like crazy. Tara and Kathleen are frantic. Why aren't you answering your phone?"

Jane shrugged. Dodging everyone's calls was completely selfish, especially with a snowstorm, but she just didn't want to face the sympathy and the platitudes. Now that word of the store closing had reached everyone in town, there was no avoiding it. Jane just wanted a couple of hours to lick her wounds on her own.

"I should have called. I'm sorry."

"Honey, we're here for you. What can we do?"

Jane looked over at Viti whose thumbs were flying over the screen on her phone. "I let your mom know you're okay and that we're with you."

"I can't believe I didn't call them." Jane leaned back in the old wooden desk chair, and rubbed her temples.

"It's okay," Viti said. "We've got you."

Tracy reached out and wrapped her arm around Jane's shoulder. "Let's go."

"Yeah, I should go home."

"Not home," Viti assured her calmly. "We're going right across the street to Claire's apartment. She has the water on for tea, and I brought all the leftovers from the shop."

Claire lived above her yarn shop in a gorgeous apartment that was like a little piece of Ireland. When she first opened the store five years ago, Jane used to go over after work for a glass of wine, or a bite to eat, but since they'd both gotten busier over the years, they weren't able to do it as often. Still, she and Claire, along with Viti, Tracy, and Gina would try to do dinner once a month. They'd missed a few, the nights becoming casualties of their busy lives.

Tracy stood, and grabbed Jane's coat from the hook. "Come on, girlfriend. Let's get you out of here."

Jane was going to object, but she didn't have the energy. That, and she knew that if Tracy had her mind set on something, there was no use in fighting it. They shut the lights and locked up the store. These were good friends, and she hadn't trusted them with some really important pieces of her life. Did that make her a bad friend? Or was she too stubborn for her own good?

With Viti on one side and Tracy on the other, they trudged through six inches of wet snow covering Main Street and into the small vestibule right next to the front door of Harbor Knits. The building was one of the oldest in town, dating back to the late eighteenth century. When it was first built, the large brick structure had a general store on the first floor, and small apartments and rooms on the second and third floors for sailors who used to crew boats based in the harbor. The town was originally called Derby Harbor after an English earl who was honored with the land, but the name was changed around 1800 when sailors insisted angels guided their boat through rough seas and safely home. After a while, the name Angel's Harbor stuck, and then finally, it became Angel Harbor.

There was no good reason for her to have the town history running through her head, but she had been steeped in nostalgia all night, looking at old photos of the store from when her grandfather started the business and made a go of it. The pity party would get her nowhere—maybe she needed a bit of the mettle shown by those sailors who relied on faith and their shipmates to get them home.

Once they stomped the snow off their boots, they headed up the narrow steps, with Tracy leading and Viti bringing up the rear. She didn't know what they were going to talk about since the sale of the store was done. There was no way to solve a problem that had already reached the point of no return.

"Gina couldn't make it. She's at *The Nutcracker* with her sister," Viti informed her. "But she wants a full report. She's bringing you truffles tomorrow."

Jane didn't know how to respond to the news of truffles, although the gesture was pure Gina. For her friend, food was love. No doubt, Jane's taste buds would be happy. Her butt? Not so much. They reached the first landing and light from

Claire's apartment flooded into the hall, bright and cheerful. The warm yellow glow was sprinkled with color, a tell-tale sign she had her Christmas lights on.

"Come on, hurry yourselves. I have tea steeping." Claire's bright Irish lilt echoed in the stairwell. When they reached the landing, she didn't hesitate and pulled Jane inside. "What were you thinking hiding out in that dark store? Everyone was worried sick about you." Claire was pulling off Jane's jacket like she was late for dinner. "Truly, Jane. I have no words for you."

That was a lie considering the way Claire was giving her the business.

"Sit yourself down, and I'll get you some tea."

Jane settled into a large, comfortable floral chair near the window and dropped her head back, allowing her to see the snow falling outside. It was letting up, with only a few flakes visible in the streetlight. "I'm going to be okay, you know? It sucks, but I'll survive. I just needed some time."

"Understood," Viti said. "And if I wanted to sleep on a bench in my bakery, I could do that. I don't have people waiting for me at home, however. You do."

She was right, of course. It was so out of character for Jane, it was no wonder her mom was worried. "I know."

Jane accepted the large white mug from Claire. It was filled with the most delicious-smelling brew. Even in the beautiful apartment, with her friends there for support, Jane had felt like she might jump out of her skin. Hopefully, the tea would help, as the scent of peach, mint, and lemon began to soothe her frazzled nerves. "Thank you. It smells wonderful."

Tracy sat on the side of the sofa adjacent to the chair. With an ease that came with over fifty years of friendship, she reached out and took Jane's hand. "I get that you're hurting, but you don't have to deal with this alone."

"I don't know if that's true. This is my problem. I'll survive, but…" Of course she'd survive. Broken hearts weren't fatal, but the heaviness in her chest told her it was going to be a long way back. "It sucks. I have no idea what I should do."

"Jane, dearie," Claire said softly, passing her a box of Viti's famous snickerdoodles. "Why don't you tell us what's really upset you?"

"Really upset me? Do I need something else?" Jane immediately regretted her snippy comment, especially since her friends were being wonderfully understanding. With a sigh of resignation, she reached in the box and took a cookie. As she bit into the slightly crisp outside, the buttery cinnamon goodness filled her mouth. The act of chewing gave her some time to think. Not that she needed it. For the past few days all she did was think.

Swallowing, she looked each one of her friends in the eyes. They were all so different, with backgrounds as diverse as the quilt squares Claire was sorting for her next class. "I…I don't like myself very much right now. I've been bitchy and inconsiderate. I have a list of apologies to make, but I am going to be fine. I have money put away. I won't be homeless or anything. I just won't have…my store. My whole life was wrapped up in the shop. Tara is going away to college, my mother will be gone, and I don't know what I'm going to do."

Tracy nibbled the edge of a chocolate chip cookie. "You're allowed to feel like crap. I know I do, but taking your crap out on the people who love you is counterproductive. You know that."

"I know." That was one of the reasons she hadn't gone home. Jane had been hell to live with for the last few days, and she felt guilty bringing all her baggage down on her mom and Tara. On top of that, she'd blown up any hope of a relationship with Danny, and that made her heart hurt more than she thought possible.

Claire put the quilt squares in a box and then sat on the floor with a skein of soft green yarn in her lap. Rhythmically, methodically, she began rolling it into a ball. Jane knew they had contraptions for that particular job, but Claire was most at peace when her hands were moving. She started by wrapping the end of the yarn around her fingers, not too tight, and then every twenty spins around her hand, she turned the ball forty-five degrees to her right, and kept wrapping. Even watching the movement was soothing.

No one was talking, they were all waiting for her. "I wish I knew how to fix it. I always know the right thing to do, and I just can't see a way forward."

"When do you have to be out?" Viti asked. Her voice was tinged with what sounded like dread. Jane could relate.

"My lease isn't up until the end of February, but the company that bought the building wants to offer me an incentive to leave earlier. I thought about relocating, but I don't know where to go."

"I heard one of the realtors in town is moving to bigger quarters," Claire offered. "But their storefront is half the size of yours. I doubt downsizing is what you had in mind."

"Elena stopped in and told me they were moving, but she agreed that it was too small." Jane played with her fingers, wondering if she should share the rest. "She showed me Sail House, though."

"Really?" Tracy's whole face perked up. "Oh, that would be some project. I'd love to get my hands on the old girl." By trade, Tracy was an interior designer, which was how she met her husband, who was an architect. She hadn't been in the business for years, leaving full-time work when she had her kids. But she'd found a way to flex her creative muscle at the store. Along with designing all the seasonal decorations, she kept the art and design section full of the best books and magazines.

"Well, I have some money, and if the incentive from the buyer is good, I could probably swing the sale."

All three women looked up, hopeful. So hopeful that Jane hated to burst their bubble. "But I'd need at least a half million dollars to bring the building up to code, and get it in shape to act as a retail space. I can either buy it, or renovate it. I can't do both."

She'd spent the last three days trying to figure out how to save her business, not just for herself, but for the town, and for Tara. The idea to relocate was the only one that was even remotely feasible.

"There has to be a way," Tracy said. "What about those crowd money things..."

"Crowdfunding? That's a lot of money to raise online." Viti rose to get a macaron from the box. She rolled her eyes when she bit into her own creation. "God, I'm good at this."

"Jane?" Claire had been sitting quietly, taking in all the information while winding her yarn. She'd wrapped the whole skein now, and she held the ball of yarn in both her hands. She was gentle, not applying too much pressure or tension. "What happened with Danny?"

The question caught her totally off guard. "I'm not sure I know how to answer that."

"He came in the store today, poor man. He was at a loss for what to get his sister and nieces for Christmas. He settled on some lovely throws. He also bought each of them some knitting lessons and a basket of supplies. He wanted to give them a gift they could enjoy together."

"Did he?" Her belly tightened just listening to Claire. "That's very thoughtful."

"Truly, it was. He's really quite lovely." Pulling a pair of long needles from the bag next to her, her friend started to cast on, continuing to talk while her hands worked. "He looked troubled though. Sad. Like, oh I don't know…like he lost the love of his life." Claire glanced up only for a moment, long enough to lock eyes with Jane, before putting her focus back on her work.

"He said that?" Her voice came out on a whisper, barely there because of the emotion welling up inside her.

"He didn't have to. That kind of sadness is deep, and his eyes were giving up secrets."

Jane saw those eyes the other day at her house. He'd apologized for not telling her, but she wasn't hearing him. She'd lashed out at him. So afraid that he would end up as another heartbreak, Jane pushed him away. "He's been back a little over a month. How can I love him like this? It doesn't seem possible."

Claire smiled gently. "It's not always about the time, but the place we are in our lives."

"He was gone so long…"

Tracy grasped her hand even tighter than before. "Jane, you've loved him since you were in high school. Your feelings are older and quieter now, but he's your guy. He's always been your guy. You just need to accept it, and then you can figure out how to move past what happened."

"I wouldn't forgive him. He should have told you." Viti didn't have any of Tracy's sentimentality, or Claire's softness. Three days ago, Jane would have agreed with her. Now, she was weighing what she really wanted.

"I guess I have to figure out if he's worth the risk." The last month had been magical. The years and distance between them melted away, revealing feelings that sparkled like something precious, but also grounded her like a strong anchor. How she felt about him was calm and settled, completely different from the desperate yearning of her twenties.

Not that it mattered, because right now, her heart ached. Losing him was the worst part of everything that had happened and Jane wondered if there was enough magic in the universe for her to get him back.

Chapter Seventeen

WITH BOOKSTORE CUSTOMERS, Christmas Eve was always hit or miss. Usually it was pretty quiet, but today Jane had seen a flutter of activity right before closing. A man had just come to town on a surprise visit to see his parents for the holiday and he had no presents for his folks, his siblings and their spouses, and nothing for his passel of nieces and nephews.

Jane was able to take care of all his gift needs and wrap every last present. He'd just left a very happy man and promised he'd be back next year for help with his list. He'd need more presents next year, he told her. Two of his sisters were expecting.

Jane smiled, even though the thought of next year wasn't of twinkling lights and happy customers, but a great empty void, an existence without the colors and light of all the Christmases past.

Still, the man's visit had been refreshing. Not being a local, he didn't know the store was going to be closing by February 1st.

Three days ago she signed the agreement with the new owners to move out a month early. It was no small amount of money they'd offered, but she still hadn't deposited the check, not quite ready to make it final.

It was a nice break that her last customer of the day hadn't offered condolences, or platitudes. He was just concerned about getting gifts for the people he loved. It was actually the perfect ending to a day that had been incredibly sad.

With a light snow falling, and the afternoon light beginning to fade, Jane decided to close for the day. It was Christmas Eve, and whatever was happening to her personally, she had her family at home. She and Tara and Mom would go to midnight mass and then tomorrow have Tracy's whole family for Christmas brunch. She was looking forward to their traditional gatherings, even though the day wasn't going to include the man who had stolen her heart.

Like a self-fulfilling prophecy, Jane had been right to be concerned about her growing feelings for Danny. Completely in love with him, she was broken-hearted knowing it was over, and she had no one to blame but herself.

With a flick of her wrist she turned the sign on the door to closed and threw the deadbolt to make sure no one else wandered in.

Tracy, who usually worked the morning of Christmas Eve, had asked for the day off. Her kids and her parents were back in town, and she was hosting everyone for Christmas Eve dinner.

It would be a good time if Jane could shake the headache that had been annoying her since this morning with its dull, persistent throbbing.

She put the cash in the safe, powered everything down, and resolved to come in early the day after Christmas to square up the books. It would have been easy enough to do the ten minutes of bookkeeping, but it could wait. Other than her last customer, there had only been a few sales, and it was time for her to go home. Chloe obviously agreed, as Jane's canine friend was waiting by the door, leash in her mouth, ready to take her walk.

Thankful she hadn't driven today, Jane stepped out into the cold Christmas air. Filling her lungs with a deep breath, she hoped the time outside would clear her mood and help her shake off a very annoying headache. It was only four o'clock, but with the shorter December days and the heavy cloud cover, it was already starting to get dark. Christmas lights were flicking on all up and down Main Street. It was a charming scene, picture-perfect in so many ways. Jane only wished she felt like celebrating.

Across the street she saw a young couple strolling hand in hand, each of them clutching a shopping bag. Over near the candy store, two children bounced in front of a man, probably their father, dragging him inside for a last-minute sweet treat.

Jane pulled her coat around her and the ache in her chest grew more acute. She'd probably built her last holiday book tree, told her last Christmas story, and put up her last menorah. The season was a bellwether for what was to come. An era was ending. She was going to lose it all—the people, the community—all of it would be gone.

There were those who told her to be grateful. Lovely people who reminded her to look at the blessings in her life. It was true; she had many, including her daughter and her mom, and her friends. She had a home and her gorgeous doggie. She had her health. All of these things were important. Over and over she told herself, things could be so much worse, that she was, indeed, very fortunate. But that's not how it felt, and all the advice, while well-meaning, didn't help.

She couldn't even think about Danny. That kind of heartbreak was too much for her to bear along with everything else. She hadn't seen him in ten days. He'd called and left a message, but Jane couldn't even bring herself to listen to it. Today, she was surprised to see his niece, Ella, who stopped in with a small gift. Jane hadn't opened it yet, saving it for when she was alone, as she fully expected to cry.

Chloe walked beside her, leaning into Jane's leg as they moved up the sidewalk. No doubt, the dog sensed Jane's mood. It made Jane wonder how Chloe would deal with the change in routine. A fixture in the bookstore since she was a puppy, it was as much a part of Chloe's life as Jane's. She figured the dog would once again prove to be more adaptable than her human.

"I'll be okay, Chloe girl. I promise." Chloe looked up, her soulful brown eyes filled with doggie love. "We'll find something new to do together. Maybe we should take a road trip after Tara heads off to school. Where do you want to go?"

The idea of packing the dog in her truck and heading out into the great unknown had its appeal. There were plenty of places in the United States and Canada that would be fun to explore.

In no rush to get home, Jane stopped to gaze into store windows and wave to friends just closing up shop. Turning, she looked down Main Street, admiring all the decorations, which cut a glittering path right to the harbor. This was such a joyful time of year, but again, Jane felt the deep sense of loss squeeze her heart. Since the news came out about the building being sold, friends and neighbors stopped in. Some were in tears, others were angry, vowing to fight for her with the village council.

Unfortunately, there was nothing to be done. It was too late. The house was zoned commercial, the new owners vowed to keep the exterior authentic, and any improvements would be just that, improvements. Plans included replacing the windows, and making the porch a little larger so folks could eat outside in nice weather.

The big restaurant group that bought the building was going to put in a trendy brunch bistro that would serve breakfast and lunch only. It sounded like a fun addition to the downtown area that wouldn't do any harm to existing businesses.

Except hers.

The owner of the group reached out to her and tried to mend fences. Not that it mattered, but she did find out the details of the sale. Apparently, Colton Van Velt, the man she'd met the previous summer, and the Homestyle owner were prep school friends. They'd seen each other at a reunion and hatched the deal. Colton had no idea when he offered the building next door to the restaurant group, that they'd want the bookstore too. Colton saw dollar signs and the entire deal was kept quiet. Wanting to generate a little goodwill, the restaurant leadership team offered a big incentive for Jane to move out before her lease was up. She took it, naturally. Jane had never seen a check that big, and it would come in handy since she was going to be unemployed for the first time in her life.

Jane didn't have a clue about what came after. Elena had continued to scout for new retail space but hadn't found anything in the vicinity that didn't need massive amounts of time and money to make it work.

In the short term, she'd store everything. Furniture, stock, and the café fixtures would be tucked away until she could formulate some kind of plan. That plan might include selling everything off, but she needed time to think about her options. If only she'd saved all the money she'd sunk into the physical building. It sure would have helped her now.

Water under the bridge, her dad would say, or he'd make some comment about hindsight being twenty-twenty.

Indeed it was.

Just as she passed the theater, Chloe stopped and gave a little woof. She was fully alert, with her ears erect and the hair on her back standing up. This was unusual since she and Chloe walked this route home at least three times a week. The dog knew every house, every shrub, and every squirrel and chipmunk in the neighborhood.

"What is it, baby?"

Following the dog's gaze, Jane looked to her right and saw a figure move on the porch of Sail House right at the edge of town. Had it finally been sold? There were lights on inside, and as she moved closer, the front of the house lit up, like someone flipped a switch, startling her with a blaze of colored and white twinkling lights.

The roofline, the trees and shrubs, the porch rails and pillars were decorated for Christmas. Wreaths adorned the windows and doors and there, standing on the top step, was Danny.

His hands were tucked in his coat pockets and he wore a sweet, but nervous smile. "Hiya, Janie." His voice was low and full of emotion, and as he descended the porch steps, Jane was tongue-tied, completely taken off guard.

"Danny?"

Choe barked in greeting, her tail wagging like she hadn't seen him in years.

"I was wondering when you were going to come by." His voice was low, gentle, like he might talk to a nervous animal, or a crazy woman on the verge of snapping.

"Have you been waiting for me?" It was a nice to think he had. It lightened her mood ever so slightly.

"Maybe."

Jane took a step toward him. *Why was he here, at this house?* "Maybe?"

He was on the path now, closing the distance between them. "Of course I was waiting for you."

"I see. Why?" Jane's heart picked up a steady beat. He looked so handsome and unsure, backlit by the Christmas lights and dusted by snow swirling around them.

"I'm going to screw this up, so please know that everything I do or say comes right from my heart, but the stakes are kind of high, so I'm nervous."

"Okay." Her own heart had gone from a steady beat to a series of wild thumps in her chest. Her stomach was currently occupied by a flock of butterflies. Her woo-woo must have kicked in, because Jane felt like something life-changing was about to happen if she let it.

"I love you, Jane. I love you so much I ache from it. I learned the hard way that I can't be the person I want to be without you. I can't even think about it."

Chloe lay down on the walk by his feet and tilted her head back to listen. Jane stepped closer, letting the heady scent of him surround her. "Oh, Danny. Are you sure? I'm crazy in case you haven't noticed."

"Very sure. If you know nothing else, know that. I love you. And you're not crazy."

He'd told her before, at her house, but she was too stuck in her own head to listen. Thank God he'd said it again. Tears spilled from her eyes, and Jane didn't even try to stop them. If Danny was going to show his heart, she could show hers.

"I'm sorry I didn't tell you when I found out the building was being sold. I should have right away and trusted you to know what was best. I tried to fix things, but keeping you in the dark was wrong."

"I wish I had known, but your heart was in the right place. I'm not used to having someone look out for me like that. I always feel like I need to be strong for everybody."

"I know." He reached out and took her hands in his. "And every single person you touch is better for it. I know I am, but who's going to take care of you, Janie?"

Her breath hitched, and tears slowly found their way down her cheeks. Danny didn't wait any longer for her to come to him; he took hold and pulled her in.

"I don't have words to express the impact you've had on people, but you need to lean on those of us who love you. We're here, and we're not going anywhere."

She turned her face into his hard chest and tried to absorb what he'd just said. Her breathing was coming in great gulps, the cold air feeling heavy in her lungs. "I was so blind—I knew what was coming, whether you told me or not. It was easier not to admit it. I feel like such a…a failure. Like I let everyone down. I don't know if it's logical, but that's how it is."

"You're not a failure. You are the furthest thing from it."

She held on to him, unsure if she could stand on her own. His warm body provided so much more than physical support. He was her person. He'd always been her person and she was so very grateful to have him back.

"Janie," he whispered, "you didn't fail. The building being sold is awful, but that wasn't your fault."

"Why does it feel that way?" She sniffled and held on to him like a buoy in a storm. He was her anchor, her lifeline, and only now—with the snow falling and the lights shining—did she understand how much she needed him.

"You're so tough on yourself." He rubbed her back, soothing her without any judgment.

"It's special, Danny. There's something magical about it, and now it's going to be gone."

"People adapt, Jane. We learn and grow. Look at me. But there's no blame here. Nothing we did, or could have done, would have changed anything. It sucks."

"You don't think so?" She looked up at his kind eyes.

"Nah. It was a done deal when I found out right after Thanksgiving. It doesn't change that I should have told you, though. I messed up."

People often apologized because they had to. Danny

apologized because he meant it.

"I want to help," he said quietly. "Will you let me?"

"I love you. So much. I shouldn't have pushed you away. I just felt so helpless."

"Jane Fallon, you are many things, but if I've learned anything, helpless is not one of them."

They stood there, with the dog between them, holding each other tight. Jane didn't know how long it was before she opened her eyes and once again caught sight of the house behind him. It was almost a hundred and fifty years old and showed its age, but with the big windows, a wraparound porch, and gingerbread trim, the house had amazing character and great bones. It was large, set on a decent-size lot for this part of town. It had been a law office at one time but it hadn't been occupied for several years.

"Do you want to tell me what's up with the house?"

"House?"

"Yeah, you know. The one behind you?"

"Oh, right. That house. Let's talk about that." He took a deep breath and stroked a finger across her cheek. "I bought it."

Shocked was an inadequate description for what she was feeling. If he had dropped a case of books on her head, she wouldn't have been more surprised. "I'm sorry. Did you say you bought it?"

"It's going to contract right after Christmas. I need a place to live when I'm here, so I'm going to convert the top floor into an apartment. It's huge."

Live here?

"You're still planning on staying? Not going back to

Hawaii like your agent said?"

"Only to pack," he said without any hesitation. "Would you be okay with that, though? If I stuck around?"

He was really staying? "Are you sure? It's not very exciting here."

"You're here. I want to be wherever you are. But if you're having second thoughts about us, if you want some distance, just tell me. I screwed things up so badly, I'd understand. But I'll wait for you. I will."

"You're staying, you're really staying?"

"I don't want to leave you again. I meant what I said."

Without another second's hesitation, Jane took his face in her hands and kissed him. She tasted his supple mouth, absorbed his now familiar scent, and for the first time, Jane had no doubts. It was magical. It healed. This kiss, unlike the others, didn't speak of lost moments and missed opportunities; this kiss was about their future, it was a promise. It was a testament to her faith in him. *In them.* After all this time, Jane had her soul mate, and his warmth and strength spread through her like she was being wrapped in a lush blanket. Jane felt safe, protected, and loved. She felt so loved it brought fresh tears to her eyes.

Finally, Jane felt a gentle reminder that they weren't alone. Chloe nudged between them, bringing them back to earth.

"That was nice," he whispered.

"I could get used to it." She could. Danny was a very skilled kisser. It made her wonder what other skills he might have.

"I want to show you something else. I don't deserve it,

but I need you to trust me. Will you come inside?"

At this point, she'd have followed him anywhere.

"I like what you've done with the place," she teased. "You said you were going to make an apartment upstairs. What about the rest of the house?"

With her hand in his, Danny pulled her to the front door. There was an urgency, an excitement, to his movements and she was getting excited along with him. *He was buying the house?* In a million years she never would have thought he was going to buy a house. And one that needed so much work? That was even more of a shock. Something was up, and while Jane was happier and more hopeful than she'd been in months, questions still floated through her mind.

"I have a plan," he said as he opened the door. "I'm curious to hear what you think. Whether or not it happens is totally up to you."

They entered a large foyer with a grand staircase that curved its way to the second floor. A Christmas tree was set in the center of the space, soaring at least twelve feet in the air. It was decorated with white lights; glass globes of red, gold, and green; sparkling stars; and books. *Books?*

Blown glass ornaments of books in all sizes and colors dotted the tree. It was like an homage to her shop. Beautiful, festive, and joyful. It was lovely, and as sad as she was about losing her beloved store, this was truly a beautiful gesture.

"Oh, Danny. This is stunning. It's beautiful. Thank you!"

"Thank you? Oh. The tree. Right. It looks nice, doesn't it?"

"Nice?" It was way more than nice. He kept hold of her hand and pulled her down the hallway. "Where are we going?"

"You'll see. Come on."

Before she could say another word, Jane entered a large open space that she realized ran from the front to the back of the house and in it was another beautiful Christmas tree, along with everyone she knew. *Everyone.*

The room was bursting. Among the faces she saw Claire, Viti, Robert from the pet store, and Gina. All of the local merchants had gathered, as well as the customers she'd known over the years who had become dear friends. This was her large extended family, here to say goodbye.

The bookstore meant so much to the town, it was gratifying to see all this love in one place. It was heartbreaking, but to be able to pay tribute to something that had been part of the fabric of Angel Harbor for so long was, indeed, touching. Jane would have thought she was all cried out, but tears started to leak out of her eyes.

In the crowd she spotted her mother and Tara, and Tracy with her family. Dan's sister and brother-in-law were there with the kids. Jane pressed a hand to her heart and gazed around the room. Then, through the blur of tears, her gaze settled on a large sign attached to the wall.

New Home of Harbor Books

Coming Soon

"I don't…I don't understand."

Then it hit her.

Jane's breath left her lungs. She dropped Chloe's leash

and bent forward, the reality of what was happening hitting her all at once. He bought the house.

He bought it for her.

"I can't believe you did this. I can't..."

Stepping to her, Danny dropped a hand on her back and brought her back to standing. With her hands in his, he smiled, kissed her softly, and to her shock Jane saw the hint of a tear in the corner of one of his eyes.

"All of this? All the people? I didn't do that—you did it, Jane. I bought the building, sure. But this is a *partnership* if you'll have me, and this is the crew that's going to help you get your new store up and running. *If that's what you want.*"

"What do you mean? My crew?" The question was sincere. She had less than six weeks to vacate her store. She'd rented a storage unit, but her big plan was to have a company come in eventually, and sell the fixtures after she'd sold off or donated her stock.

Gina stepped forward and touched Jane's arm. Her big brown eyes dominated her face, but it was her gentle smile that calmed Jane's nerves. She was the sweetest person, and she'd been a wonderful friend. Gina was smart and creative, and just as invested in Angel Harbor as Jane was.

"Jane, if you're ready to give this a shot, you have all of us to help you. Do you see Dave over there?

Jane followed Gina's gaze and she waved. Of course she knew him.

"Did you know Dave is a cabinet maker?" she asked. "You helped him pick out books for his mother who recently moved to a senior living center and was having trouble adjusting. He didn't know what she might like, but once a week, you would pick out titles for her. If you saw something come in that she might like, you put it aside, not even knowing if he was going to be back. His mother cherished every book. To thank you, he's going to build your shelves and storage. All you need to do is get him the materials. Claire is going to help Tracy with decorating. The two of them are going to work with your vision to create a store that feels like home."

Jane was overwhelmed. These people, her community, were rescuing her. Just when she thought she had lost everything, her neighbors proved her wrong.

"The gentlemen from the hardware store are donating all the paint and supplies," Claire said with her light Irish brogue. "And, bless them, they're going to come after work to do the painting, install any hardware, and hang all your pictures."

Two large men, with black hair and coal dark eyes, raised their hands. "Miss Jane," one of them said, "I'm Rafe Espinoza, and this is my brother Marco. I don't know if you remember us, but when we were young and had just arrived in this country, you let us stay at the store after school when our mother was working in the diner."

"Oh my goodness! Yes! I do!" She remembered those two sweet, scared little boys whom she'd seen sitting in a small booth at the diner while their mother finished her lunch shift. She was perfectly happy to have them come sit in the children's room to read or do some homework.

"I own a landscaping business," Marco said. "And Rafe is a contractor. We'll be donating our time and labor to help with the renovation. It's the least we can do."

"Excuse me?" She was stunned. She hadn't seen these men since they were in high school. That had to be at least ten years ago.

Big and handsome, the Espinoza boys shared the same broad smile. "We've never forgotten how nice you were to us," Rafe said. "You helped with our homework, and with our English. You made us feel like we belonged, and we'll never forget it."

"I don't know what to say," she gasped. "I don't deserve this."

One by one people came forward to tell her how they would help, and why. Stories of what Jane had done for the town, of how she'd helped people came flooding out. Donations of materials and labor, free advertising; those who couldn't do anything else volunteered to help her pack, move, and unpack. One customer owned a large warehouse, and he offered to store everything for her until she could reopen in the new location.

Finally, Tara brought an easel forward, and Tracy and her husband came with her. Her daughter, more beautiful by the day, had grown into an incredible young woman. "Now you can see what's been planned. Uncle Greg did some drawings."

Tracy's husband was an architect, but he specialized in urban design and planning. Jane didn't see a lot of glass and steel on the North Shore, but when the first rendering was revealed, Jane was sure he'd missed his calling. It was a gorgeous sweeping panoramic view of the inside of the shop as he imagined it. Bright, with large windows, shelves along the walls, and a central information counter in what was currently the foyer created a perfect environment. The space was open and airy, utilizing the high ceilings. It took Jane's breath away. The second drawing showed how the kitchen of the house would be turned into the café, as well as elevations of the renovated porch. Finally, a third showed the backyard, which included a parking area and a green space with an outdoor classroom and story area.

"These are your dreams, Jane," Tracy said. "All the things you've wanted to do over the years. There's going to be a meeting room for book clubs and writers' groups, and plenty of square footage to host book signings. This will be the destination bookstore on the East Coast."

Danny smiled, and Jane wondered when she was going to wake up. This had to be some kind of dream.

"The basement will be outfitted as a stock room and workspace, and you see that big guy over there? That's Bob. Bob?" Danny called. "Give a wave." A large balding man with a broad chest and powerful arms put his hand up. "Bob owns an elevator company. He's going to put in an elevator that goes from the basement to the second floor. No more hauling boxes, and the building will be fully ADA compliant."

"I don't know what to say. It's too much." Her voice was barely there, and awed didn't seem to cover all the emotions rushing around her insides. Nerves, excitement, gratitude, and love filled every inch of her until she didn't know where she would put any more. As Jane surveyed the room, it seemed perfect it was decorated for Christmas. It was called the season of giving, and Jane had never felt more fortunate than she did at that very moment.

"Nothing is too much for you." Danny was standing so close he smoothed the hair away from her face. "This is proof of how much you've lifted everyone up. You amaze me. Your goodness, your caring heart, the love you have for everyone in your orbit. You'll help anyone who needs it. Now it's your turn."

His declaration filled her with hope, and once again showed her why she loved this man with all her heart. He was generous and kind. An artist who painted with words and a philosopher who left a trail of wisdom behind him. Never in her life did she think she would ever find the love of her life, but here he was. The man who was perfect for her. "You saved me, Danny. You..."

"Shh." He laid a finger across her lips. "Like I said, I just bought an old house. You saved me. And all of this? The love in this room? That's all you. We believe in *you*, Jane. All you have to do is say the word."

"I love you," she whispered just for him. Then turning to the gathering, she flashed a watery smile, so grateful for all she had. "I love all of you. Thank you. Thank you from the bottom of my heart. You've thought of everything."

"Merry Christmas, Mom," Tara said, her girl crying happy tears as she held on to her grandmother.

Kathleen, also tearing up, didn't have to say a word to show how proud she was, but she did anyway. "When word got out that you needed a hand, we couldn't keep up with the flood of offers. You are much loved, my daughter."

Tracy gave her a hard hug, ever the sister of her heart. "You deserve this, my friend. Every bit of it."

"Thank you. Thank you all for being in my life."

Danny was standing behind her, his warmth and presence seeping into her. Since the day he walked back into her life, she thought about what she would do when he left again. Now she'd never have to find out. Without warning, Danny held a large white mylar envelope before her eyes. When she took it from him, Jane noticed the contents shifting inside. The weight moving in her hands. "What's this?"

He smiled down at her, dropping a kiss on top of her head. "It's my book. Your book, really. I wrote it for you."

"For me? Danny…"

"I found my words again, my passion for writing, because of you. Coming home was exactly what I needed, but only *because of you*. You're my heart, Janie. You always will be."

Jane opened the envelope he'd given her, not knowing what she was going to find inside. When she pulled out the stack of paper, she smiled. All this work, his soul was in this book, and as she ran her hand over the title page, she shivered.

The Harbor Light
By Dan Gallo

"I love the title."

"It suits. There's a lot of me in this book, but more than that, there's a lot of you. You're the light."

Clutching the pages to her chest, Jane had no idea how much that simple declaration would mean to her. On a night filled with so many extraordinary gifts, the soft affection in Danny's eyes was the only one that mattered at that moment. How did she ever get so lucky? "This makes me so happy. It's going to be a hit, I just know it."

"I hope so. My editor loves it. That's got to mean something, right? He's a mean old SOB and he said he cried."

Jane didn't realize she was crying, again, until a tear dripped on the cover page. "Thank you. It's perfect."

"You're my home, Jane. And like I said, you are the light, just like the angels. You helped me find my way back."

He rested his head against hers and sighed, and Jane let out a similar shaky breath when the cover page slipped away and she saw the dedication.

For Jane.
A beacon of hope in the darkness.
Thank you for keeping the light on.

Jane held the book close and reveled in the feel of Danny's arms as he pulled her in. Resting her head on his chest, she could hear his heart beating, strong and steady. Then, she looked to the side and saw the sea of people who were there for her when she most needed them. For years Jane had worried about her dreams going unrealized. She wasn't unhappy, but she let the question of "what if?" take up too much space in her head. Now, the past was firmly in the past, and all she could see was the road forward.

It was times like these, sacred moments that came unexpectedly, where we found the greatest clarity. Where we found love and joy and peace. Jane felt all those things—all those and so much more. Her life was rich beyond measure. Real gifts, the ones that mattered, were never found under the tree, but were found in the people who became part of our lives.

"I promise to make every Christmas better and better," Danny whispered. "Merry Christmas, Jane."

"Merry Christmas."

Epilogue

CHANGE WAS A beautiful thing. Especially when the changes brought so many riches to your life.

Sail House had been completely transformed from an elegant residence into an equally elegant store. It was more than Jane ever believed possible, and it was special because so many people had a hand in it. One year ago, Jane was facing a life in total upheaval—she never could have dreamed an outcome that had made her happier than this.

With deep gratitude, this Christmas Harbor Books would start something new. Instead of closing up shop early on December 24th, they were hosting their very first Christmas Eve open house. It seemed fitting that new beginnings required new traditions.

The staircase in the two-story foyer was draped with pine garland, glittery ornaments, and lights, which reflected off the freshly painted gray-blue walls. More ornaments hung from the ceiling, glass globes of varying sizes in gold, green, red, and silver. It was a festive constellation of color and light, and hanging from the center, directly over the customer service desk, was a crystal angel, watching over them.

The ornament was a gift from Danny. Made of artisan blown glass, with gold tips on her wings, he'd given her to Jane on their wedding day this past August.

"She'll watch over us, and our families," he said. "Just like the angels who brought the sailors home, I was brought home to you."

Behind her, she could hear his low, steady baritone filling the large entry. Glancing over her shoulder, she found him laughing with his sister and brother-in-law, so much more at ease than when he walked back into her life over a year ago. He'd gone through his own sea change, moving back to Angel Harbor, chucking his lucrative career writing crime thrillers and instead, writing what came from his heart.

His newest book—Jane's book—*The Harbor Light*, hit the bestseller lists at number one when it was released in November, and it hadn't budged from that spot, becoming this season's feel-good read. There'd been some talk show interviews that focused on how he'd done a complete pivot, and a few local tour stops, but nothing too extensive. Unlike his other books, this one didn't require a publicity tour, and he didn't want one. Danny had hit every note, writing a beautiful holiday tale about love and family that would be revisited by his readers every Christmas. Early reviews were stellar, and word of mouth carried it the rest of the way.

The movie would be out in time for next Christmas.

Jane glanced at the table filled with signed copies of the book, and couldn't help the pride and love that welled up in her chest. At times it felt like there was no room for all the love she had for him. He'd taken what could have been one of the darkest moments in her life and shined a light on all the riches hiding in the background. He made Jane see what she meant to everyone in Angel Harbor.

"Mom?" Jane turned and saw Tara rounding the corner

from the café with a plate piled with goodies. "You have got to try these."

"Mmmm." Looking at what her daughter offered, Jane eyed the small flaky puff pastries. Pinching one in her fingers, she brought it toward her mouth. The smell of the crust, combining with garlic, wine, and beef was heady. "Is this the beef Wellington?"

"Uh-huh." Tara nodded. "It's so good. Taste it."

Jane sank her teeth into the hors d'oeuvre, and felt a burst of flavor across her tongue. The seasonings were blended perfectly, the meat tender, the sauce rich and flavorful. It literally warmed her insides.

"That looks good." Jane felt Danny's warmth slide across her back. One of his large hands settled at her waist, while the other reached out and took a Wellington from the plate. This time, it was Danny's turn to be impressed. She could see it with the first bite.

"Oh, wow. That's incredible." The bliss rolled across his face. "Please tell me there are more of those."

Tara smiled. "Plenty. There's enough food to feed the entire town. Twice. This is going to be an amazing party."

Tara went off to offer her grandmother a taste, and Jane happily leaned back against the hard wall of her husband's chest. "I'm glad she made it home."

A snowstorm that sped across upstate New York and New England had dumped feet of snow near Tara's small college in Vermont. "Did you think I'd let her miss this?" he asked.

"No. Thank you for making the drive." He'd rented a big SUV to retrieve Tara and two of her friends from their snowbound dorm.

Her girl had decided against school in Dublin…for now. There was always the chance she would study abroad, or head to Europe for graduate school, but for the foreseeable future, she'd be four hours away. Tara was happy, and so was Jane.

Friends started to arrive, filling the store with all the people Jane cared about. Viti, Claire, and Gina had been the best cheerleaders. Truly, she couldn't ask for better friends. And Tracy? Well, her old friend took Jane's vision and made it happen. Working with Greg on the renovations, they put their heads together and created a magical space that wasn't just about books, but about celebrating their community.

There were antique maps, framed nautical artifacts, newspaper articles, and histories of people and places that Jane had pieced together through research. She had an entire area dedicated to the indigenous tribes that lived in the area before the land was sold to Dutch and English settlers. She found great joy putting her skills as an archeologist to work in her hometown, and it didn't escape the attention of the local university who was now sponsoring an archeology lecture series in the store every month.

"You are glowing," Danny said, dropping a soft kiss on the side of her neck.

"It's what happens when you're happy, I guess." It was the truth. Never in her life had Jane felt this content. Always on edge, wondering what bump in the road was coming next, had consumed her for so long. It was a new thing to feel such peace.

Turning her to face him, Danny leaned in for a kiss.

"You look beautiful. Have I told you that?"

Jane smiled. "I think that makes an even dozen."

Tucking her arm in his, he walked with her through the different sections. They stopped by different groups of people, the crowd that had gathered almost the same as the one from the year before—all the people who pledged to keep Harbor Books alive.

They'd put their faith in her and she wouldn't let them down. How could she when love had her back?

Once they reached the large open space that housed the café and the children's room, Danny handed her a glass of champagne.

Clinking her glass with a small spoon, she was able to quiet the room. "Well," she began, "here we are again."

The low rumble of laughter was accompanied by a few exclamations of *hear, hear.*

"I wouldn't be standing here without all of you. Your love has made this endeavor possible, and your support over the years has kept my little family whole. That Angel Harbor Books has been able to survive and thrive, is a testament to this wonderful town." Jane saw her mom, standing with Danny and Tara. They were her reason for everything. "This Christmas Eve open house is the first of what will become an annual event. Like the leg lamp lighting, the light festival, and the thousands of small traditions we have that keep the holidays special, we will keep the doors open on Christmas Eve for our friends and neighbors to come together, enjoy some food and good conversation and the warmth of this amazing town."

There was a smattering of applause, and the many wonderful smiles shining back at her assured Jane that the years to come were going to be better than she could have ever imagined. It was said that angels resided in their little village once upon a time. Looking out at the sea of faces comprised of family and friends, new and old, Jane had to believe that the angels never left.

The End

Want more? Check out another Jeannie Moon Christmas book, *Finding Christmas*!

Join Tule Publishing's newsletter for more great reads and weekly deals!

Dear Friends,

Every book is an adventure.

Bringing the town of Angel Harbor to life was no exception, but along with all the challenges, there was much joy. I based the location on a pretty, waterside village very close to where I live. I often walk along the water's edge with my dogs, shop in the stores and eat at the restaurants. The main road still has trolley tracks embedded in the pavement, reminding visitors of a time when transportation was provided to the train station a few miles away. And at Christmastime the town is magical.

Long Island (New York) is steeped in stereotypes, and some of them aren't so flattering. But for every traffic jam on the Long Island Expressway, there's a quaint village with a thriving downtown, a pretty local beach, a farmer's market, a vineyard, and of course, there's always the ocean—vast and powerful. I love setting my stories here, however, because of the people who are warm and wonderful. This is my home, and I feel such pride that my family roots go deep into the sandy soil. It's a special place and I adore being able to share it.

Christmas in Angel Harbor has been a team effort, and as always, there are a few people to thank. My agent, Stephany Evans, never hesitates to tell me the truth and always has my back. It's proven to be the perfect combination, and I appreciate her more than you know. My editor, Kelly

Hunter, knows just what to say to help be bring out my characters' deepest emotions. If there's a scene in this book that makes you cry, it's because Kelly helped me dig down and find what I needed to pluck those heartstrings. I am truly blessed to work with her. The wonderful Tracy Solheim has proven time and again, to be an advocate, a sounding board, and truly the sister of my heart. She is the friend we all need. My friend Nika Rhone generously gives of her time to offer feedback and encouragement. Thank you, m'dear.

The Tule Team, guided by the vision of the intrepid Jane Porter, has been a beacon in the sometimes difficult and confusing world of publishing. I am at home with Tule, and it's because of people like Meghan, Nikki, Cyndi, cover artist, Lee—and, of course, Jane—that I have found such joy in my writing.

Lisa Gordon and Hillary Topper…I'm so glad we found each other. Thanks for getting me seen.

Becca Syme—what do I say? I cannot thank you enough for helping me find my words again. Your wisdom, your patience, and your insight have helped me find my way back to the stories I love so much. Thank you. Thank you for everything.

My family and friends are at the heart of everything I do. My husband, children and grandchildren bring me joy each and every day. They are the loves of my life. My extended family, my wonderful friends, and my fellow Tule authors inspire me to take risks and make the next book even better than the last.

Finally, I would be shouting into the void without my

readers. Thank you for spending time with me, for each review, each comment on social media, and each email. I love hearing from you, so please keep in touch. Without you, the books might have wings, but there would be nowhere for them to land.

Stay safe and be well.

Much love,
Jeannie

Jeannie Moon
Long Island, NY
Fall 2020

Book Group Discussion Questions

Christmas in Angel Harbor by Jeannie Moon

1. Small towns often have their own personality. How does Dan's run in the opening scene, not only establish the setting, but give the reader hints about the town's inner life?
2. Memories are powerful and they can evoke strong emotions in the individual. How do the characters juggle different memories and the emotions they trigger?
3. Jane is a strong mother figure in the book, not just to her daughter, but also for Angel Harbor. In what ways does she take on the role of town mom?
4. The book takes a hard look at life changes, both the good and the bad. In what ways do our characters evolve over the course of the story as a result of the changes they must face?
5. The bookstore has a long history in Angel Harbor, how does this connect with Jane's chosen field of archeology?
6. Many of Jane's relationships are in a state of flux. Discuss the dynamics of the different relationships and how Jane is navigating them throughout the book. (Jane and Tara, Jane and Kathleen, Jane and Danny)
7. Dan's public persona is very different than his true personality. Why do you think he comes back to his hometown?
8. Discuss the connections between the shopkeepers in Angel Harbor. How does the fate of the bookstore affect them?

9. Love conquers all is a cliché, but clichés are often true. How does it play out in the story?
10. The impact of one person can be profound. In what ways does *Christmas in Angel Harbor* drive home that point?

More books by Jeannie Moon

Christmas books

This Christmas
Christmas in New York series

Finding Christmas
Standalone title

The Compass Cove series

Book 1: *Then Came You*

Book 2: *You Send Me*

Book 3: *All of Me*

About the Author

USA Today bestselling author **Jeannie Moon** has always been a romantic. When she's not spinning tales of her own, Jeannie works as a school librarian, thankful she has a job that allows her to immerse herself in books and call it work. Married to her high school sweetheart, Jeannie has three kids, three lovable dogs and a mischievous cat and lives in her hometown on Long Island, NY. If she's more than ten miles away from salt water for any longer than a week, she gets twitchy.

Thank you for reading

Christmas in Angel Harbor

If you enjoyed this book, you can find more from all our great authors at TulePublishing.com, or from your favorite online retailer.

Made in the USA
Middletown, DE
21 December 2020

29852202R00175